Jacqui Davina Penn spent her scl and plays, which her childhood pe wild imagination and a colourful life, the scene was set for an author.

She published her first novel, after winning an award for a short story. She spends her time between Kent, England, and the Andalusian hillsides in Spain. When she's not writing, she can be found walking her dogs and gathering ideas for her next book.

Also by Davina Penn

A Family for Sophia

A Second Chance for Alisha

Next Door to *Him*

Ripley

A Second Chance Romance by the Sea

Jacqui Penn

and

Davina Penn

Copyright ©2015 Jacqui Penn Davina Penn

The author or authors assert their moral right under the Copyright, Designs and Patents Act, 1988, to be identified as the author or authors of this work.

All rights reserved. No part of this publication may be reproduced, copied, stored in a retrieval system, or transmitted, in any form or by any means, without the prior written consent of the copyright holder, nor be otherwise circulated in any form of binding or cover other than that in which it is published and without a similar condition being imposed on the subsequent purchaser.

All the characters in this book are fictitious and any resemblance or similarity to persons alive or dead is purely coincidental.

For my mum, and wonderful memories of a place by the sea.

Prologue

'How's the deal with Jefferson's going? It should be finalised by now.' Richard Bradford raised his eyes from the papers he'd been working through. His partner Jerry Mayer stood before him somewhat aloof, his thinning, mousey hair swept across his bald patch.

'Should be sorted by this afternoon. There was a bit of a wait on the bank confirmation.' Jerry shuffled his feet and scratched the side of his nose.

'Good, one less thing to worry about.' Richard hated paperwork; luckily Jerry took care of all the important stuff.

'I need to go to the bank shortly. Is there anything you want while I'm out?' Jerry asked.

'A croissant and coffee from the bakery would be good. In fact, two croissants and get yourself one while you're there, the second one isn't for you.' A smile spread across Richard's lips. A croissant was his treat of the day, and as today was Friday, he felt he deserved an extra one. He patted his stomach; he shouldn't really have two, but what the hell.

Richard had built his business from scratch and now he could afford to sit back and almost let things run themselves. The deals came regularly, enabling him to keep his wife in the style she had come to expect, and allowed his wonderful, fifteen-year-old daughter Ripley, a private education at an exclusive boarding school. Ripley was, and always had been since the day she was born, the most important person in Richard's world. He loved her more than life itself and her continued happiness made all that he did, purposeful. The smile on her face always gave him a surge of joy, unmatched by anything else.

Jerry left the office a few moments later. He had been acting strangely for a few weeks now. Richard put it down to the probability his girlfriend was playing him up again. Richard went back to the paperwork and soon lost himself, scribbling notes and making phone calls.

Richard and Jerry met around twenty years ago when Richard relocated to Ipswich. They hadn't been mates back then, but Richard soon found out that Jerry could always be relied upon to pull off a deal, which brought in a quick return. Someone like that always kept one ear to the ground for a fast turnaround, so for Richard, Jerry was an asset to have on board.

Every Friday lunchtime, the partners shared a few pints in their local pub.

'Slow down, Jerry, we're not in a rush.'

'I haven't got a lot to do this afternoon, I'm thirsty.'

Richard began his second pint as Jerry finished his third. Richard eyed him suspiciously. 'Is everything alright? You seem a bit edgy.'

'I'm fine. You're not my boss; you can't tell me how much beer I can drink.'

'I wasn't, it's just not like you to drink that much.' Richard looked around the pub, feeling awkward. The theme was Charles Dickens, after the pub's name. Pictures of characters from the books adorned the walls along with artefacts from that era. The pub had been sympathetically refurbished lately to keep it dated in style but with shiny brass pumps and new seating and tables. The low lighting added to the atmosphere of days gone by.

'Anyway, I might not go back to the office today. I've got some other stuff to sort out.' Jerry held his head back as the final dregs from his glass slipped down his throat.

'Okay. I'd better be getting back. I'll see you Monday then. Have a good weekend,' Richard said, standing up. Jerry did little more than grunt. It probably was best Jerry wasn't going back to the office, too much alcohol could make him unpleasant. Richard left by the big wooden-framed, glass-panelled doors and looked back as they closed behind him to see Jerry ordering another pint at the bar. There was definitely something amiss; he'd worked with Jerry too long not to know when things weren't right.

Richard unlocked the office door and sat at his desk. He spun his chair around to look out of the large picture window. People were rushing about in the street below, no one had time these days. He considered himself to be one of the lucky ones with a thriving business. Legitimately, the firm exchanged currencies for competitive fees, but the real business was money laundering; cleaning, that was where the real cash could be made. Although the risks they took could have landed them both in prison for a good many years, they made sure they were never greedy, and things seemed to sail along smoothly. Maybe he should have a short day too. He flicked through some papers and answered a couple of calls before locking up for the weekend.

Richard's Mercedes was parked in the underground car park. For a moment he was surprised to see Jerry's car still there; surely he wouldn't still be drinking in the pub.

After an evening watching television with his wife, Richard felt tired.

'I think I'm ready to go up. How about you, Clarissa?'

'I'm going to give Ripley a call, make sure she's okay.'

'Sweetheart, leave the poor girl alone. She'll ring us if there's anything wrong. It's only a sleepover with a bunch of girls.'

Clarissa nodded. Ripley was growing up so fast and she had a nice group of friends. 'Okay.'

An hour later the phone woke them both with a start.

'I told you I should have called her. Answer it, then,' Clarissa said impatiently.

Richard reached across his bedside table and brought the phone to his ear.

'Hello. Oh hello, Tracey.' He paused to listen covering the mouthpiece. 'It's not Ripley,' he whispered. Clarissa fell back on her pillow with a sigh of relief. 'No, sorry, I can't help you. No, everything was fine when I left him. I doubt he'll ring here. Hope you find him. Yes, bye.'

He placed the phone back on its holder. 'Was that Jerry's Tracey?' Clarissa asked.

'Yes. He never went home after work. In fact, he took the afternoon off. I left him half cut in the Dickens.'

Clarissa mumbled and turned over. 'Night then.'

'Hope we can get back off, it's two o'clock. I knew there was something on his mind, dirty sod. Good night.'

On Monday morning, Richard pulled into his parking space and spotted Jerry's car was already there. He was bright and early, very unusual for a Monday. The office door was still locked, dirty bugger must have been at it all weekend. Strange he hadn't collected his car.

Jerry's mobile phone had been switched off all morning and by eleven o'clock, Richard had become concerned. He daren't ring Tracey; he was surprised she hadn't called him again. The phone rang and Richard answered the call from an important client.

'Good morning, Mr Lewis. What can we do for you today? ... Really? It should have gone through on Friday. I'll give the bank a call and see what's going on, it's probably just a computer error. I'll get back to you as soon as possible.' Damn, he couldn't call the bank, he didn't know the passwords, and he didn't know what details they'd want; that was Jerry's department. He'd have to go into the bank to sort it out. Well, at least he could pick up elevenses. He took a brisk walk into the bustling town and waited in the bank queue. After getting no help from the cashier, he was eventually shown into a side office. A dark-suited man sat opposite him, fiddling with the keys on his computer.

'I'm William Trent. Do take a seat. Would you excuse me a moment?' he said as he stood up, and left Richard sitting drumming his fingers on his knees. It was quite a simple request. Why did these places always take so long? Anyway, where the hell was Jerry? It should be him sorting this out. Richard fished in his pocket for his mobile; Jerry's phone was still turned off. He returned the phone to his pocket and resumed drumming his fingers in frustration.

'Sorry to have kept you waiting.'

'That's fine,' Richard said tartly, sweeping back his blond, slightly-too-long hair.

'It seems that the money was transferred to an offshore account on Friday.'

'Offshore? No way!'

'Here's the transfer copy.' He passed a sheet of paper to Richard.

'I don't even know who this is. There's been a mistake.'

'Jerry Mayer made the transfer.'

Richard had begun to perspire under his shirt collar. 'I know he made the transfer, but it's not to the right place.'

'I'm sorry, but there's nothing the bank can do. The money has already gone.'

'It was only done on Friday, there must be some way of stopping it.'

'The transfer was on Tuesday and it completed on Friday.'

'Tuesday! No! It can't have been!' Richard voice was raised and quivering. 'Something's dreadfully wrong here.'

'Could you speak to Mr Mayer? There may well be a simple explanation.' The suited bank employee sat bolt upright and was uncomfortably straight-faced with his spectacles perched on the end of his nose.

Richard stood in a hurry. 'How much is left in the account?'

'One hundred and seventy pounds.'

'Let me see that!' Richard yanked the screen around towards himself. 'How much was the transfer?' He picked up the copy again. 'No! This can't be happening!'

'If there's some discrepancy, I could call the police for you.'

'No, I'll sort it out, there's been a mistake that's all. Didn't anyone wonder why such a large amount was being transferred?'

'No. Large sums regularly go through this account.'

Richard stumbled from the room and headed for the main doors in a daze. What to do? The account had been cleared out; what the hell was going on? Jerry! He had to find Jerry. He walked back to the car park and climbed into his car, looking across at Jerry's car still in the same position. Bastard! Where the hell are you? When I find you, I'll kill you!

He pulled up outside Jerry's semi-detached house. All the window blinds were pulled down. Richard kept his finger on the bell and rapped the knocker loudly with his other hand. He peered through the letterbox.

'I know you're in there. Jerry, get out here now!' There was no response so Richard kicked open the side gate and went down the alley to the back of the house. He rattled the locked kitchen door and then thumped it, almost breaking his wrist. He ran his hand through his hair and took in a deep breath. What now?

He turned to walk away and saw a woman in the adjoining garden staring at him over the bushes.

'Have you seen Jerry today?'

'No, they left on Saturday for a surprise holiday. He hadn't said a word to Tracey. I said I'd look after the dog; it was too late to book him into kennels.'

'Did they say where they were going?'

'It was somewhere exotic...' She looked thoughtful for a moment. 'Fiji, I think.'

'Very exotic!' Richard turned and walked back down the side of the house.

'Who should I say was looking for him?' the woman called out to deaf ears.

Richard sat in his car and thumped the steering wheel. He took off his tie and undid his top shirt button. Cleared out! Fucking bastard! He had to take control and think what he was going to do. He could start again, he started from scratch before and at least there were still a lot of clients who hadn't been affected so they wouldn't know anything had changed. The first thing was to change the bank account.

His head spun as he started the car and pulled out of Jerry's road straight into the path of a lorry. The sound of crumpling metal and the squeal of the lorry's brakes bore into him as he tried in vain to turn the wheel. As the bonnet rose up, bending towards the windscreen, an incredible pain shot through his leg. Everything around him swirled in slow motion as the car came to a halt.

For a moment silence prevailed. Was he dead? He forced his eyes open and saw people standing around and heard them speaking in a robotic fashion as he drifted in and out of consciousness. The lorry loomed over the front of the car like a menacing predator.

Richard heard himself groan as someone tried to move him; in the distance sirens rang out.

'Richard, it's Clarissa. Can you hear me?' She sounded distant and he was too tired to open his eyes. 'Richard, come on, wake up.' The bloody woman wasn't going to shut up. He peered from squinted, slit eyes. 'Oh thank God!

Don't try and move, you've had loads of injuries. Do you remember the accident?'

Another female voice spoke. 'He needs rest. Why don't you go home and have a rest yourself?' The voice was that of an angel.

'Okay. Will you call me if he needs me?'

'Of course.'

'I'm going home, Richard. I'll come back later.' A damp kiss landed on his cheek, before he heard the clicking of heels on a hard floor getting farther away. Richard's hand was lifted into the air and his wrist was held for a moment, then gently lowered back onto the bed.

'Thanks,' he said hoarsely.

'Don't talk. Have a rest now.'

When he managed to open his eyes, the room was in semi-darkness, lit only by a night light. He was alone. Then, as his eyes focused, he noticed Clarissa sat in an armchair in the corner of the room. He closed his eyes and suddenly the horror of the day returned to him. Shit! He was ruined. His head thumped and his body ached. He couldn't remember an accident; that was the least of his worries. He couldn't tell Clarissa what Jerry had done; she had warned him about getting involved with such a bad character. What she didn't realise was that someone *clean* would never pull off their deals and bring in the money to keep her in the style she expected. This was a problem he had to sort out for himself without her knowing. He'd never hear the last of it and he had enough to cope with.

'Oh, you're awake. How are you feeling? The doctor said there shouldn't be any lasting damage. Shall I pour you some water? There's juice if you'd prefer, but it's not very cold. You broke your leg and two ribs, that's why it's best not to move. Broken ribs are so painful. Well, I don't know that myself, but that's what the doctor said. He's a nice young man, seems to know what he's talking about. Oh, and you had concussion.'

'Clarissa, please be quiet.'

'Oh, that's nice. So how are you feeling? I bet your leg hurts.'

His leg didn't hurt, or if it did, he couldn't feel it. He closed his eyes and after trying twice more, Clarissa took the hint and kept her mouth shut. She meant well, but he had far too much on his mind to listen to her babbling on. How much was in his personal account? He hadn't a clue; that account took care of itself with everything on direct debit. There might be enough to last a couple of months until he got back on his feet again. He had to sort out the firm first and get some money turning over. Then he'd hire someone to look for Jerry. Fiji! He should have kept a closer eye on everything, but Jerry had been really clever. He'd managed to build up complete trust and then went in for the kill when the firm was thriving and the bank balance was bursting. Fuck! Part of that money was a payment Steve Lewis was waiting for. It was an extortionate amount of money to find, how the hell would he be able to do that? He closed his eyes as he thought through all the other clients with money in the system. Water filled his eyes. He couldn't do it! It just wasn't possible. No one would touch him now, not once word got around. His heart quickened and his breathing became rapid.

'Are you alright? Shall I get someone?' Clarissa asked.

'No, leave me alone, I'm fine.'

'You don't sound fine. I think I'd better fetch someone to have a look at you.'

'For fuck's sake, leave it!' He lowered his tone, realising he was being unreasonable. 'Sorry, no, I don't need anyone.'

'I know you're in pain, but there's no need to be rude.' He saw her blink away a couple of tears before wiping them with her fingers.

'Sorry. I didn't mean to shout. I need to get out of here.'

'The doctor said...'

'I don't give a shit what the doctor said, I'm out of here in the morning. I've got stuff to sort out.'

'Let Jerry sort it out. It's about time he took some responsibility.'

'Responsibility isn't his strong point. Get some sleep now.' He closed his eyes.

Richard left hospital on crutches the following afternoon, twenty-four hours after the accident. He had been instructed not to put any weight on his broken leg and he had to go for another x-ray in a week's time to confirm if he needed an operation. Great!

'Why do you have to go to the bank? You've only just left the hospital.'

'I know that and I want to go to the bank. Now if you wouldn't mind dropping me off, I can try out my crutches down the high street and then I'll meet you in the car park.'

Clarissa was miffed as she dropped him off. Whatever was the matter with him? He must be suffering to be treating her so badly, but then, he couldn't feel that bad if he was going to the bank. Maybe she'd park the car and have a quick look in the shopping centre; Richard would be ages yet.

An hour later, and armed with several bags, Clarissa made her way back to the car. She could see Richard standing there, leaning against it. She raised one hand to wave, but there was no response. He must still be in a bad mood. She'd rise above it; the shopping therapy had raised her spirits.

Richard scowled as she drew closer. 'What the hell have you bought now?'

'Tut, tut! We're a little out of sorts today. Is everything hurting?'

'No, it's not. You need to stop spending money.'

'What do you mean? You're really touchy today. I know you've had an accident, but...'

'Clarissa, there's no money! Get in the car. Now!'

She threw the bags onto the back seat and did as she was asked, for once not questioning his command.

Richard had had a difficult time at the bank. The business account had quickly gone into overdraft, as he hadn't had the foresight to cancel anything when he was in there the first time. Unfortunately, it was the end of the month, when all the regular debits came out. His personal account was no better with a balance of only a few thousand pounds. Normally, every three months a bonus payment went in and that had been due to be paid the following week.

As they drove home, Richard explained. Clarissa kept shrieking in disbelief and had to be constantly reminded to keep her eyes on the road. This must be the worst day of his life and there was little he could do about it. He dreaded having to go into the office the following day. He'd have to be honest and hope he could keep some of the business going.

The following weeks were filled with attempts to manage the rapidly increasing debts with nothing coming in, and little support from clients, some of whom had worked with his firm for years. They didn't blatantly put him down, and most were quite polite about letting him down gently.

'You're going through a bit of a tough time, of course we'll try to support you. We've only gone with someone else while things look dodgy.'

'Of course we'll come back to you once things are up and running again.'

Why could no one understand that he couldn't up and run again with no one trusting him with their money? Word had got around so fast he hadn't had a chance to drum up any business, before the excuses began. If only he hadn't had the accident. If only Jerry hadn't had full authorisation on the accounts. If only...

He felt the world was closing in around him. Clarissa had all but said *she told him so*, the bank had suggested his best option was to go bankrupt, and he couldn't afford Ripley's school fees. So far Ripley knew nothing of the disaster which was about to tear her world apart. He didn't even have enough money to pay an expensive electricity bill, which until now he'd never even noticed.

One Friday evening, Richard sat staring blankly at the television, totally unaware of what he was watching. The phone rang.

'Phone,' he called out to no one in particular. These days he never answered it. Too many people he owed money to had managed to get his home number. 'Phone.'

'I'm in the bath and Ripley's out,' Clarissa yelled back.

He reluctantly crossed the lavishly furnished lounge and picked up the receiver.

'Hello.'

'Richard, it's May.'

'Hello May, this is a surprise.'

'Yes, well you won't be pleased with what I have to say.'

'That doesn't surprise me.' He hadn't spoken to his sister for twenty years.

'I can't manage this place anymore. Gill died last year and the place is too big for me. You know I'm over sixty and my health isn't what it used to be.'

'I don't know what you expect me to do about it. My business has gone down and we've got no money.'

'I expect you to get down here and look after the place, or it'll fall down to the ground.'

'We could sell it. It's been in our family for generations, but that doesn't mean much these days.' His mind churned over the situation. If they sold the old place, at least he could buy somewhere in Clarissa's name when the bank took his house back. Now might not be a sensible time to be nostalgic. 'I suppose we could sell if that's what you want.'

'No, of course it isn't, but I can't manage any more. The place is falling down around me and I'm not having strangers doing work, not while I'm here alone. Money's no problem, but you need to come and sort it out.'

Same old May. Creating unnecessary problems. 'Look, I'll ring you back later, let me think about the best options.' His mind was a whirl of ideas, but he had to think them through first.

Clarissa appeared in the lounge wrapped in a bath robe, and a white towel around her hair.

'Who was on the phone?'

'May. Says she can't manage the old place anymore. Apparently Gill died last year and now she's struggling.'

'Where's Gill's lad gone then?'

'No idea. I've been thinking.' Richard looked at her with a certain expression on his face she'd seen many times before.

'No, Richard. Don't even consider it as an option.'

'You don't know what I was going to say.'

'I have a pretty good idea. There's no way we could go there and anyway, things have been alright here, we've managed.'

'Clarissa, face facts, things aren't alright. We're going to lose the house, you know that. We could go there on a temporary basis while it's being done up and sold, then at least we'll have some money behind us again.'

'Why do we have to go and stay there while it's being sold?'

'Basically, because we have no money to begin anywhere else. We'd only get a pittance for it at the moment and May won't have any work done while she's there alone, you know what she's like.'

'I'm not happy, Richard.'

'Nor am I! We can't pay next month's school fees; things are going from bad to worse. We have to give it a try. May has all the family money to do the place up, it's our only option.'

'I never really understood how she ended up with control over everything.'

'That's why we fell out. She persuaded mum to sign it over and then stuck her in a home. Anyway, we have the current issue to consider. What do you think?'

'Do we have a choice?'

'No.'

'We'll have to try it then. Ripley won't be happy.'

'She'll be fine. She'll be leaving that school in the summer anyway and going to college or somewhere.'

Ripley returned home from school the following weekend and Richard broke the news.

'We can't leave!' Tears began to trickle down Ripley's flushed cheeks. 'There must be something you can do, Dad.'

Richard's heart ached. 'Your mum and I have worried over this for months now and I'm sorry to say there is nothing else we can do.' Richard looked at his daughter sadly. He hated it when she cried and he'd put this moment off for weeks, knowing the inevitable tears would fall. As he dragged his hand through his thick, wavy hair he tried to think of something which would lighten the moment, but there was nothing forthcoming. No good would come of the present situation.

'You don't even like Aunt May. You haven't spoken for years.'

'Believe me, I don't want to do this either… None of us do.'

'No, we don't! This is a nightmare for all of us, Ripley,' her mother said haughtily. 'Your father's made a few mistakes in his time, but this one tops them all. I told him Jerry wasn't to be trusted. What he's done to us is despicable.'

'That's enough, Clarissa. Ripley doesn't need to hear your bickering about Jerry, not now.'

'When do we have to go?'

'Easter. That'll give us a few weeks to sort things out.'

Ripley nodded. She had to be brave. She could see the hurt in her dad's eyes. Her mother, as usual, blamed him for everything. Dad would never hear the last of them having to move in with Aunt May. Ripley had never met her eccentric aunt and wasn't looking forward to living with her. There had never been anything good said about her. According to her dad, Aunt May had lost her marbles a long time ago. She lived in the family house, on the cliff tops in a place called Crompton, in Kent.

'I'm going upstairs; I have some school work to finish.' She slowly climbed the stairs, went into her room, closed the door and sobbed. Her sheltered, privileged life had fallen apart and the future, for the next few years, looked grim.

Chapter 1

The house where Ripley had grown up had been stripped of all the furniture and now stood bare and empty, awaiting new owners. Ripley's father, as usual, had been shrewd enough to sell before he went bankrupt. Ripley looked back one last time from the window of the car, as they pulled out of the driveway. A lump came to her throat and although the back seat of the car made her travel sick, she was glad her parents couldn't see the tears welling in her eyes.

Her mother sat, stony-faced in the front passenger seat, while her father drove, impatient with every other driver on the road. No one uttered a word for the first hour.

'I'm starving. How about stopping for a bite? There's a service station at the next turn-off,' Richard said, breaking the silence.

'I could do with a coffee,' Clarissa answered. 'How about you, Ripley?'

'I wouldn't mind a smoothie.'

'Not sure if smoothies will have reached Crompton yet. You'd better make the most of the modern world while you still can,' Richard chortled.

'Don't wind her up. Of course they'll have smoothies there, take no notice of him,' Clarissa said as she shot her husband a look of disapproval.

The removal lorry had arrived in Crompton on schedule, ahead of them, and the family could quite clearly see the men sitting in the cab as they pulled into the driveway.

'They can't have unloaded already, surely,' Richard said, climbing out of his car. The man in charge jumped down from the cab of the lorry and walked towards him.

'The lady of the house won't let us in. We've been here hours.'

'Oh no! I'm sorry about that. I'll go and have a word.' Richard walked along the gravel path leading in between two cobbled stone walls, up to the large, old door, and pulled the handle. The bell could be heard clanging away inside. Did May really have to be cantankerous this early on in the move?

A shrill, irritated voice came from within the house. 'I've told you. My brother is on his way and he won't be pleased to find you here. Now go away before I call the police.'

'May, it's Richard. Open the door. The men are the removers.'

Ripley stood at the side of the car stretching her arms out. The house was old and quite daunting, with large, dark, dirty windows and 'Cliff Top Manor' inscribed above the door on a wooden frame. The rickety roof tiles had several patches where they'd been replaced and a chimney had smoke billowing out and hovering above the building. Ripley counted seven upstairs windows, including two in an annex which stood out at one end. Downstairs were three larger wooden-framed windows in dire need of a coat of paint. A statue of a man stood tall and proud in the shade of a large oak tree. The manor looked mysterious and Ripley couldn't wait to get inside. She wouldn't have been surprised if a bent-over butler with a walking stick opened the door. Instead, a thin woman with her white hair parted in the middle and curled at the ends stood before Ripley's father. There was nothing to indicate they were related, much less brother and sister.

'These men have been trying to break in all afternoon.' She held her walking stick in the air and waved it at the removal men.

'They aren't breaking in, they are delivering our furniture,' Richard said.

'Furniture. There isn't any room for furniture. It's all full up now. Who are they?' she said, motioning her stick towards Ripley and her mother.

'Come on you two. Come and meet May. This is my wife Clarissa and this is our daughter Ripley.'

'Ripley! What sort of name is that?'

Ripley studied the woman's face. There were quite a few wrinkles and not a spark of life in her dull, green eyes. 'I'm pleased to meet you, Aunt May. I've heard a lot about you.'

'All bad, I expect. This one wouldn't have a good word to say about me,' May said, nodding towards Richard.

Clarissa cleared her throat. 'Richard, are you going to get the men started? They'll be here half the night at this rate.'

Ripley liked her aunt's openness, but she could see the disapproval in her mother's face already. There could be a lot of entertainment in this old house, which was to be home for the foreseeable future.

May turned, walked into the house, and Ripley followed, leaving her parents outside to talk to the removal men.

The house resembled something from the old films. A spiral staircase with hefty wooden bannisters wound its way around to the upper floor. Ripley stood in the entrance area which had several big wooden doors leading off, a couple of portraits and a tapestry.

May looked Ripley up and down. 'You've got the lovely dark hair my mother had, and her green eyes. You can show yourself around. I only use the blue sitting room and the kitchen.' May looked past Ripley as the men started bringing in the furniture. 'I don't know why your father brought all that stuff with him, there's no room.' She shook her head. 'I'm going to sit down.'

Ripley watched as the woman slowly made her way down a short passageway, muttering away to herself before finally disappearing into a room and slamming the door behind her. There was silence apart from the sound of men talking amongst themselves as they lifted the furniture up the stairs under the supervision of her father.

Ripley opened the door closest to her. It was heavy and squeaked with age as it swung slowly back on its hinges. The shutters on the windows were closed so Ripley could barely see anything apart from the light the doorway allowed. She fumbled around and found a light switch.

When the light came on, Ripley gasped at the sight before her. It was a library, fitted with shelving from the floor to the ceiling, each shelf crammed with books. She walked in and began scanning the titles. There were some first editions and leather-bound sets all in mint condition. The familiar names of famous authors, mostly deceased, stared out from the shelves.

Intrigued, she walked across the hallway and opened another door leading into room, double the size of the library, its contents covered by white sheets. She pulled back one of the corners and saw a luxurious leather sofa. The cover fell back into place as she raised her hand over her mouth in shock. Her eyes had fallen on a dark wooden coffin in the corner of the room.

'There you are.'

Ripley let out a piercing scream and then calmed herself. 'Oh Dad, you made me jump. Look over there. A coffin.'

'That'll be empty and waiting for May. It's a bit of family tradition to have a coffin made in advance. Don't ask me why. I remember my grandparents having theirs ready and waiting in the barn.'

'That's awful. Would you just check it is empty? I won't be able to sleep if I'm not sure.'

Her dad walked across and tugged on the lid. 'Oh no! May must be keeping this corpse for some reason.'

Ripley raced from the room and almost knocked May over.

'What's all the noise? I hope you're not one of those loud young ladies, it's not befitting.'

'No, sorry. It's a coffin in there which startled me.'

'Richard, you can keep your hands off, that one's mine. Get your own made.'

'I'll find a safe place in the shed for it tomorrow.'

'You'll do no such thing. All those creepy crawlies, you don't know what'll get in there.'

'I don't think you'll know much about it by the time you're in there.' He laughed.

'Richard, don't be facetious. That has sat there for years and it's not going anywhere now you're here. It was bad enough when our poor mother died having to listen to your whining and whinging on about everything.' She turned and stomped her way down the hall back past Ripley, as though the girl was invisible.

'What happened when your mum died?' Ripley whispered, looking to make sure May had gone out of earshot.

'That was why we fell out. First she put mum into a home without consulting me. She said I wasn't around to help look after her, so therefore it wasn't my decision to make, and secondly, she made sure mum left everything in her name and nothing in mine.'

'Why would she do that?'

'I could never understand why mum would have done that, but May ended up with power of attorney and could do what she wanted. As it happens, it's worked out in my favour, because when I declare bankruptcy, they can't touch the house or the inheritance.'

'But why would she have put Gran in a home?'

'May called it dementia, but I knew there was nothing wrong with mum. As it happens, she died a month later. Of course I went ballistic and blamed May. That was the last time we spoke. Still, that's all a long time ago and now we all have to try and get along under the same roof.'

Ripley smiled. 'That might be easier said than done. She's a bit cantankerous, isn't she?'

'She's set in her ways and unfortunately she expects everyone around her to conform. We'll stick together and have some fun. Give me five.' He brought the palm of his hand up in front of Ripley. She slapped her own palm on it and they laughed. 'Come on, I'll show you your new room. It's the one I had as a child.'

The stairs creaked as they climbed upwards. The removal men passed on their way down.

'Any chance of a cuppa?'

'Sorry, I should have offered. I'll sort it out in a moment,' Richard said. They were now walking along a dimly lit corridor. 'Here we are. Now don't be expecting too much. It'll be alright when it's done up a bit.' He opened the door. Two small leaded windows looked out to the back of the house. Ripley could see two horses with their heads over the stable door peering out. There was a clump of trees to the left behind the stables, and to the right a barn. Through the middle she could see a glimpse of the sea.

'Oh Dad, it's perfect. I don't care about the room, the views make up for everything.' As she spoke she glanced around the dusty bedroom. A single bed stood in a corner facing one of the windows and there was a matching wardrobe and chest of drawers.

'We'll get this old furniture moved out, you'll feel better once you've got your own stuff.'

Ripley walked over to the wardrobe and opened a door. She spluttered as dust cascaded around her. There were a multitude of old spiders in the corners and it smelled musty.

'Yes, I think my own furniture would be better. Will we have to fight Aunt May before we can shift this stuff though?'

'Probably. That'll be half the fun. What say you, shall we have a little wager on who wins?'

'Dad, that's terrible... I back May.'

'That isn't loyal of you. I wanted to go for her too!' They were still laughing as they went back downstairs.

'I'm glad you two are finding something to laugh about. Have you seen the kitchen?' Clarissa whined.

'Can't say I have for about twenty-two years. It can't be that bad, my mum turned out wonderful meals.' Richard dutifully followed his wife down the passage to the rear of the house.

A door opened and May stuck her head out. 'Oh, it's you dear. Ritly, come in here and let me see you properly, you do so remind me of Mother.'

Ripley dutifully followed May and found herself in a sitting room with blue velvet curtains hanging at the edge of a large picture window.

'What a lovely view of the garden from this room,' Ripley said as she went to have a better look. Dusk was falling and the shadows of the trees made a spectacular sight.

'That's why I choose this room in which to spend most of my time. Your father never had any time for views and he had the best view from his bedroom. I pleaded with him to swap, but he wouldn't. He wouldn't have given me anything, even if he didn't like it himself.'

'I've got that room now and I love it.'

'I told him you should have it. I'm used to where I am now, far too old to change. But for you, Ritly it's perfect.'

'My name's Ripley.'

'Oh, I see. Strange name. Do you like it?'

'I suppose I'm used to it. A lot of my school friends liked it. Well, at least all the ones with boring names did. Aunt May, would it be alright if I had my old bedroom furniture in my bedroom?'

'Of course, you must. It'll make it feel more like home for you. I'll tell those men to get it done straight away.'

Ripley smiled to herself as May left the room. That had gone well, much better than she'd thought it would. May re-entered the room.

'Tried to tell me they wouldn't have time. I told them, if they hadn't spent so long sitting around in their lorry they'd have finished by now.'

Was she being serious? 'Thank you for trying. Maybe Dad can do it tomorrow.'

'Oh no, they're doing it. I told them I want it done or there'll be no more tea.'

'Did they have tea? Dad told them he'd make one, but he might have forgotten.'

'Oh well, we should go and put on the kettle.'

The sound of raised voices came from the kitchen.

'I can't live here Richard, it's unreasonable to make me. The kitchen's filthy and there are no cupboards, just an old pantry full of God only knows what. The whole lot needs throwing out, we'll all go down with food poisoning. And as for your sister, she's rude and arrogant.'

'Oh my dear,' May said, as she walked into the kitchen, sounding totally in control, 'by the time you've been here a while you'll come up with many more words to describe me, but at the moment they'll do. The pantry houses all the basic ingredients needed for good healthy meals. You will not throw anything away while I am alive. Ritly dear, would you put the kettle on the stove?'

Clarissa watched as May left the room. 'You never said a word, Richard. The least you could have done was stuck up for me.'

'Clarissa, you need to stick up for yourself, I'll have enough of my own arguments to sort out with her.'

'She's alright, actually,' Ripley said. 'She's organised for the removal men to put my furniture in my bedroom.'

Her parents stared at her for a moment. Richard raised his eyebrows. 'That's it then. Anything we want, we send Ripley in!' he said gleefully.

Tears fell down Clarissa's cheeks faster than she could brush them aside. 'I don't know how you can be so jovial; this is a nightmare.'

'Come on, don't cry. We'll get it all sorted out. We need to think of it as an adventure into the unknown,' Richard said as he put his arm around her shoulder.

'I hate it. The house is creepy as well as dirty and I'm sure I saw a mouse run under the pantry door.'

'We can sort out a new kitchen in no time. Don't forget, money is no problem here, it's all in the trust for maintenance. Anything you want we can have. Ripley, would you come and help me upstairs for a minute? Clarissa, I promised the men some tea. Could you do the honours?'

'So I'm a char woman now.'

Richard ignored her and went back upstairs with Ripley. He led her into a large double bedroom at the front of the house. 'This is our room. We need to get all this old stuff out of here quick before your mum ventures up the stairs and puts her oar in. Grab the end of this.' Together they carried most of the furniture down the landing to another smaller room. 'I'll get the men to help with the heavy stuff, thanks love.'

'It's not that bad here. Mum just takes a bit of time to get used to new ideas,' Ripley said.

'I know, but to be honest, I think it'll take years for her to get used to this. I've let you all down.'

'No you haven't. None of what's happened is your fault and we all have to get used to it.'

'You're a good kid, Ripley. I'm so lucky to have you. Come here.' Ripley walked into his arms for one of his famous bear hugs. 'I love you.'

'I love you too, Dad.'

'Come on, I'll show you the stables and some of the gardens.'

The view from Ripley's bedroom window did not compare with the enormity and beauty of the place once she stepped outside. Flower beds and bushes were randomly placed, adding colour and depth. There was a fenced paddock and tall trees lined a pathway.

'What's down there?'

'It leads to the beach. It's getting a bit late now, but I'll take you down there in the morning. Are you getting hungry? We could drive into Crompton and see what's on offer these days.'

'Sounds good to me. Do you think Aunt May will want to come?'

'I doubt it, but you could ask her; we have to be seen to be making an effort.'

As they went back up towards the house a young man was walking towards them. He had brown tousled hair and dark, lively eyes.

'Good evening, and who might you be?' Richard asked.

'Good evening, I'm Joe, pleased to meet you. I'm Gill's son. I stayed on at the cottage to help Mrs Bradford when my mum died.'

Richard cleared his throat. 'Very decent of you. Thank you. I thought the grounds were looking in good shape. I thought May might have had someone from the village up to help her when your mum passed away. Sorry about that.'

'Thanks. No, she won't let anyone up here.' He looked at Ripley and smiled.

'I'm Ripley. Do you look after the horses?'

'Come on Ripley, we'd better be getting down into town for some dinner, times getting on.' Her dad sounded impatient.

'Oh, okay. Nice to have met you, Joe.' She felt a small flutter pass through her.

'And you. Bye.'

'I'll go and find your mum,' Richard said. 'You ask May if she's coming.'

Ripley and her mum sat in the back of the car on the way to the town. Apparently, May had to sit in the front, as the back seat made her queasy. Clarissa sat with her lips pursed, looking out of the side window.

'It's quite a way from the town then, too far to walk,' Ripley said, trying to lighten the atmosphere.

'Joe used to cycle everywhere when he was young. You'll need a bike, Ritly,' May said.

'Her name is Ripley,' Clarissa spat. 'Ripley!'

'Here we are, beautiful Crompton,' Richard said, brightly. 'I'll park in the car park and we can walk to find somewhere to eat.'

'I only want something small,' May piped up.

'You can have whatever you want,' Richard answered amicably. Clarissa muttered something under her breath.

'I'm starving,' Ripley said.

They walked along a narrow street, only just wide enough for two cars. There were two pubs on the corner of another street. 'Come on, I'll show you the seafront, it runs adjacent to this road.'

'I thought we were coming out to eat,' May moaned, following the small group.

They turned up a steep path and were soon looking down onto the sands. A harbour nestled in the curve of the pier with small boats bobbing up and down with the waves.

'Oh wow! This is beautiful,' Ripley said. 'Oh look. There's a black horse paddling.'

'That's Joe, on Filou. He brings one or the other down here most evenings, weather permitting of course,' May said, standing still to watch him. They all stood taking in the scene.

'I like it here,' Ripley said. 'I really like it here.'

'Good job. We're here for the foreseeable future,' Richard said. 'It's not a bad little place.'

'Little place is about right. There's nothing here,' Clarissa hissed.

'I've never lived anywhere else; I wouldn't want to. Life is what you make it. We could all spend our lives moaning,' May said, trying to sound diplomatic for once. Richard and Ripley raised their eyebrows at each other.

'Come on then, let's find somewhere to eat,' Richard said as he walked on along the seafront. At least Ripley was happy, she had been his biggest concern; the rest of them could get on with it.

Chapter 2

During the night, shadows flickered and bounced around the bedroom walls, floorboards creaked and there was a scratching sound coming from the corner of Ripley's room. A couple of times she was sure she heard voices she didn't recognise. Daybreak brought a welcome relief. Ripley threw back her quilt and pulled her dressing gown out from her suitcase. She went to the window and looked around the gardens. Her eyes fell on Joe, undoing the stable door. His hand went up to the horse's mouth with what looked like a treat of some kind. He disappeared inside the stable out of sight for a few minutes and then reappeared leading the white horse out to the paddock. He returned a few minutes later and gave Filou a treat before leading him into the paddock. He patted Filou's head and closed the paddock gate before disappearing between the trees. Ripley went downstairs and found her aunt already in the kitchen with the kettle on the agar slowly whistling.

'Good morning, Ritly. Another early riser like me. Did you sleep well?'

'Good morning. No, there were a few creaks and strange noises. I'm sure I heard a man's voice. I think I was awake all night.'

'That would have been the Major you heard. He comes most nights. You've got the gift.'

'What do you mean? What gift?'

'I'm the only one who's ever been able to hear the Major. No one else has ever seen or heard him, but now there's you. It's a gift and not everyone has it.'

'Who is the Major?'

'Major Hanks. His family owned this house before our family. There were no heirs, so when he died it was sold to your great great-grandfather. The Major often visits, always in the still of the night. He's a wise man, you should always take notice of what he tells you.'

Ripley looked at her aunt. Did she seriously believe that some man was coming to her room and talking to her at night? There had been strange voices; maybe she'd fallen asleep and dreamt them. 'Shall I make some tea?' It seemed her aunt was oblivious to the continuous whistle of the boiling kettle.

'Thank you, dear. I suppose you think I'm a mad old woman talking about ghosts. They've all thought that over the years, but you'll see. They don't have the gift, so they never saw or heard a thing.'

Ripley concentrated on making the tea. She wasn't sure she wanted to be gifted. A strange man appearing in her room at night would frighten the life out of her.

'I saw Joe putting the horses out to graze this morning, he's up early.'

'Yes. He has to be at the hotel by six-thirty to do breakfast. He works hard, that lad, always has. Terrible shock for him, finding his mum like that. Heart attack, they said, and she was gone. She used to help out in the house and kept the flower beds looking good. Joe took over all of the gardens when she went.'

'Do you ever ride the horses?'

'Not any more. I go and see them every day and have a little chat. Do you ride?'

'No, I sat on a donkey on the beach once, but dad had to get me back down because I screamed every time it moved.'

'Oh dear. I'm sure Joe will teach you, if you're interested. You make a good cup of tea, Ritly. Pop some bread under the grill if you're hungry, I'm going up to get dressed before the mob come down.'

Ripley watched her aunt leave the room. Was she an eccentric old lady on the way to losing the plot, or was the house haunted? Either way the prospects weren't good.

She made herself some toast and found some jam in the pantry. Hopefully her mum would have slept well and be in a better frame of mind this morning. She heard someone on the stairs; the creaking was going to become a familiar sound.

'Morning Dad.'

'Good morning, how are you?'

'Tired. There's a lot of strange noises at night.'

Richard nodded. 'One of the joys of these old houses.'

'And I heard a man's voice.'

Richard raised his eyebrows. 'Oh Ripley, you're beginning to sound like May already. She always used to hear voices.'

Ripley laughed. 'She still does. Haven't you ever heard them?'

'No! Any water in that kettle?' He lifted it for a moment before placing it on the heat. 'Your mum wants me to take her to look for kitchen units this morning. You can come with us, or stay here, up to you.'

Ripley smiled. 'I'll stay here and explore the grounds. I haven't seen half the rooms yet either.'

'Okay. Do you want to come into town for breakfast before we go?'

'No, I've had toast. Do you really think this place is haunted?'

Richard shook his head and frowned. 'No, I don't, and please don't say any of that sort of stuff in front of your mother. It might tip her over the edge.'

'Oh. No better this morning, then?'

'Worse. She said she slept okay and woke up in a nightmare.' Ripley smiled knowingly at him and went off to get dressed.

A while later, Ripley unbolted the door and walked out into the gardens. The grounds were vast and there were no neighbours as far as she could see. Filou put his head over the fence as she passed by, and she patted his nose while keeping a careful eye on his mouth.

'Sorry, I haven't got a treat for you. Maybe later.' She followed the path alongside the trees and ended up on quite a steep slope. She took a deep breath. She could smell the sea. After a while the path opened out onto a golden beach with lots of large rocks.

Ripley sat down on the cold sand, took off her shoes and tucked her socks into them. She rock-hopped towards the sea which was lapping gently against on the shoreline. Her toes touched the water and she leapt back in surprise, falling onto her bottom. The sea was freezing and now her bum hurt. She pulled herself up and pushed her foot forwards to test the sea again. It was no better the second time; it was only Easter, but the sunny morning had given her a false sense of summer and warmth.

She continued along the water's edge, taking care not to get too close. There was a bend up ahead; she was intrigued to find out what was around the corner. The bend turned out to be farther away than she had thought. She walked on and on, oblivious to the time.

Only a few more yards and she would probably be at the nice little beach and harbour they'd seen the previous evening. She began to turn the corner only to find it was a large bend spreading out around the cliff face. It couldn't be much further to the beach in the town. If she could ride it would be lovely to bring one of the horses along here.

At last she rounded the curve, only to see another expanse of beach, and rocks spreading out as far as she could see. Feeling tired, she turned and made her way back along the beach. After what seemed forever, it suddenly dawned on her that she had no idea where the path was which led up to the house. She kept walking. Eventually she decided she must have missed it and turned back to walk in the opposite direction.

She was lost. She must have turned back too soon. She turned again. Her feet were getting sore and her legs were aching. She walked on, searching the cliff for a pathway to the top.

Thank God! There it was, her shoes neatly waiting for her. She breathed a sigh of relief and sat down to put them on. Her tiredness had lifted with the relief of finding her way back at last. The trees swayed above her head as she re-entered the gardens. There were a few buildings over to the left she hadn't spotted before. They looked like sheds of some description. As she walked towards them a huge turkey raced across the yard towards her. She turned, let out a scream and ran for her life. She heard a shout and turned to see Joe in hot pursuit of her assailant.

'Get on the floor,' he yelled. Ripley lay down on the ground as fast as she could. The turkey ran past.

'It throws him when you get down. I found out when I fell one day.' He held out his hand and pulled Ripley to her feet.

'I thought he was going to kill me. He's pretty big.'

'He'll be okay once he knows who you are. We don't get many visitors here.' A nearby dog had slept through the commotion, but now stretched its legs and stood up yawning.

'There are lots of animals.'

'Come on, I'll show you around. There are two horses, two dogs, three cats, four chickens and two geese. Oh, and one turkey.' He had a grin which lit up his whole face.

'Quite a menagerie. I didn't know my aunt liked animals. She's opposite to my dad; I've never been allowed to keep a pet.'

'She said they had nothing in common, her and your dad. May calls him a townie. She's a good woman, always been kind to me, and to my mum when she was here.'

They reached the stables. 'Meet Filou,' Joe said. 'Give him a stroke if you like. Oh, and he likes people who carry sugar lumps in their pockets.'

Ripley liked Joe's smile.

They walked on and were now at the chicken coop. It opened out into a run and the chickens were all busy, pecking away at the seed and vegetable cuttings scattered over the ground.

'I like my aunt, we seem to get along okay so far. She says the house is haunted. Where's the other chicken?' Ripley asked.

'Probably laying an egg in the hen house.' He bent down. 'Yes, look, bend down and you can see her. Any minute now she'll start cackling.'

Ripley bent down to take a look.

'You're right. May knows the house is haunted; she's forever talking about the Major. Rex, the dog you haven't seen yet, was off his food and she made me take him to the vet because the Major had told her he was ill. I argued that he'd only been off his food for one meal, but she insisted. The vet said he had an infection in his stomach, gave him antibiotics and he was back to normal by the following day.'

'It could have been a coincidence.'

'Yes it could, but there's been a few things like that. He told May my mum should go for a check-up and she refused. May went mad and the next day mum died. It was a bit weird, no way was that coincidence.'

'So you believe in the ghost then?'

'I have to. What he's told May has been more than coincidence over the years. Here's Rex. Come on boy, what have I got for you?' The cats were sleeping in the sun and the geese honked in the distance. The chicken let out several clucks. 'You can go in and collect the eggs if you're going back to the house. Only if you want to.'

'Yes, I want to do everything,' Ripley said. 'I love it here already. There's no comparison to living in a town.'

'I wouldn't know, I was born here.'

Ripley went into the hen house and collected four eggs. 'I'll take these back and maybe see you later.'

'I'll be around. See you.'

Ripley found her aunt snoozing in an armchair by the fire in the sitting room. She quietly turned to creep away.

'I'm not sleeping, only resting my eyes. Come in. Have you had a nice time?'

'The best day ever, apart from getting lost on the beach and a turkey trying to catch me.'

May laughed. 'You're getting into country life then? How does it suit you so far?'

'I love it. You've sort of got a farm by the sea, it's beautiful.'

'I'm so glad you're happy. Your dad never appreciated the beauty of the place. Our mum always said if he had any say in it, he'd knock it down and build a block of flats. That's why she left me in charge of the finances, and the property. Your dad accused me of manipulating her, but that was ridiculous. She'd signed it over to me years before she lost her marbles. I had to send her to that home, she needed proper nursing. You know, she used to store all the rubbish, refused to throw anything away. The whole house began to stink where she hid food and all sorts… The dog mess was the final straw, but I won't bore you with that. Do you fancy a cup of tea? Your mum and dad have been gone a long time.'

Ripley and May chatted while they drank their tea in the kitchen. 'That's the front door. They're back, I wonder what delights they've bought. I suppose your mum has to have her home comforts.'

Richard and Clarissa came through to the kitchen. 'There's nothing decent around here, we had to go all the way to Canterbury,' Clarissa said wearily.

'Did you find anything?' Ripley asked.

'Yes, but they can't fit it until next week, so until then, we'll have to manage as best we can.'

'I've managed for nearly sixty years, I'm sure you'll cope.' Clarissa raised her eyebrows. 'I don't want to cope, I want a decent kitchen.'

May raised her eyebrows and put on a false smile. 'I'll reheat the kettle, if that's good enough for you.'

Clarissa let out a huff and left the room.

'She needs some time to adjust. She'll be okay,' Richard said, sounding uncertain of his own words. 'So, how's your day been Ripley?'

'Brilliant. I found the beach, got chased by a turkey...'

'A turkey! Why the hell have you got a turkey, May?'

'He's a pet.'

Ripley carried on after hearing the defensive tone of May's voice.

'I collected the eggs from the hen house, stroked a couple of dogs and patted a horse. My day was wonderful.'

'At least one of us is happy then. Shall we get a take-away tonight? We'll try and get organised with some proper shopping tomorrow, mind you, I can't see your mum cooking until she gets her new kitchen,' Richard said somewhat apprehensively.

'I can cook. I have some pork chops in the fridge and plenty of potatoes. Ritly, would you go to the veg garden and pick whatever you all like?' May asked.

'May! Her name is Ripley,' Richard said.

'You'll have to give me directions. I didn't see a vegetable garden today,' Ripley said. She didn't hold out much hope of her aunt ever breaking the habit of calling her Ritly, but she didn't mind as much as her parents did.

That evening they sat around the large dining table with seating for ten people. May had shown Ripley how to place the cutlery and glasses, making sure it was polished to a shine.

Ripley's long walk along the beach had given her a hearty appetite. Richard emptied his plate as though he hadn't eaten for a week, but Clarissa pushed her food around eating practically nothing, then made her excuses and went upstairs to have an early night.

Ripley helped May clear the table. She ran the water to wash up while May dried and put the crockery away.

'The Major says your mum will have trouble settling down here. He's usually right about such things.' Neither of them had noticed Richard enter the kitchen.

'Don't fill her head with your crap, May! You can make up what you want, but don't put that sort of rubbish into Ripley's head.'

'It's not rubbish and I don't make it up. Ritly already knows that.'

'Just leave her alone, do you hear me?'

'You can't stop me talking to the girl, not while she's in my house.'

'*Your* house! This isn't your damn house; it belongs to both of us.'

'Yes, through my goodwill, but if you care to look at the paperwork, Mother left it to me.'

'Only when you stuck her in a home and manipulated her!'

'The Major said there'd be trouble letting you come back here.'

'Shut up, May! Ripley, leave that and go to your room, please.'

Ripley could hear the raised voices for at least an hour after she went upstairs. She sat looking out of the window, watching the branches of the trees gently swaying in the breeze. Tomorrow she would walk along the beach in the opposite direction but be more careful to note her surroundings.

Would she hear the voices again tonight? Joe believed in the Major. Would Ripley soon be convinced of the truth, or would a part of her always doubt an eccentric woman with good perception? There were no such things as ghosts. Tonight she would try to pay more attention if she heard the man's voice again. There had to be some other explanation.

Chapter 3

The rain tapped rhythmically against the window pane. Ripley kept her eyes shut for a few minutes listening to the sound. The room felt cool as she threw back the quilt, sat on the edge of the bed and stretched out her arms. She pulled on her dressing gown and drew the belt snugly around her waist before padding across to the window. This morning the horses were still stabled, but she could see a golden Labrador leaping through the puddles after Joe, who was walking away from the house towards his cottage. She lifted the latch on the door and made her way along the landing to the bathroom before going down to the kitchen.

'Good morning, dear. How are you this morning?' May asked.

'I don't remember falling asleep. The first thing I heard was the rain hitting the glass this morning.'

'It began around midnight and hasn't given up since. What are you doing today?'

'I was going to explore the other end of the beach, but now it's raining I don't know.'

'You can't let a few drops of rain stop you. As long as you're dressed right, the rain's a wonderful asset to any exploration. The Major says this'll be in for the next couple of days. Oh, we'd better make sure no one hears us talking about the Major. Your dad got quite upset last night. Poor love, he hasn't got our gift, and he's missed out all these years.'

'Shall I make some tea?'

'Yes dear. I'll go and get dressed.' Ripley watched as her aunt tottered out of the room in her fleece dressing gown with a full-length, flowered nightdress flapping around her heels. Ripley shook her head thoughtfully. *The Major says it'll rain for a couple of days.* She should start a diary and see how much of what he predicts actually comes true. She couldn't blame her father for thinking it was nonsense, but May was harmless and if visits from the Major kept her happy, so what? Ripley filled the teapot and gave it a stir, as May had instructed her the previous day. She felt intrigued by the way May still lived in a world which had changed without her; she was so different from her brother.

After toast for breakfast Ripley searched through the bags which were still packed in the bottom of her wardrobe. At last, she found the yellow Wellington boots in the last bag but one, along with a raincoat. She tied up her hair in a ponytail, dressed in warm clothing and made her way back downstairs.

'Where are you off to dressed like that?' Clarissa asked as she came down the staircase.

'Down to the beach.'

'Don't be ridiculous, you'll catch your death of cold in this rain.'

'I've got warm clothes on. I'll be fine.'

'I bet May put these stupid ideas into your head. People who live out in the sticks like this have no idea about looking after themselves.'

'I'll see you later, Mum.'

'Richard, tell her, will you? Look at her going out to the beach in this weather.'

'She looks pretty much dressed for it, if you ask me,' Richard said, coming down the stairs behind his wife.

'You never would have let her out in weather like this before we moved to this hell-hole.'

'Clarissa, chill out, will you? People walk along the beach in all sorts of weather.'

Clarissa stomped off in the direction of the kitchen, muttering to herself about living in the dark ages.

'Have a good time, love. See you later, and for God's sake don't come back with a chill, we'd never hear the last of it.'

Ripley smiled. 'See you later.'

By the time she reached the bottom of the slope, Ripley realised she was going to be too hot with her scarf around her neck. She removed it and tied it around the fence post. Today she would have no trouble finding the path back to the house.

She walked briskly, hopping over rock pools, aiming for the sand in between the rocks. The cliff face was edging further towards the sea, maybe at some point the two would meet and the beach walk would end. She looked up at the white, chalky cliffs and spotted a cave. It didn't look like a difficult climb, there were only a few rocks to get over. She'd never seen a cave before.

The rocks were trickier than she'd thought, but finally, after a lot of slipping and sliding on the wet surface, she made it into the cave opening. It was pitch black inside and she could only see a few feet in front of her. The floor was uneven so she edged herself along the wall for some stability. She sneezed and had to duck as several birds took off, only a few feet above her head. Ripley was suddenly frightened and turned around to leave the cave and return to the relative safety down on the beach. Next time she'd bring a torch.

As she reached the cave opening, she saw to her horror that the waves were now covering the rocks she'd only just climbed. The rain was harder than it had been and blew into the cave entrance with a vengeance. She stood back and tried to keep herself calm. Would the sea come straight into the cave? Should she make a dash for it and hope for the best? Tears of fear ran down her cheeks; she felt herself tremble. She bent down to the floor of the cave beyond where the rain was falling. It was dry. At least that meant the sea didn't rise into the cave, so she was safe. Unless it had dried out since the last high tide.

She looked down once again to the sea below and wondered if she should try to escape while she had a chance. The waves seemed to be higher and more ferocious than before. She couldn't risk it. She'd have to sit tight and hope for the best. She had no other choice.

Back at the house, Clarissa had decided that they needed to shop for proper food. Richard downed the last of his coffee and they headed out to the car. The next town, Whiteleaf, had a Waitrose supermarket and Clarissa insisted nowhere else would do. Richard obligingly started the car and headed for Whiteleaf. They found Waitrose situated at the far end of the town.

'Let's have a quick look around the town while we're here. At least it'll keep us away from your sister a bit longer,' Clarissa suggested.

'I bet they've got a coffee shop which sells croissants for breakfast,' Richard answered, suddenly happy about looking around the town.

May sat in her favourite armchair reading the newspaper. Her head kept nodding forwards as she tried to keep her eyes open. She was fighting a losing battle and dozed off to sleep, snoring gently.

At two o'clock, Richard and Clarissa returned home. For once Clarissa was in high spirits after spending more than she should, and they were laughing.

May awoke with a start. How long had she been asleep? She glanced up at the clock. Lunchtime had passed already. How did that happen? She heaved herself out of the chair and then, hearing her brother in the kitchen talking to his wife, she sat herself back down and resumed reading the newspaper.

'Ripley, have you had lunch?' Clarissa called up the stairs. 'Ripley?' Receiving no reply she climbed the stairs. Ripley's room was empty. 'Richard, is Ripley down there?'

'May, have you seen Ripley?'

'No Richard, not since she left for the beach this morning,' May called back from her sitting room.

'Clarissa, are her boots and coat in the bedroom?' he called back up the stairs.

'No.'

Richard left the bag he'd been unpacking. 'Okay. No need to panic. I'm going to look for her.'

'She can't still be out on the beach, she left hours ago. Where would she have gone?'

'Clarissa, calm down. I'm going to find her.'

Clarissa heard the door slam as she raced down the stairs. 'Richard, I'm coming with you. Shouldn't we call the police?'

'Shall I put the kettle on?' May asked, coming into the hallway.

'Do what you want. She should never have gone out in this terrible weather. I'm going to help Richard.'

Clarissa hurried down the front steps and crossed the driveway aggrieved she couldn't see Richard anywhere.

'Richard! Where are you?'

'I saw him going down towards the beach,' Joe said, walking towards Clarissa pushing a wheelbarrow. 'Are you alright?'

'No. Ripley's been gone for hours. She only went for a walk on the beach. We need to find her, anything could have happened.'

Joe rested the barrow onto the ground. 'Okay, I'll help.' They reached the end of the path and saw the scarf wrapped around the post. 'Look, it'd probably be quicker if we split up. You go that way and I'll go this,' Joe said.

'Okay.' Clarissa began walking along the rocky beach. Why ever Ripley wanted to spend her time down here was a mystery. She drew Ripley's scarf around her head and battled the wind and rain in her face as she made her way cautiously between the rocks.

'Ripley! Ripley!' she yelled at short intervals. How she hated this place. They never should have come here.

Richard had headed off in the same direction as Clarissa, but was a good way ahead of her. There were a couple of dog walkers he spoke to who hadn't seen anyone matching Ripley's description. *Bloody hell Ripley, where are you?*

After walking for what seemed like miles, Richard turned back. They'd have to call the police if she wasn't home. Why had he let her go alone? He'd grown up in this area and it held no dangers, but to a town girl like Ripley? She wouldn't have gone in the sea. He shook his head, pulled his collar up around his neck and made his way back along the beach to the house.

'Clarissa, what are you doing out here? Is she back?'

'No she's not and I'm looking for her the same as you are. If anything's happened to her Richard...'

'Come on, don't get upset. We'll get back to the house and find her sitting with May drinking tea.' He wished he felt as confident as he sounded. 'Here, take my jacket, you're soaking.' He wrapped his jacket around her shoulders and linked her arm through his. They made their way back to the house trying to shield their faces from the wind and steady rain.

Joe made his way along the beach. He should have told Clarissa to call the lifeguard. If Ripley had walked in this direction she could easily have been cut off by the incoming tide. That was the trouble with townies, they were never aware of the dangers around these parts. The rain was heavy and the wind had picked up. He kept his face down as he trudged along. He could see the end of the beach had been covered by the sea. All he could do was call her name, at least the cliffs would echo and carry his voice a fair distance.

'Ripley! Ripley!' he shouted. He then made a sound like an Indian warrior. The sound would be easier to hear. He waited a moment. Was that his own echo, or another voice?

He made the sound again, this time with a distinctive tune. A different tune called back. He looked up and saw Ripley's face peering around the entrance to a cave. How had she managed to get up there?

'Stay still and get back from the edge,' he bellowed. The tide will turn soon and I'll come and help you.' He saw Ripley's hands go up to show she didn't understand him. He gestured towards the sea and waved his hand trying to indicate the sea would be going out soon. He circled his thumb and finger in a circle and held it in the air. Ripley's thumb went up. She understood!

Ripley sat back in the cave, out of the treacherous weather. She was going to be alright. A couple of tears of relief fell down her cheek; she must have been here hours. No one would ever understand how wonderful it was to hear Joe's voice, she literally felt her heart lift.

The sea was receding quickly and as the last few waves covered the rocks beneath, Joe scrambled up to her.

'Thank you. I was so frightened and then I heard your call. I've been stuck up here for hours.'

'So no one told you to watch the tide?'

'No. I didn't realise it would come up so high. I climbed up to have a look in here and it only seemed like moments before the water was swirling below me and the waves were crashing into the rocks.'

'At least you had the sense to stay up here. It would have been dangerous to climb down.' Joe looked out of the cave. 'Okay, I think you'll be alright to get down now. Your family are really worried.'

'Oh God! This'll be my mum's excuse to leave this place. She hates it here.'

'And how do you feel?'

'I love it, and I never want to live anywhere else.'

They cautiously climbed down the cliff and soon reached the safety of the sands.

'I have to admit it was frightening up there when I thought I might die, but at the same time it was wonderful listening to the gulls and hearing the waves lashing against the cliffs.'

'I'm glad you can see the beauty. Some people go through their whole lives with blinkers; they can't see anything. Tomorrow I'll introduce you to the horses properly. We could go out for a ride.'

'I've never ridden a horse.'

'You've never ridden? I couldn't imagine not ever riding, you've missed a lifetime of fun. It'll be fine, George will be perfect for you, he's old and plods on forever.'

Ripley laughed. 'Plods on forever, sounds about right for me.'

They chatted as they walked and Ripley felt as though she'd known Joe forever.

When they arrived back at the house Ripley opened the back door and Clarissa came rushing through the outhouse, crying.

'Ripley, thank God you're alright! The police are here and the lifeboat... Oh Ripley!' She flung her arms around her daughter and held her tight as her father rushed towards her.

'Are you hurt? Where were you?' he asked.

'In a cave and Joe found me.'

'A cave! Ripley what were you thinking? I knew this place would be bad for you. It's dangerous Richard, we can't stay.'

'Clarissa, she was exploring; it's what kids do. She's home and safe, nothing to worry about.'

'Don't patronise me, Richard! I want to leave here and live in a proper, safe environment for our daughter. I want what's best for her.'

'Mum, this is what's best for me. I love it here, there's no comparison between here and where we used to live. I don't want to leave. I'll be more careful in future, I'm sorry I worried you.'

May appeared in the doorway. 'The police have gone. I knew you'd be fine; the Major would have told me if you were in danger. Come through and I'll make you a nice cup of tea.'

'That'd be lovely. Thanks, Aunt May.' Ripley followed May, leaving her parents in the outhouse.

'Why do you let your sister spout off such rubbish? I want to leave. Ripley doesn't know what's best for her, she's still a child.'

'Clarissa, you know our financial position at the moment. We have to bide our time and make the best of it until we can move on. Ripley's not a child, she's a young adult who's perfectly capable of knowing her own mind.'

'I might have guessed you'd take her side.'

'There aren't any sides. Come on, let's go and have a cup of tea, it's been a trying time for us all.'

'Your sister didn't think so. She'll be reading the tea leaves next.' Richard raised his eyebrows knowing he was fighting a losing battle.

'I'm having a cup of tea. You do what you want.'

Clarissa went upstairs and sat on the edge of her bed. She'd never felt so miserable. Why couldn't Richard see sense? How had they ended up in this awful position? Richard should never have trusted Jerry, she'd told him so many times, but it was the same situation as they were in now. Richard couldn't see what was staring him in the face. She had to think of a scheme, some way of getting them out of here and back to normal life in town.

A few tears slid down her cheek. There was no alternative. There was no scheme she could come up with. She had to start being realistic. Whinging on wasn't going to solve anything; they had no money and nowhere else to live. This hell-hole was home for the foreseeable future and she had to get on with it. Sod Richard, and Jerry, and May, sod the lot of them. A barrage of anger swept through her like a thunderbolt. Why hadn't Richard done anything about Jerry? He'd let him swan off to some tropical island to live a life of bliss while they had to suffer the consequences of his scam.

Clarissa dried her eyes and looked in the mirror. She looked a bit puffy-eyed, but that'd be in her favour. She walked downstairs.

'There you are. Would you like some tea now?' Richard said, jovially.

'No, I wouldn't. Richard, is Jerry going to get away with what he's done to us, or are you intending doing something about him?'

'Don't worry yourself. I'm taking care of things; he won't get away with anything.'

Richard had someone on the case who had already located Jerry. Now he had to decide what to do about him. There was little chance of getting the money back. Jerry would have that securely tucked away. In a one-to-one confrontation, Richard wasn't confident he'd be the one to walk away. He toyed with the idea of paying some heavies to do the job for him. He needed time to think, but Jerry wouldn't get away with anything.

Ripley could see her father was worrying and thought she'd lighten the subject. 'Joe said he'll teach me to ride. I'm having a go on George tomorrow,' she said.

'Oh, you'll love George,' May said, 'He's a lovely horse to learn on.'

Clarissa broke into a scowl. 'Horse riding! Ripley, you could fall.'

'I have a hat for you, Ritly. Don't worry Clarissa, we grew up on horseback and it didn't do us any harm.'

'May, I don't care what you did, I don't want my daughter participating in dangerous sports.'

'Mum, I'll be careful. I'm really looking forward to it.' Why did her mother always try to spoil everything? Ripley's world had opened up and she was enjoying it. Her mother was not going to spoil things for her any longer.

Chapter 4

Ripley woke at dawn and leapt out of bed to look out of the window. The stable door was open and she could see some movement. She hurriedly dressed and quietly made her way down the stairs.

May startled her. 'Where are you tiptoeing off to at this hour?'

'Oh, Aunt May! You made me jump. I'm going riding with Joe.'

'And I suppose you thought you'd sneak out before your mother came down and put a stop to your fun.'

'Mmm, something like that.' Ripley looked embarrassed.

'I don't blame you. You have to be two jumps ahead with that one. The hat's there for you, but you need some breakfast first.'

'But...'

'No buts. The horses can't be ridden for an hour after they've eaten anyway and Joe's only just finished doing them.'

'Oh, okay.'

'Tea and toast, or how about some eggs?'

'Eggs please.'

'There's a riding jacket there for you as well and the jodhpurs might fit. I was as small as you once upon a time.'

Ripley hurried over to the chair and picked up the jacket. 'It's lovely. I'm really going to look the part. I'll go and try the jodhpurs on.'

She came back into the kitchen a few moments later looking like a professional rider. 'Thanks, Aunt May.'

'Well don't you look wonderful? Try the hat for size.' Ripley put it on and her aunt fixed the catch. 'Perfect. Now you only need to be able to get on the horse. George will do the rest.'

Ripley sat down at the kitchen table and put salt on her eggs. May looked at Ripley and for a moment she felt a touch of envy that she didn't still ride, then she frowned. 'Ritly, you really need to take the hat off for breakfast.'

Ripley smiled. 'I love you, Aunt May.'

'And I love you. I have to admit the thought of one of today's teenagers coming to stay here was a bit daunting, but you're a pleasure through and through. Things couldn't have turned out any better. Eat up. Your eggs are getting cold.'

Ripley tucked in while her aunt went upstairs to dress. She washed the dishes, put her riding hat back on and stood admiring herself in front of the mirror in the hallway. Her other boots would look better. She dashed upstairs to change and then went out to the stables to find Joe.

'Good morning. You look the part,' Joe said. 'I shall have to go and get dressed up myself.'

Ripley laughed. 'No you don't. Wear what you always do. Aunt May gave me this stuff and I couldn't really disappoint her by not wearing it.'

'Of course not. I'll be back in a minute and then we'll have a go at getting you on board.'

'I can't wait. I feel like a child waiting to open Christmas presents.'

Joe smiled as he walked away. Ripley was going to be fun to have around, not like some girls, all giggly and stupid. He changed and glanced in the mirror. He should have a shave really. He whipped off his jacket throwing it to one side and went to the bathroom.

Ripley saw him walking through the trees towards her. He had a sort of rough, sexy look about him which she hadn't noticed before. He was quite good-looking with his tousled brown hair.

Joe led George out of the stable and into the yard. 'Meet George.'

'The name suits him.'

'Right, hold the reins in both hands,' he said as he passed them to her. 'Left leg in the stirrup and then hoist yourself up. Put your right foot in my hands and I'll help you.'

Ripley lifted herself up and threw her leg over George's back. She'd done it! 'That wasn't too bad.'

'Not at all.' Joe fastened his hat and climbed on Filou. 'Just touch your legs gently into his sides and he'll start to walk. It feels a bit wobbly but you'll soon get used to it.'

Ripley followed the instructions and George took off at a slow pace. She held onto the reins for dear life.

'Relax, he'll keep at this pace all day. How do you like it?'

'I love it, although I feel really hot and wish I hadn't got this jacket on.'

'Do you want to stop and take it off before we leave the grounds?'

'No, I might get cold when I calm down a bit.'

'It's down the track to the beach then.' They began making the descent.

'I didn't notice it was this steep before. I feel as though I'm going to plunge over George's shoulders.'

'You're fine. Don't look down, look straight ahead. Lean back in the saddle. You might have to push yourself back against the pommel to keep your leaned back pose, otherwise you'll pitch over the front of your saddle.'

Ripley followed the instruction, and only felt safe once they had reached the bottom and were on the sands. They set off at a leisurely pace along the beach.

'Tell me if you want to go back. I usually go right onto the sands at Crompton.'

'That's fine with me. This is like a dream come true. We saw you on the beach the first night we arrived and I felt so envious. Thank you, Joe.'

'You're welcome. My mum used to love this ride.'

'How did your mum get to know Aunt May?'

'It was your dad who offered my mum the job. May needed someone to help around the house and to take care of the gardens and animals. She didn't want a man around, so your dad asked my mum and he sent her a cheque every few months for the work she did.'

'My dad paid? I never knew that, but I suppose it saved him from having to make an appearance and do anything himself. That way he was doing his share. He's a bit crafty at finding ways around awkward situations.'

'He sent more money once I was able to work around the place too. It worked well for all of us. May had the help she needed and we had a lovely place to live and some regular money coming in. It's not easy to find work around here.'

'You work in a restaurant now, don't you?'

'Yes, and I go to college one day a week. I take my exams in a couple of months' time, then I'll be at the restaurant full time.'

'So do you ever get any time to yourself?'

'I don't need it. The things I do around the farm are what I love, so it's more like a hobby than work.'

'I don't know what I'll do later on. I definitely want to live here forever, but I might have to convince my mum.'

They rode along the sands until they came to Crompton main beach. The horses paddled for a while, then Joe suggested a rest. He jumped down easily and then helped Ripley. He tied the horses to a metal ring used to tie boats up on the harbour wall and then sat down on the beach and took off his boots.

'Fancy a paddle? It's lovely and refreshing when you've had boots on.'

'Okay, I'll try it, but the other day it was freezing.'

'You have to give it time for your body to adjust. If you can get past that point it's great.'

Ripley wasn't entirely convinced, but took off her boots anyway and followed him to the water's edge. She shrieked as the first wave lapped over her feet, then took a deep breath and braced herself for the next. He'd been right, it felt so good once the shock was over.

'Do you fancy an ice-cream?' Joe asked.

'Sounds good.'

'Do you want to look after the horses or go for the ice-creams?'

'I think I'd better go for the ice-creams.'

'See where it says trays of tea for the beach? They do a double scoop with a flake there.'

Ripley couldn't stop smiling as she walked to the café. She could never have imagined spending the Easter holidays like this. Shame she had to go back to school next week. She dreaded going to a new school, but then, she had also worried about moving to Crompton.

She walked back to Joe with a cornet in each hand. He was stroking George's nose.

'There you go, double scoop with chocolate flake,' she said. They sat on the beach savouring each lick and taking advantage of the morning sunshine.

Richard sat in the tea rooms near Whiteleaf harbour munching his way through his second croissant. Deep in thought, he stirred two sugars into his coffee and stirred it longer than necessary. Although he hated to admit it, Clarissa had been right. Jerry was living the life of Riley at his expense and it had to be stopped; he'd got away with it for too long. He had set the cogs turning, but for some reason hadn't made the final call to confirm. He must be getting soft in his old age.

He ordered another croissant and coffee which allowed him more time to think. He paid his bill, complementing the ladies behind the counter on their cabinet of delicious-looking cakes, then went to sit on the harbour wall to make a phone call.

The boats were bobbing around with the wash. There was only one man in sight mopping down the deck of his boat. Richard watched as the chap squeezed out the mop and then picked up the bucket and went below deck. Richard lifted his arm in the air and launched his phone out into the sea, smiling with satisfaction as the last few air bubbles disappeared.

A desk for his home office was the next item on his agenda for the morning. Calmly he walked back along the harbour wall, taking in the scenery and whistling to himself.

Ripley and Joe unsaddled the horses, put on their blankets and stabled them.

'Thanks Joe, I've had a great time, although I have to say I ache.'

'You'll soon get used to it. You're welcome to join me anytime. See you later.'

'Have you collected the eggs today?'

Joe noticed the look of hope on her face. 'No, not yet.'

'I'll get them.'

'Okay.' Joe smiled as he walked away. Ripley was turning into a country bumpkin so soon. He'd brought a couple of girls back to the farm over the years, but none were ever interested in what he loved. That might be why Joe had never had a serious girlfriend. He'd only been to the cinema, or played ten-pin bowling a couple of times, but then he tired of them.

Ripley walked into the kitchen and stacked the eggs in the basket. The new ones went on the right hand side.

'Hello, Ritly, how did you like riding?'

'Oh, Aunt May, it was fantastic. We rode right onto Crompton sands and ate ice-cream. George is wonderful. We paddled in the sea and Joe, well, Joe's wonderful too.'

'The Major said you two would get along fine, but he said there might be trouble ahead.'

Ripley looked at her aunt's serious face for a moment. Did she want to know more about some sort of trouble a ghost had predicted? 'I'm starving. Shall I make some sandwiches? I'll go and see if Mum and Dad want some.'

Ripley found her mum on her bed with a headache. 'No, I couldn't eat and your dad's gone to buy a desk for the study.'

'The ride was great. We went...'

'Not now, Ripley.'

School began a few days later and Ripley was shown into her registration room which was alive with girls chatter and giggling. They were mostly in groups and although a few turned to look, no one approached her. She sat down at a vacant table and began to look through her bag, trying to look busy. The door opened and a teacher called the group to register.

'You can't sit here, this table's taken,' a girl with long dark hair and big brown eyes told Ripley. Ripley stood and looked around.

'Oh hello, sorry, didn't see you there,' the teacher said. 'You must be Ripley.' She looked down at a sheet of paper on her desk. 'Yes, Ripley Bradford. Right girls, make Ripley feel welcome. We've all experienced a first day here, so do what you can to help. Have you got a timetable, Ripley?'

'Yes.'

'Show me. A, okay someone from A to show her around?' There was silence and then a meek voice from the corner offered.

'Thanks Hannah. Stay with Hannah, she'll make sure you know the ropes. Right, register, we're running late.'

Hannah was a timid, blond-haired, pretty girl. Ripley followed her around for most of the time in silence. Even when she was asked open questions, Hannah seemed to be able to make her answers short and to the point. She showed no enthusiasm. Hannah was happy to keep her head down in her books ignoring the people around her.

The bell sounded for the end of the day and Ripley packed away her books and pencil case.

'Thanks for helping me out today,' she said to Hannah.

'You're welcome. I'll see you tomorrow.' At least Ripley would still have Hannah to tag along with; no one else had spoken to her. Everyone else seemed to be in little groups and an invitation to join in was not forthcoming.

Her dad leaned across the seat and opened the car door as she approached.

'How did you get along?'

'Okay I suppose. They aren't the friendliest people I've ever met. No one really spoke to me.'

'In small towns like Whiteleaf, people sometimes take a while to accept newcomers. Give it time. What about the lessons?'

'They were okay. I hope Joe's riding tonight.'

A week later, Ripley learned it was better if no one at school spoke to her. A couple of girls asked her where she had come from and what school she went to. Ripley mistook their questions as a sign of friendship, but they only wanted the information to taunt and tease her with later.

'Boarding school, how posh! Lowered herself to mix with the likes of us commoners.' Ripley laughed off their comments as the girls giggled and left her standing, feeling like a fool. Hadn't she been told not to say she'd been to private school? Why had she thought they were being nice? Why did they have to be so mean and bitchy?

On Saturday at lunch time, Ripley returned home from riding with Joe and saw a police car parked at the side of the house. Aunt May was in the kitchen.

'What's going on?'

'The Major said there was trouble brewing, but wouldn't expand. The police and your dad have been in the drawing room for about half an hour.'

'I'll ask Mum what's happening.'

'She's in her room; with a headache, I shouldn't wonder.' May raised her eyebrows. Ripley smiled.

'I'll go and see.'

Sure enough, her mum was in her room. 'Why are the police talking to dad?'

'I have no idea and I have a dreadful headache. I'm fed up with all of this; I've had nothing but headaches since we moved here.'

'Can I get you a drink or anything?'

'You could pull the curtains closed.' Ripley did as she was asked and then returned downstairs. May had made tea and toasted teacakes for her.

Ripley had an awkward feeling as she ate. Her dad had been strangely quiet since the move to Crompton. She had thought it was due to her mum's constant whingeing and whining, but now she wasn't so sure.

Eventually Ripley heard her dad showing the police to the door and she went through to the hall.

'What did they want?'

'Nothing for you to worry about.'

'Come on, Dad, I'm not a child.'

Clarissa came down the stairs. 'What was that about Richard?'

He stood for a moment and looked at both women then cleared his throat. 'Jerry has been found dead at his home and nothing was stolen, so they are questioning anyone who knew him.'

Clarissa let out a puff of air. 'They can't possibly think you would have flown to Fiji unnoticed.'

'No. I think it was just routine enquires. They knew he'd run off with the firm's money. I imagine Tracey told them about me when they asked if she could think of anyone who might hold a grudge.'

'Well, I don't like to speak ill of the dead, but maybe karma played a hand. He got what was coming to him. So what about the money? Will you be able to do anything about getting some back?'

'I don't know. I'll have to make some enquires of my own.'

Ripley went up to her room and listened to a CD as she worked through her homework. She couldn't concentrate. Jerry had been around since she could remember. Maybe it wasn't only her dad he'd cheated. The thought of him being murdered frightened her. She closed her books and went for a walk outside.

Joe was mucking out the stables. 'I'll give you hand,' she said.

Joe passed her a large fork and she began loading an empty wheelbarrow while he pushed a full one to the manure heap. As she plunged the fork into the straw her spirits lifted.

'Nothing like hard work to loosen the cobwebs,' Joe said playfully.

'How do you know there were any cobwebs to loosen in the first place?'

'Because May told me you might need a bit of a lift today.'

'The Major, I suppose?' Ripley tilted her head to one side and took a deep breath. 'I'm going to start making a chart of all the things he predicts. I do think I believe in him, but I have a nagging doubt, probably due to my dad's scepticism.'

'I think you'll find most of what he says is right. I've lived with it for years,' Joe said. 'The ghost of Cliff Top Manor is coming to get you.' Joe made his voice quiver and brought up his arms over Ripley's head, wiggling his fingers about in a ghostly fashion.

Ripley laughed. 'Funny enough, it doesn't frighten me. I would have expected to be a nervous wreck, living with a ghost, but I only find it intriguing.'

'I think that's due to your aunt. She speaks about him like he's one of the family.'

'I think she likes him better than the family.'

'Come on, it's a lovely afternoon. Let's go for a walk along the beach and find some shells.'

They strolled around the rocks and searched the water's edge for shells. Some were quite pretty.

'Oh, look at this one. The mother-of-pearl is beautiful,' Joe said, holding out a shell. Ripley took it and studied the colours for a moment before handing it back.

'Why can't I find one as beautiful as that?'

'You will, I've got quite a collection at home. You'll have to come and have a look.'

'I'd love to.'

They picked up a few more shells and then made their way home.

'Do you want to see the shells now?' Joe asked.

'Might as well. I want to see your cottage; I imagine it to be really quaint.'

'I don't know about that.'

Joe turned the handle and the front door opened. 'Don't you lock it?'

'There's no need. Who's going to want anything from in here?'

Ripley looked around in awe. The table and chairs had been carved from logs and the wooden shelves around the walls held endless trinkets such as oddly shaped rocks. Pictures made from dried seaweed and sand hung around the walls.

'Are all these things you've found or made?'

'I never buy much.'

'You actually made the table and chairs?'

'It was an old oak tree which used to stand in front of the house until one night an awful storm brought it down. Luckily it fell in front of the house and not on it.'

'And look at these shells; they can't all have come from here.'

'Every one of them.' He put his hand in his pocket and pulled out the collection he'd found that day. He carefully placed them with the others on a homemade stool in the corner of the room. 'Which is your favourite?'

'That one.' It was the mother-of-pearl shell Joe had found earlier. 'Which is yours?'

'This is one my mum gave me when I was small. It might not be the most beautiful, but I can remember her giving it to me like it was yesterday. I must have only been about four or five.'

'How lovely. It must have been hard... when... you know.'

'I thought my heart would break. It was only this place that kept me going. I used to throw myself into everything and lost sight of the real world for a time. I used to come back to the cottage at the end of the day invigorated and ready to deal with everything, and then by the next morning I'd be in floods of tears again.'

'What about your dad?'

'Never knew him. Apparently he was a sailor and drowned at sea before I was born.'

Ripley walked back to the house inspired by the way Joe lived. He wanted for nothing, virtually lived with nature's resources and was the happiest person she knew. He had made such a huge impact on her life; the world through Joe's eyes was certainly different.

Chapter 5

Ripley's family had lived in Crompton for four months and nothing much had changed. Clarissa still whined at every opportunity. May harped on about the Major and wound Ripley's parents up, and her dad was still on the quiet side. The girls at school had bored of tormenting her, but Hannah was still the only friend she had. Hannah had visited Ripley's home only once and Ripley had never had an invitation to Hannah's. The afternoon had been stilted and Ripley thought Hannah had probably felt out of place, so didn't invite her again. The constant and wonderful thing in her life was Joe. They spent time together every day and it was the time Ripley loved most of all.

Ripley's sixteenth birthday fell on a Saturday and she chose to ride with Joe in the morning, go to the beach, swim during the afternoon and invite Joe to a special dinner her mother had organised for that evening.

'You want Joe to come to the restaurant with us?' Clarissa said haughtily. 'He's hired help; can't you choose someone from school to come with us?'

'I don't want anyone from school. I want Joe to come.'

'We'll have to see what your father says.'

'It's my birthday, surely I can decide who I share it with.'

Ripley went to the stables, early as usual, and found Joe with the horses ready to go.

'Happy birthday, Ripley. I've got a present for you in the cottage, when we get back.'

'Joe, you shouldn't have got me anything. I love all that we do together, I don't need a present.'

'It's nothing grand.'

They walked the horses on their normal route into Crompton and had ice-cream on the beach.

'Every time we do this, I think how lucky I am to have such a wonderful life,' Ripley said, running her tongue around the drips along the edge of the cornet.

'I still appreciate it all and I've never known any different.'

They returned home along the beach, stabled the horses and walked down the track to Joe's cottage. Ripley's eyes fell straight on the small package on the table. It had been wrapped in leaves and tied with string in a bow. Joe crossed to the table, picked it up and handed it to her.

'I hope you like it.'

'I'm sure I will.' She pulled the bow undone and unwrapped the leaves. She gasped when she saw the present. A necklace of tiny shells with the mother-of-pearl one she'd chosen as her favourite, hanging down. 'You made it? You really made this?'

'Yes, it was a bit fiddly, but I got there in the end.'

'Joe it's beautiful. Thank you so much, this is the most beautiful thing I've ever had.' She flung her arms around his neck and kissed his cheek. He took her in his arms and gave her a squeeze.

'Happy birthday. I'm glad you like it.'

'Like it! I love it!' She looked into his eyes. 'Thank you.' Their eyes met and neither moved nor blinked. They held the gaze for a moment before their lips met. The passion they had restrained for so long was now obvious.

'I love you, Ripley.'

'I love you, Joe.'

Joe looked into her eyes. 'You are the best thing that's ever happened to me.'

'We must be the best thing that's ever happened to each other then.' Their lips met once more in a passionate embrace and Joe ran his hands down her back. Ripley felt as though she would melt. She took his hand and led him into the bedroom and onto the bed.

'We can't, Ripley.'

'I love you, Joe, and I want to.'

'I don't think we should.'

'Why? We've waited all this time and I'm sixteen now.'

'I haven't ever… you know.'

'Nor have I.'

'I haven't got a… you know.'

Ripley let out a nervous giggle. 'I'm on the pill to control my periods.'

He looked into her eyes and kissed her. She undid the top button of her shirt, followed by the second. Her bra was now on display and Joe gave an involuntary shudder of uneasiness as he wrapped her in his arms.

At seven-thirty that evening, Clarissa, Joe and Ripley climbed into the back of the car, while May sat in the front next to Richard. The adults tried to make small talk all the way to the restaurant, but Joe and Ripley were in a world of their own. Ripley sat between Joe and her mum with her arms crossed, holding on to Joe's arm with the hand which couldn't be seen. Every now and again Joe turned to look at her and squeezed his arm onto her hand. Both of them were oblivious to the cool mood of Ripley's parents.

Aunt May kept the atmosphere at the table light with her stories of childhood, mostly remembering things Richard didn't have a clue about.

'You must remember going down to the parlour and eating cereal at two o'clock in the morning when we were going on holiday?'

'No, I can't recall that.'

'We thought it would save time in the morning and we could climb out of bed and go on holiday immediately. Mother came down, gave us both what for and sent us back up to bed.'

'Nope. Don't remember that at all.'

'What about when you rolled in the cow pat just because you didn't want to wear a shirt to go to school? It was stained green forever, and Dad made you wear it.'

'I never did!'

'Yes, you were a right one for mischief in those days. Mind you, the Major says not a lot has changed.' Ripley snorted back a giggle and Joe knocked his knee against hers under the table. Richard scowled.

At the end of the meal, the waiter approached carrying a cake with sixteen candles burning brightly on the top and all the restaurant customers burst into song with *Happy Birthday*. Ripley blew the candles out and closed her eyes to make a wish. She looked longingly at Joe when she opened her eyes. The look didn't go unnoticed by her mum.

'Shall we save the cake until we get home? It's getting late, I expect May's getting tired.'

May shook her head. 'I'm not tired; I had a rest this afternoon.'

'No, let's have cake now,' Ripley pleaded. 'I don't want today to end.'

Clarissa looked at her daughter's face. There was something different today, but she couldn't decide what it was. Maybe it was that beautiful blue dress she was wearing. It certainly was flattering, made her look grown up. She'd have to try to find a way of steering Ripley away from this boy. She was spending far too much time with him.

An hour later they pulled up at home. 'I'll quickly check the horses with Joe before bed, back in a minute.'

'What, in that dress? Ripley...' Clarissa said. Ripley had already walked away and didn't look back.

The horses were fine. Joe took her in his arms and kissed her tenderly. 'I've never been to a restaurant as posh as that before. The food was out of this world.'

'We don't go often, only special occasions really. You made today so special for me, Joe.'

'Your necklace caught the light as you moved, made you look even more beautiful.'

'I'd better go before Mum sends out a search party. I love you, Joe.'

'Love you, Ripley. See you tomorrow, sleep well.'

'And you.' She was now half-way across the yard and heading towards the house.

'There you are. You shouldn't be out here in the dark at this time of night,' Richard said, trying to sound stern.

They walked into the house to be met by Clarissa in the hall.

'You're spending too much time with that boy, Ripley, and it has to stop. He's not of our social standing and you're going to pick up bad habits.'

'Social standing! Mum, I don't go to private school now and I don't care about social standing. I like Joe as a friend and he's the only one I've got.'

Clarissa's face tightened. 'Ripley, you need to pull back. It's not good for you.'

'Your mum's right, Ripley. He's not good enough for you.'

Ripley burst into tears. 'I've had a lovely day and you have to spoil it don't you. Thanks a lot! I'm going to bed!' She stomped upstairs leaving her parents in the hall.

May stood with her ear to the door listening and shook her head. She'd never heard anything so ridiculous. They weren't fit to call themselves parents, breaking Ritly's heart like that; couldn't they see she was in love? May had seen it months ago. There was nothing wrong with Joe. He was a polite, well-mannered youth and you didn't get many like that these days. Richard and Clarissa were going to lose their daughter if they didn't watch out.

Ripley fell onto her bed and wept. Why had they spoiled her birthday? This had been the best day of her life. She ran her fingers around the shells on her necklace. Her parents had given her money to choose what she wanted. That was okay, but it hadn't required much thought. May had given her a framed photograph of George which Ripley loved. She looked at him standing proud on the shelf and smiled. She wondered what Joe would be doing now. He was probably fast asleep.

Joe couldn't sleep. He was in love with the most beautiful girl in the world and she loved him. He hadn't been able to tell her before today, he'd been frightened of losing her friendship. Today had been like a dream come true. She was young; he had to be careful not to scare her off. She meant everything to him. He lived every minute waiting for a chance to see her, if only from a distance. He sat on the beach looking up at the stars. When you wish upon a star... I wish, I wish, I wish. He threw his hands up in the air and shouted.

'Thank you, thank you, whoever you are, thank you!' He laughed at his own stupidity, pulled himself up and walked slowly back to the cottage. His mum would have loved Ripley as much as he did. He loved everything: her walk, her chatter, but most of all he loved the dimples that constantly appeared in her cheeks when she smiled.

Richard had more important issues to worry about than his daughter. The police had questioned him twice more at the station. Clarissa knew nothing of the interviews and that was how Richard intended it to stay. Apparently the police had arrested someone for the stabbing, but had to release him due to a lack of evidence.

'I've never heard of him. This is a complete waste of time when you should be out there looking for the culprit.'

Two officers sat opposite him with serious expressions. 'We're doing that, and our enquiries are leading us closer and closer to those responsible. Rest assured, we will find the perpetrators.'

Richard left the station feeling uneasy. They didn't have anything on him, they couldn't have. He didn't like the way they said *perpetrators*; up until now they had said they were looking for one man. The payment had been made in cash, there could be no comeback on that. The police were clutching at straws. They had no evidence that could point to him, he had nothing to worry about.

Richard sat in his usual breakfast café making his way through the coffee and croissants. The women who ran the shop no longer asked what he wanted; they already knew his order would be the same as always. Richard sat at the customary table in the corner of the room where he had a good view of everyone entering and leaving. Not that he knew anyone, but some of the faces were becoming familiar as regular clientele of the café.

Today he was waiting for someone to join him. He glanced at his watch; Mick Hacho was already five minutes late. Mick had been introduced to Richard by a trustworthy mutual acquaintance and he had been the middle man he used for the cash payment. Richard ran the last piece of croissant around his plate to mop up the remaining crumbs and after licking his lips, put it in his mouth. He'd wait another five minutes.

The door opened and the burly frame, topped off by a mass of dark curls belonging to Mick, entered the tea rooms. He lifted his hand to acknowledge Richard, walked over to the table, held out his hand to shake, and sat down.

'I haven't got long. So are you clear? The most important thing is to get a receipt when you cash in, or the whole exercise is pointless.'

'Yes, yes, I know that. So I'll meet you in here again on Friday.'

Mick looked around at the other customers. Two old girls sat with a pot of tea in front of them waiting for it to brew; they took turns at the sugar and milk. A man sat alone reading the newspaper, fiddling with his moustache denoting his concentration. The women behind the counter were chatting as they busied themselves. Mick pushed a brown envelope across the table and Richard put it into his inside pocket.

'This place seems okay. Friday then, same time,' Mick said, as he pushed the chair back and stood. He nodded and left Richard watching as he disappeared through the door. Richard thought it best to leave a few minutes gap before he left, so he ordered another coffee, but managed to resist another croissant.

Ripley woke, threw back the covers, leapt out of bed and rushed to the window. Joe must be in the stables; she could see the door ajar. She pulled on a tee-shirt and track-suit bottoms and quickly brushed her hair before heading off downstairs.

'Good morning, young Ritly. Are you stopping for breakfast or do you have other pressing matters?'

Ripley smiled shyly. 'I'm going to help Joe with the horses, then I'll be back for breakfast.'

'Off you go then. It's lovely to see you youngsters in love.'

Ripley gave a nervous giggle. Aunt May couldn't possibly know, surely the Major wouldn't talk about such personal issues. Oh my God, now she was starting to sound like her aunt. What a ridiculous idea! A ghost gossiping!

'See you later.'

'Yes dear. Don't leave breakfast too long.'

Ripley hurried out to the stables. 'Good morning,' she said to Joe, who was filling the feed buckets. He stopped and stood to look at her.

'Good morning, how are you?'

'Happy! How about you?'

'Happy is an understatement for how I feel. I'm deliriously, ecstatically in love and it feels magnificent.'

Ripley laughed. 'Well now you put it like that, I feel jubilant, rapturous love.'

Joe put down the feed bucket and took two steps towards her. He gently lifted her chin and kissed her tenderly.

'What are we going to do about Ripley and this boy? She's only sixteen; he's much too old for her. We should never have moved here, Richard, I knew there'd be trouble.' Clarissa and Richard were still in bed on the Sunday morning after Ripley's birthday.

'Clarissa, there isn't any trouble. It's quite natural for a girl of Ripley's age to mix with boys, and anyway, I think she's more interested in the horses. Ripley is innocent, to her he's just a friend. You're reading far too much into their friendship.'

Clarissa pulled herself up onto her pillow and faced her husband. 'So you think it's okay for her to spend all her free time with him?'

'As it happens, yes I do. She's having the time of her life here in the country, it's nothing to do with him. He's showing her around the place, and she'll soon tire of him.'

Clarissa scowled. 'I think I'll encourage her to invite Anna for a long weekend. She hasn't even kept in touch with her since we've been here.'

Richard sighed. 'Anna's history. Ripley has a new life now and Anna probably has new friends.'

'I think I'll suggest it.' Clarissa threw back the covers and pulled on her robe. 'You can't see what's happening before your very eyes.'

'Whatever you say.'

'You never listened to me over Jerry and look where that got us.'

'Please give it a rest, Clarissa. Do what you want.' Richard sat on the edge of the bed and stretched his arms. 'Do you fancy going out for Sunday lunch?'

'Not really. There are no decent restaurants around here.'

Richard knew he was fighting a losing battle. Ripley wasn't interested in Joe. He was an employee and she was taking advantage of his riding skills to teach her a thing or two about the horses. Why couldn't Clarissa see that? She always had to read more into every situation and create a problem. He went through to the bathroom and ran the shower. A dribble of lukewarm water came through. He'd have to get on to the repairs that needed doing around the place. He'd phone a plumber first thing Monday morning.

Chapter 6

Clarissa began to mentally note the time Ripley spent with Joe, and a week after Ripley's birthday, she decided to put a stop to the liaisons. She collected Ripley from school and they drove to a local shopping centre. They sat in the car park.

'What are we looking for? I'm going out for a ride with Joe.'

'I thought it might be nice to do a bit of shopping and mooch around a bit.'

'Mum, I'd rather go riding; there's nothing I need.'

'Ripley, you have to stop spending so much time with Joe. He's nice enough, but he's not the sort for you to be fraternising with.'

'Mum, I'm not fraternising with him, he's my friend and he's the only one I've got.'

'I was thinking about that. Why don't you invite Anna to stay for a weekend?'

'Anna won't like the horses, or the beach. It wouldn't work.'

'How about inviting someone home from school, broaden your horizons a bit?'

'My horizons have been broadened and I like the way things are. I don't need anyone else.'

'I'm not going to fall out with you over this. I don't want you spending all your free time with that boy.' Clarissa sat, stony-faced, glaring at Ripley.

'His name is Joe. You and Dad took me away from everyone I knew, miles away, and now you want to stop my friendship with the only person who makes me happy here! I'm not going to stop riding and I'm not going to stop seeing Joe! Can we go home now, please?'

Clarissa started the car and pulled out of the shopping centre.

'I only want what's best for you. You're only sixteen and I'm your mum. You need to do as I ask Ripley, or we're going to fall out.'

'I am sixteen and I'm old enough to make my own decisions. You can't stop me riding!'

'I don't want to stop you riding, I want you to mix with your own sort.'

A while later they pulled up at home. Ripley climbed out of the car, stomped into the house, went up to her room and looked out of the window. Good, Joe was already tacking the horses. She felt hot and angry. How dare her mother try to stop her friendship with Joe? Her own sort? What was her own sort? Her mother lived in some sort of ridiculous land of snobbery. Ripley would never be like that. Joe was the nicest, kindest, most wonderful person she knew and her mum couldn't take that away. She pulled off her school uniform and put on her riding clothes.

Ripley met her mother on the stairs. 'I've told you you're not going riding. You must have homework to do?'

'No, I did it at lunchtime.'

'You're not going Ripley!'

'I am! You can't stop me!' Ripley pushed past Clarissa and ran out into the yard with tears of anger rolling down her cheeks. Her mother was hateful! Why did she have to always find fault?

'Ripley, come back here right now!'

Ripley heard the call but didn't look back. She couldn't let Joe see her like this. She ran the opposite direction to the stables and ended up at the chicken house. Around the back was a pile of grass cuttings; Ripley sat down and sobbed. Why was her mother so horrible to her? A surge of guilt ran through her mind. If her mother knew what had happened with Joe she would be right to stop the relationship, but there was no way her mother knew; she was just being difficult.

Joe would be wondering where she was. She dried her eyes on her sleeve and went to the stables.

Richard couldn't have been happier; his life had certainly changed for the better. Every afternoon he drove to a casino, a different one each day, and gambled money away, along with his fellow punters. For him the money meant nothing; after all it wasn't his money.

'You lose a bit and you win a bit.' Mick had said, as he handed over the first envelope. 'You need a receipt for the winnings and you get ten per cent. You use different places. The money's dirty and once it's got a receipt it's clean. Easy!'

The first afternoon was daunting. Richard had never had so much cash in his pocket. He tried the roulette table and lost appallingly. Black jack, he had to have more luck with that. He collected his chips and crossed the casino to take a seat next to a Chinese man who nodded at him. Richard nodded back feeling as though everyone knew his cloak and dagger operation. What if he didn't win anything, if he lost all the money? He should have asked more questions.

He felt his hand shake as he placed his bets. The cards weren't on his side. Now what? He walked back over to the roulette table and placed his chips on the table. The croupier called for no more bets and the wheel spun. Richard's heart raced as he watched her drop the ball onto the wheel. All around him everything seemed to fade into insignificance. Red nineteen! Oh yes! That's more like it. Richard placed another stack of chips on red nineteen along with several other stacks on other numbers. He rubbed his hands together. Here we go! Black twenty eight. That'll do nicely. After three hours at the tables Richard cashed in his chips and remembered to get a receipt. This must be the best job he'd ever had.

Richard met Mick Hacho once a week to exchange money. The meetings were always short and to the point which suited Richard, he found Mick rather intimidating.

At last Richard was on the way back up and the money he earned was hidden from Clarissa's beady eyes. She'd have spent it before he'd even counted it. He intended to get a bit behind himself and then look for another opening.

Joe turned when he heard Ripley behind him.

'I thought you were going to stand me up,' he said lightly, and then noticed her tear-stained cheeks. 'What's happened?'

'Nothing much. My mother thinks we're seeing too much of each other and she forbade me to come and ride today.'

'Ouch! That's not good news. What are you going to do?'

'No one will ever stop me riding, or seeing you.'

'I don't want you falling out with your parents over me, but I couldn't bear not to see you. It's probably because I'm a lowly land worker, not good enough for you.'

'Don't say things like that, Joe. You're as good as anyone else and I love you.'

'Come here, my poor little Dimps.'

Ripley's face broke into a smile. 'Dimps?'

'I love your dimples. Sorry.'

'I quite like it. Dimps. There's sort of a ring to it.'

'Dimps it is then.' He put his arms around her shoulders and drew her close. 'You know, when you finish studying we could go anywhere you like. I could always get work somewhere else.'

'Joe, you wouldn't be happy away from the Manor, but it's a nice thought.'

'Dimps, I'd be happy anywhere so long as you were by my side.'

'Joe, they're not going to keep me away from you, ever.'

Richard returned home to find Clarissa in bed with a headache.

'No, don't turn the light on. Richard, we have a problem with Ripley and that youth. She deliberately disobeyed me and went to meet him. Totally ignored me. You'd better sort it out.'

'What do you want me to do? We've already been over this and I thought we decided to trust her judgement.'

'We never decided that at all. So you're going to let it carry on?'

'I don't know what you expect me to do. If I banish her from seeing him, she'll go behind our backs. She won't be able to give up the riding and to be quite honest, why should she over a whim of her mother's?'

'It's not a whim, Richard, and I find that accusation very insulting. You should be on my side over this.'

'There are no sides. I'm going down to make a curry.'

'I couldn't eat a thing.'

'Suit yourself. Hope your headache gets better soon.'

He exhaled as he walked down the stairs. Clarissa didn't have enough to occupy her. He picked up the Yellow Pages and began to thumb through it. Clarissa could oversee the work on the house; she would spend her time bullying and ordering the builders about and give him and Ripley a break.

Ripley and Joe had ridden out along the roads on the edge of the fields. The wind had been too forceful for the beach and the fields weren't much better.

'The trouble is we'll be in headwind going back, maybe we shouldn't go too far,' Joe said.

'Suits me, I'm freezing,' Ripley shouted back above the sound of cars driving past. They turned back and were soon stabling the horses.

'Do you have to go indoors straight away? I've bought hot chocolate,' Joe said as he tried to read her expression. She looked happier than when she'd arrived.

'No, I don't want to go home yet. Hot chocolate sounds good.'

Back in his cottage, Joe put a match to the fire he'd set earlier and filled the kettle.

'It'll warm up soon. Can't believe it's June and we've got weather like this.'

'Summer in England and I'm freezing,' Ripley said. Joe wrapped his arms around her. 'I feel better already.'

They fell back onto the sofa in an embrace. Joe ran his hand down her back, sending small tremors through her body. She relaxed as he gently loosened her clothing, removing one piece at a time. He ran his finger around the contour of her breasts and then slid his finger down her stomach. He pulled at his trousers.

Ripley felt lightheaded as he entered her. He moved slowly and deliberately, looking into her eyes as he pushed. She couldn't keep her eyes open. She floated away on a cloud, her body feeling weightless.

Once dressed again, they sat on the sofa, each clutching a mug of hot chocolate. 'I'm boiling,' Ripley said.

'Come on, Dimps, you were freezing just now.'

Ripley thumped him playfully. 'I love being with you, Joe.'

'Not as much as I love being with you. I'll sleep here on the sofa tonight and imagine you still next to me.'

'I'll sleep in my bed and wish my teddy was you.'

'You have a teddy?'

Ripley looked embarrassed. 'I've had Fred since I was a baby. Don't take the mickey.'

'I'm not.' Joe stood, went to the bedroom and opened a cupboard. He returned carrying a furry donkey. 'I've had Henry since I was a baby. He's had to stay in the cupboard since you've been visiting.'

Ripley laughed. 'Ah. He's so sweet. Did your mum buy him for you?'

'No, actually he was a present from May. It had to have been an animal, coming from her.'

'I'd better be getting back before they send out a search party.'

'I'll walk you back. You know where I am if it gets tricky.'

'Thanks Joe.'

They kissed under cover of the oak tree by the house and Ripley sneaked in hoping her mum wasn't around.

'Boo!' Her dad stood before her, laughing.

'Very funny. Where's mum?'

'In bed with a headache. I hear there was a bit of a situation earlier.'

'Mum had a situation. I didn't.'

'Ripley, do you spend so much time with Joe because of the horses?'

'Yes, and he's a good friend.'

'Okay love, that's what I thought. Curry for dinner; it's one of my specials.'

'Mmm. Can't wait, it smells good. I'll go up and have a quick shower.'

'Don't wake your mum.'

'I won't; do you think I'm stupid?'

Richard smiled and watched as Ripley climbed the stairs. She was a chip off the old block. Imagine if she'd turned out like Clarissa and he had two highly strung women to deal with. A slight shudder ran through him. He shook his head and headed back to the kitchen where the curry simmered away on the stove. He lifted the lid and let the aroma fill the air. Perfect. He reached into the cutlery drawer and pulled out a spoon. Delicious. Ripley would love this one. He hadn't seen May, so maybe he would have Ripley all to himself tonight; a rare treat.

May sat in her favourite living room armchair and dozed off. She leaned out of the bedroom window and waved as the Major crossed the gardens. 'It's alright, you can come up. They're all asleep.' A few moments later she heard his footsteps outside her room. She opened the door as quietly as possible. 'Come in before one of them spots you. They lurk around practically every corner; it's not as safe as when I was here on my own.'

'How are you doing with your houseful of family? How's that brother of yours treating you?'

'He's alright, I can hold my own with him, but his wife is a trouble maker. She upset Ritly today, said she should stop seeing Joe. I don't know what's wrong with the woman. I'm so glad young Ritly has come into my life; she's a lovely girl.'

'The girl needs to be careful, her heart will be broken.'

'Joe wouldn't do anything to hurt her.'

There was a tap on the door and May woke up with a start. The Major was gone.

'I must have dozed off.'

'I'm making a cup of tea, Aunt May, would you like one?' Ripley asked.

'What time is it? I thought I was in bed and you were all sleeping.'

'It's about seven. Dad cooked a lovely curry.'

'Oh dear, curry doesn't agree with me at all. My digestive system can't tolerate all those spices. I'll make something later. Tea would be nice.'

May sat deep in her thoughts until her niece returned. Ripley put the two mugs of tea on the table and went back to close the door. May loved these moments alone with her niece. Her brother and his obnoxious wife would never come knocking on May's living room door. Only Ritly would choose to see her when she didn't have to.

'Now dear, come and sit next to your old aunt. Are you alright?'

'You heard mum then?'

'She won't be able to stop young love and more to the point, she shouldn't want to. Joe's a good chap, you won't go far wrong with him, although the Major sees trouble ahead.'

'Joe loves me.'

'I know he does, dear. I've seen the way he looks at you. It's all in the eyes, you know.'

Ripley smiled. Her aunt was the only adult who understood and she'd never been married.

'Was there ever anyone special for you?' Ripley asked coyly.

Her aunt looked around the room and whispered, 'Can you keep a secret?'

'Absolutely.' Ripley moved in closer and gazed into the now aged face. May adjusted her glasses.

'Jimmy Graham, he used to deliver the vegetables from the greengrocer in Crompton. Ritly, he was the most handsome man I'd ever seen. Tall and dark, with a twinkle in his eye. He made me laugh so much there'd be tears running down my cheeks. There only needed to be a certain look and I was off. They were the happiest days of my life. We used to meet on the beach and we'd walk for miles.'

'Did Grandma and Granddad know?'

'No, Mummy and Daddy wouldn't have liked him. He was what they called a rough diamond. Not so different from your dad. Maybe I shouldn't have said that. Ritly, you won't repeat it, will you?'

Ripley giggled. Her dad always liked people to think he was whiter than the driven snow. Ripley knew differently and obviously so did her aunt. 'No, I won't repeat anything. What happened to him? Jimmy, I mean?'

May's eyes sank into darkened pools. 'He was ill. Born with a weak heart, not that it stopped him doing anything he wanted to. He knew how to give a girl...' May took a deep breath and was away on another planet for a moment. 'Well anyway, he became so ill and eventually they couldn't help him. I visited him every time I could. He lived in a council house right in the middle of St. Patrick's estate. They were a family who knew how to love, they always made me feel so welcome. I always felt embarrassed that my parents wouldn't, or maybe couldn't accept people so graciously. I called in one evening and he was gone. I grieved for months but couldn't tell my parents what was wrong. My heart felt like it'd been ripped out. No one could have matched up to my Jimmy. He was a breath of fresh air who'd entered my life and then slipped away without saying goodbye.'

Ripley felt tears stinging her eyes. 'So your mum and dad were a bit like mine when it came to suitable friends?'

'I'm afraid so. For whatever reason, fate sometimes deals us a formidable hand, but Ritly, there is always a reason.' They each picked up their tea and sipped it. May was back with Jimmy and Ripley was somewhere in the future with Joe, hoping it would be in a place by the sea with horses.

Chapter 7

School broke up for summer and Ripley knew it would be the best summer of her life. Joe worked split shifts at the restaurant most of the time, so they would spend the afternoons riding, or swimming. Ripley had reluctantly told her mum that she spent a lot of time with Hannah, freeing up her time to spend with Joe. She couldn't bear the constant arguments and questioning.

Richard had gone away for a few days and had been unusually cagey about where he was going. 'I'm going to look at a business opportunity.'

'What's the point? The bankruptcy court will take any profit you make,' Clarissa said.

'The point is that I have to be doing something. I can't sit around here all day staring at the walls.'

'That's a laugh. You're never here. You've left me to deal with all those ghastly builders and you haven't even put in any ideas or anything. I don't see why I'm doing it; it's your house.'

'Yes, well we're all trying to do our bit.'

'Your sister doesn't do anything. She shuts herself away all day and leaves it all to me. You disappear out and I'm left coping with it all.'

'Do you want May to help you? I'm sure she wouldn't mind putting in a few of her own ideas. I thought you'd like making a few changes of your own.'

'No, I don't need her help. Don't say anything, I'm better off without her opinions, thank you very much.'

'Alright Clarissa, as long as you're sure that's what you want.' Richard walked away smirking to himself. He was proud of the fact he had learned how to manipulate situations within the household to his own advantage and somehow still come out on top.

He planned to stay in a different area to use other casinos. His face was familiar in the local ones so he had to break away to widen his field. Staying away for a few nights would enable him to spend some more time with his latest mistress.

The day he'd met her, Miranda had been on a winning streak when Richard joined the table. When hanging his jacket over the back of the chair, he carefully removed his wallet and placed it in his trouser pocket. She was quick to notice the wad of cash making his wallet bulge. Her eyes sparkled. She had a mission, and now it seemed easier to accomplish. Miranda placed a few chips on two numbers Richard had already favoured. Her lucky thirteen came up and she cast Richard a winning smile, which he warmly reciprocated. 'I think I'll follow your numbers again, if you don't mind,' she flirted, blinking her long, false eyelashes at him.

'Not at all. It's nice to have some good-looking company,' Richard said, and quickly berated himself for such a corny chat-up line.

During the next hour the flirtatious remarks continued until Richard went to cash in his chips. 'I'm going to the restaurant for something to eat, would you care to join me?' he asked.

'That would be lovely. I'll just pop over and tell my friend.' Richard went to the cashier and carefully put the winnings in his wallet.

After sharing a fish platter and salad, Richard went back to Miranda's house for a drink. Miranda lived alone in Queensgate, which wasn't far from Cliff Top Manor. Richard had been captivated by the splendour of the property. She was obviously a woman of means. Over the following weeks Richard had met with Miranda regularly, and often went back to her place to finalise the day in the best way possible.

Recently, Mick had suggested a trip to another area, at the firm's expense. He explained that being seen too regularly in one establishment would draw unwanted attention. So with little explanation to Clarissa, Richard was on his way to spend a few days at a luxurious hotel with Miranda.

Ripley and Joe spent all their free time together and Ripley was dreading returning to the school in ten days' time, although she hoped the sixth form would be better.

'It's been so lovely seeing you so much. Now it's going to be back to studying and horrible routines,' she moaned.

'We'll still see each other every day, like it was before the holidays. You don't think I could go without seeing my girl every day do you?'

Ripley nodded in agreement. Neither of them could stay away from the other, and it wasn't all about the sex. The sex certainly brought them closer, but what they enjoyed most was the love they shared. Their unspoken understanding was beyond explanation and both believed they had found a soul mate with whom to share the rest of their life. It never mattered that they were young and would be ridiculed if they let their feelings become known to the adult world. They knew the truth, which was all that mattered to them.

They were sitting on the sofa in Joe's cottage, sharing a can of coke. Joe put on a Bryan Adams CD and they sang to each other as 'Everything I Do' played. Joe gently pulled Ripley to her feet and they swayed in time to the song. Then he led her into the bedroom, where he began to slowly peel off her clothes. She melted with his touch and lost herself as he made love to her with the sound of Bryan Adam's 'Heaven' drifting through the room.

Ripley grabbed the sheet over herself when the front door of the cottage burst open and a moment later Clarissa stood in front of them shouting and screaming.

'You bastard! She's sixteen! Ripley, get out of here now. How could you? I knew it, I knew you were lying to me. Get out, NOW!' Clarissa raced over to the bed and started thumping Joe as he bent double trying to protect himself and cover his manhood.

'Leave him alone,' Ripley shouted. 'We love each other. We're not doing anything wrong.'

'We'll see what your father has to say about that. He trusted you. Get dressed.' Clarissa was becoming breathless. 'And if you know what's good for you, you'll get out of here as fast as you can before Richard finds you,' Clarissa screeched at Joe. She turned and went through to the living room. Ripley appeared a few moments later, followed by Joe.

'This isn't Ripley's fault. You're right, she's too young and I should have left her alone,' Joe said.

'What are you saying, Joe? Why are you saying that? You love me,' Ripley argued between her sobs.

'Yes, I do love you and I don't want you being blamed for what I've done.'

'Don't worry yourself over who'll be blamed. Richard will blame you and your life won't be worth living,' Clarissa spat. 'Come on, Ripley.' She took Ripley's arm and dragged her out of the cottage. Ripley glanced back at Joe. He mouthed *I love you,* as she was pulled through the door.

Joe could hear Clarissa's scathing criticisms as they walked back to the house.

'Wasting yourself on that no-good gardener. What the hell were you thinking? I knew it, I knew it all along. Well my girl, you've really done it this time. No more going out for you.'

'You can't stop me seeing Joe,' Ripley said, still crying. 'I'm sorry I lied to you about where I was, but you gave me no choice.'

'Can't stop you? We'll see about that. We'll be leaving this hell hole as soon as your father returns.'

'Leaving? To go where? Dad said we had to stay here for now.'

'Don't back-chat me, Ripley. Your dad won't have a leg to stand on over this one.'

At that moment, Ripley hated her mother and felt she had just been waiting for an excuse to get them all out of Cliff Top Manor. Her dad would find a way so they could stay, she was sure of it, but what would he do about Joe? Maybe he'd relieve him of his duties around the farm and find someone else. Whatever happened, they couldn't keep her a prisoner forever.

At midnight, Ripley crept down the stairs and used a torch to find her way along the path to Joe's cottage. She tapped on the door and was relieved to hear his footsteps drawing closer.

'Joe, it's me,' she whispered. He opened the door and Ripley fell into his arms. Joe looked behind her up the pathway and pulled her inside.

'Are you okay?'

'Yes, but my mum's going to try and make my dad move away from here. I can't bear the thought, Joe.'

'Would your dad move? What about May?'

'Joe, I just don't know.' She began to cry. 'I heard mum on the phone to dad, he's coming home tomorrow. I'm frightened about what he might do.'

'He wouldn't do anything to you, would he?'

'No, but he might be unstoppable if he got hold of you. Oh Joe, what a mess. He might sack you.'

'It'd be no more than I deserve. We can still see each other. I'll wait at the clock tower on Crompton sea front every afternoon at four o'clock. You could meet me straight from school when you go back.'

'At least we'd still see each other. I could run away.'

'Where would we go? When I'm qualified, and you've finished school, we could definitely go away from them all.'

'I'd like that, Joe. You're all that matters to me.'

'I'll find a way for us to be together no matter what.'

'I know we'll be together. We have to be sensible for a while and then...'

'And then, you and me, always and forever.'

'I'll get out when I can to meet you at the clock tower.'

'I love you, Ripley. More than you'll ever know. Remember that whatever happens.'

Ripley nodded. Joe slipped her arm through his and took her back up the path. He kissed her tenderly. 'Remember, clock tower at four. I'll be there every day,' he said in a hushed voice.

Ripley turned and quietly crept in through the back door. She waved and Joe blew her a kiss before going back to the cottage. 'I love you,' she whispered into the night, before closing the door and hurrying up to her bedroom.

The next morning Ripley watched from her bedroom window as Joe fed the horses and led them out to the field. She waved and, after looking around, he waved back and smiled. He held up four fingers. She also held up four fingers, held them to her mouth and waved a kiss his way. He responded by mouthing *I love you.*

Ripley drew a deep breath. Maybe she could promise never to have sex with Joe again and persuade her dad to let Joe stay. Until now she'd always had her own way where her father was concerned. However, she'd never been caught naked in the gardener's bed until now, so this was new ground. This time she had pushed her luck a bit too far and knew that, for the first time ever, her dad would be furious with her.

She looked at her watch. May would be in the kitchen with the kettle boiling. Ripley tiptoed down and opened the door.

'Good morning, young Ritly. What a lot of argy bargee yesterday. Whatever happened?'

'Mum caught me with Joe when I should have been with Hannah.'

'A lot of fuss over nothing as usual then.'

'To be fair, Aunt May, we didn't have any clothes on.' Ripley watched her aunt's face turn to a frown and then quickly lighten.

'Oh Ripley. You're not alone. Jimmy and I were caught out once by his parents; it makes it all so much more exciting, don't you think?'

Ripley thought it over for a moment. 'Were they as furious as mum was? You must have heard her.'

'Yes, I did, and no they weren't. I think by then they realised he didn't have long and they were glad he was enjoying himself. Although his mum did ask me not to do it anymore because of his weak heart. We laughed about that for a long time after. It's a bit different for you though.'

'Mum's going to try and make us leave here, I know she is, and Dad is bound to sack Joe.'

'That won't be his decision. Joe has grown up here. I couldn't manage the place without him. As for leaving, I'm sure it won't come to that no matter how much your mum insists. Your dad is strong and he knows where he's well off at the moment.'

'I do hope you're right. I couldn't bear to leave here, and life without Joe would be terrible.'

'Come and give your old aunt a hug. We'll sort something out.'

Ripley was in her bedroom when she heard her dad return home.

'Where is she?' he bellowed. Ripley felt a sudden pang of fear. Her aunt had lifted her hopes and now she knew it was useless to hope for a good outcome.

'She's in her room. I've told her she's grounded,' Clarissa answered.

'We're leaving in two days' time. You'd better start packing,' Richard said authoritatively.

'Two days?'

'Get packing, Clarissa, we're out of here.'

Ripley's hand went up to her mouth. She'd run away. She wasn't going anywhere with them. Aunt May would let her stay here. She heard the back door slam and slipped to one side of the window to peek out. Her dad strutted down the path towards the cottage like a man on a mission. Half an hour later he returned and stomped up the stairs to crash through her bedroom door.

'No more, Ripley, do you hear me? I trusted you, I believed you and you really let me down. It was so good and you spoiled it. We're leaving in two days. You'd better help your mother pack.'

'I'm not going. I'm staying here with May.'

Richard's face turned thunderous. 'You will not stay here. You are coming with us and I'll not hear another word about it.' He slammed the door as he left, enforcing his final decision.

Ripley knew better than to argue. It would only make matters worse. Tonight she would creep to the cottage once everyone was asleep, and make a plan with Joe.

She sat on the edge of her bed unable to sleep, watching under the door for the last light to flick off. At last the house was in darkness and Ripley crept along the landing. She could hear voices coming from May's room and guessed the Major was paying a visit. She wondered if the Major already knew the outcome of this awful situation. Was he telling

May that Ripley was creeping past her door at this very moment? Even if he was, May wouldn't worry and certainly wouldn't tell her parents.

Ripley unlatched the back door and stole along the path by the light of her torch. She tapped on the cottage door and waited.

'Joe, it's Ripley. Let me in. Joe.' She knocked a little louder this time. 'Joe!' No sound came from within the cottage. She tried the handle and it turned, allowing the door to swing back into the living room. 'Joe, it's me, Ripley.'

The bedroom door was open and the bed empty. 'Joe, where are you?' She flicked on the light. The cottage echoed in silence. She stood for a moment, taking comfort from the smoothness of the mother-of-pearl on her necklace. Ripley went back through to the living room and turned on the light. On the mantelpiece above the hearth she saw an envelope with her name scrawled across it in capital letters. She grabbed it down and ripped it open.

Darling Ripley,
I had to leave, I'm so sorry.
I love you Dimps and I always will.
Be happy, I'll never forget you.
Love as always now and forever,
Joe xxx

Ripley read it through over and over again. It made no sense. He made it sound as though she wouldn't see him again. He couldn't mean that. It suddenly hit her. Of course, he wanted to make it look to her parents as though he'd gone and wouldn't be seeing her again. This letter wasn't written for her, but for her mum and dad. Ripley heaved a sigh of relief, and clutching the letter to her chest she made her way back to the house. Wonderful Joe, he thought of everything. Where would he have gone, and why so quickly? Maybe her dad had threatened him, or told him he had to go immediately. That would be it! Poor Joe.

At first light Ripley looked out of her window and saw the stable door open. He hadn't gone, he was feeding the horses. She pulled on her clothes and ran downstairs, not caring who heard her. Out of breath, she rushed into the stable, then stopped dead.

'Oh May, what are you doing here?'

'Ritly, thank goodness. Grab that bucket for me, I didn't realise how heavy it was.' Ripley took the feed over to Filou, who nudged her arm and then delved into the bucket. 'Your father sent Joe on his way before I could do anything about it. I hope he'll ring later so I can tell him to come straight back. That boy's been here with me since he was born, Richard had no right...' Her aunt's eyes were tearful.

'Don't worry, he's meeting me at the clock tower at four. We could both go.'

'Four, you say? Well that ties in nicely with the opticians. You can come with me; we'll call a taxi.'

'Oh brilliant. I was so worried I wouldn't be able to get out. Thanks, Aunt May.'

'You're welcome. Now help me get the horses into the field, will you?'

'Don't worry, you go and put the kettle on. I've done the horses with Joe lots of times.'

May hobbled away, back to the house. That interfering brother of hers. At least by this afternoon she'd have Joe back.

May looked up as Ripley entered the kitchen half an hour later.

'You know your dad was going into town to that agency to find me someone else. He's intent on taking you away from here. I don't understand his plan. If he thinks Joe is gone then why take you away? Where will you live?'

'I don't know any more than you. He told me I had to help pack and we were leaving in two days. I said I was staying with you and his expression frightened me; I've never seen him so cross. I can't stop thinking about Joe and where he spent the night. This is all my fault.' Ripley began to cry.

'Now then, don't get upset. You'll see him later and all will be well.'

'Did the Major say it would be alright?'

'To be honest, he didn't have a lot to say. He was more evasive than usual. Kept going on about there shouldn't be secrets in families.'

'I couldn't exactly tell my family what was going on, could I?'

'Que sera, sera. Whatever will be, will be,' May said thoughtfully. 'What a mess and just when everything had settled down. We might be better to find out if your dad is serious about leaving before I ask Joe to come back. Time is a great healer; with Joe out of the equation, Richard might realise his decision to leave was made in haste.'

Ripley thought for a moment. 'I think you're right. If Joe came straight back there would be no chance of staying. Dad might have calmed down this morning.'

The door opened and Clarissa, still in her dressing gown and looking irritated, grunted as she made herself a coffee and then proceeded to leave the room without a word. May raised her eyebrows and sucked her lips. The front door slammed shut. Ripley rushed into the lounge and, pulling back the curtain slightly, saw her dad driving away at high speed. He obviously hadn't calmed down at all. She returned to May, who was deep in thought now sitting in her armchair, clutching her cold, empty tea cup.

'Dad's gone out. He must still be mad with me. I wish it was four o'clock already; Joe will have come up with a plan, I'm sure of it.' May nodded with a look of sadness.

The scenario took her back to years before when Richard had suddenly left for no apparent reason. It had seemed as though he had a mission to follow then and the scenario was now playing itself out again. May hadn't understood it then and didn't understand it now. Deep down she knew Richard was taking his family and scuttling away instead of facing up to his troubles. Couldn't he see that Ritly would fall in love with whomever she chose and there was nothing her parents could do about it? There was nothing to be gained by running away. How she would miss her young niece. Ritly was the closest family she'd had since her mother passed away. Her heart ached at the thought of losing her niece so soon after getting to know her. Joe out there and alone. Something had to be done; this was a horrible situation.

Chapter 8

May and Ripley stood at the clock tower on the seafront at precisely four o'clock. Ripley fiddled with her necklace, willing Joe to show up. The clock gave a chime for half past four. May had sat on a bench and Ripley had repeatedly walked from one side to the other searching both ways along the seafront for Joe.

'How about going to the restaurant and seeing if he's been held up?' May suggested. She had an awful gut feeling about this. The Major had said Ripley's heart would be broken and once again it appeared he had been right. Joe wouldn't have gone and left her, not when they'd made an arrangement. He wasn't the type to let anyone down, especially not Ripley.

'Okay. But what if we miss him?'

'You go and ask at the restaurant and I'll wait here.'

Ripley didn't need telling twice. She shot off towards the restaurant as though her life depended on it. The doors to the restaurant were closed. She went into the reception area at the hotel next door which was run by the same family.

The girl behind the desk smiled brightly as Ripley entered the foyer. 'Good afternoon.'

'Good afternoon. I wonder if you could help me, I'm looking for Joe who works in the restaurant kitchen.' Ripley could feel her heart pounding in anticipation.

'Joe didn't turn up for work this morning; I was just about to call the number we have for him to see if he was coming in tonight.'

'Oh. I see.' Ripley's heart sank. Where was he?

'It's the first time he's ever let us down.'

'Okay. Thanks for your help.' Ripley slowly walked back to the clock tower with tears flowing relentlessly.

May saw Ripley's subdued stance in her walk and then the tears streaming down her face as she came closer.

'Not there?' May said, shaking her head.

'He hadn't turned up for work this morning. Where could he be?' Ripley sobbed. 'I really thought he'd be here.'

'I know you did, poppet. Shall we go home?' Ripley looked up and down the seafront, and May sighed. 'It's nearly five.'

Ripley nodded. 'I'll come back tomorrow. He said he'd be here every day.'

'We'll go to the phone box and call a taxi.' May was thoughtful for a moment. 'I hope he's alright,' she said, thinking aloud. Ripley went hysterical and fell into her aunt's arms.

'It's all my fault. He could be hurt, or anything.'

'I shouldn't have said that. He'll be fine, he's a strong young man.'

'Not if my dad did something to him.' Ripley blew her nose into the handkerchief May had given her. 'Dad was cross enough to have done something awful, I know it.'

'No. Come on, Ritly, you're letting your mind run away with you. Richard wouldn't do anything; he's not a violent man.'

'Jerry, dad's partner, died after what he did to dad and the police have been questioning him about it.' Ripley took a deep breath, trying to stop her tears.

'Ritly! That's an awful thing to say.'

'But it's true. I heard dad on the phone to a solicitor about it. What if Joe...'

'Let's go and ring a taxi. All this sort of talk is frightening me.' May shook her head and squeezed her hands together.

Ripley put her hand on her aunt's shoulder. 'I'm sorry, I didn't mean to worry you. I have my mobile.'

'I'll have a word with the Major. He'll know what's going on.' Ripley put her arm through her aunt's and they slowly made their way to the roadside.

The taxi arrived and Ripley saw her aunt into the back seat. 'I'm going to walk back along the beach.'

'You can't. Your mum and dad will go mad if you don't arrive home with me.'

'I have to make sure he's not lying hurt somewhere. I don't care what they say. They can't make anything worse than it is now.'

May turned herself and watched out of the back of the car, as Ripley turned and went down the steps to the beach. This was one hell of a mess. May felt sickened, remembering her own heartbreak when Jimmy had died. Somehow, not knowing where Joe was seemed worse.

When Ripley returned home, she went straight up to her room and closed the door quietly. Her mind was buzzing with fear and dread. She had walked the length of the beach and found nothing to indicate Joe had met with foul play. Maybe he'd turn up tomorrow. Inside she dreaded the truth she had to start facing. If he had any intention of turning up, he would have been there today. Why hadn't he gone to work?

She looked out of the window, across to the paddock. The horses were gone and the stable doors were shut.

She heard footsteps approaching and there was a tap on her door.

She hurried to sit on her bed. 'Yes, come in.'

Richard walked in. 'We're leaving tomorrow morning, so make sure all your stuff is packed.'

'Tomorrow morning! Why? Why do we have to go? Joe isn't even here anymore.'

'He decided it was for the best if he left.'

'He decided! You mean you told him to go! What did you do to him? Where did he go?'

'I didn't do anything. Look Ripley, we're out of here in the morning. Get your stuff packed, or leave it here. Your choice.' His voice was soft and showed no anger, only sadness. He turned and left the room.

Ripley couldn't understand. If he wasn't angry anymore, why did they have to leave? Who would look after the place? Where would they go, and where was Joe? She pulled a bag down from the top of her wardrobe and began to toss her clothes into it. Let them leave! No way would she go with them. She'd go missing like Joe, and then demand to stay here when she eventually came back. This was the only place Joe would ever return to, she had to be here.

Waiting for the lights to go out seemed to be becoming a regular occurrence. When the house fell silent and dark, Ripley headed down to the kitchen for some provisions from the kitchen before setting off for the beach. She walked along the path and could see the cottage over to the right. On an impulse she walked over and opened the door. She felt close to Joe when she was here. She turned on the light and shot back against the wall as a scream broke the peace. Ripley saw a movement in the bed and leapt towards the door before realising it was a man and woman sitting up and looking bewildered.

'Who are you?' Ripley asked.

'We might ask you the same question,' the man said crossly.

'I live at the house.'

'And we live here,' he said.

'I told you to fix that lock on the door,' the woman said.

'You live here?'

'We've taken over the grounds and the horses as from today.'

'You can't have...' Ripley broke down into tears. 'Joe... Joe was supposed...'

The woman threw back the covers and pulled on a robe. 'Look love, we don't really know what's going on. The agency called us and told us it was an immediate start. All our references were in order. Sorry if we've done someone else out of a job.'

'So who hired you? My father?'

'Richard Bradford. He owns the big house apparently,' the man chipped in. Ripley nodded, her mind in a whirl.

'I'm sorry to have bothered you.'

Ripley sat on the beach in turmoil. In two days her life had turned into a nightmare. Joe had gone, new people had taken over his job and here she was sitting on the beach crying. She'd never cried so much as she had in the past hours. Joe wasn't coming back. Her dad must have really frightened him, or worse. Had he taken any of his belongings with him? She cast her mind back to the previous evening in the cottage; she couldn't remember if his things were still in place or not. She had to find out.

Scrambling up from the sand she rushed back along the beach and up to the cottage. The lights were out once again, but she needed to know. She knocked.

'For fuck's sake. What now?' The man was shouting. Ripley was already shaking with nerves, but her need to know drove her to wait. The door flew open.

'What?'

'I'm really sorry, but I think something might have happened to my friend. Were there any belongings in the cottage when you took over?'

'No, it was empty apart from kitchen stuff and the like. Now can we get some sleep around here?' He slammed the door and Ripley heard him groaning on about mad women as he turned the lights off. So someone had emptied the cottage. She surely would have noticed if all Joe's things had gone, but she was no clearer knowing if he had taken anything, or nothing. She went back to the beach and sat pondering her options.

After no sleep and a restless night on the beach, Ripley decided to go home. There was nowhere to go and her parents were sure to call the police. She sadly and slowly picked up her bag and sauntered along the beach. In her wildest thoughts she still held the vision of Joe turning up, but somehow she didn't believe it now.

The kitchen light was on; that'd be May as usual at this early hour. Ripley walked into the kitchen and dropped her bag onto the floor. Her aunt looked up at the sudden noise.

'Oh Ritly, there you are. Thank goodness. The Major said you'd be back.'

'You knew I ran away?'

'The Major lets me know what's going on. I'll make us a nice cup of tea.'

'Dad has new people in the cottage. A couple.'

'I know. I met them last night. It won't be the same. Joe was so reliable and easy to get along with. Oh Ritly, I don't know what I'm going to do without you.' A tear rolled down her cheek.

'Please don't cry. I know they won't let me stay with you, but I promise I'll visit every holiday.'

'You'll have your own life. All this will fade as soon as you're settled somewhere else.'

'You don't seriously believe I'll ever forget you, or this place, or anything. I feel empty inside at the thought of leaving. Did dad say we were still going?'

'Yes, I'm afraid he's never sounded surer of anything. I don't know what's got into him. He's found some housekeeper who's coming Monday to Friday, as well as the couple in the cottage. It might have been better if my parents hadn't left so much for the running of this place; then he wouldn't be able to up sticks and run off so quickly again.'

'What do you mean, again?'

'Your dad suddenly ran off when he was in his twenties. There one minute and gone the next. No fight, or row, just gone. Mummy was beside herself, thought something dreadful had happened to him. Ritly some things are meant to be, that's what the Major says. He's been cagey over this and says there are some family issues he can't get involved with. He can be very old-fashioned sometimes. Now, I've something I want to give you.' She shuffled across the room and pulled open a drawer in the dresser. 'This is for you.'

She handed Ripley a charm bracelet. 'I always felt as though it brought me luck; I'm sure it'll do the same for you, Ripley.'

'Thank you. It's beautiful.' She fastened it around her wrist. 'It's got a J on it.'

'Joe gave me that one when he was sixteen. Said it would remind me of our rides out along the beach. Ripley, things have strange ways of turning out for the best.'

'You called me Ripley, twice.'

May laughed. 'I know your name, I like to wind your mum and dad up, and it somehow stuck. I'm still a bit devilish at heart. Time for tea, and you could do with eggs for breakfast after being out on that beach all night.'

Ripley looked at her aunt pottering over the stove. Surely the Major must know something about Joe.

'Aunt May. Couldn't the Major...?'

'I know exactly what you're going to say and the answer is no. He won't tell me anything. That's what I meant when I said he won't get involved in family business. Stubborn old fool.' She raised her eyes to the ceiling and frowned. 'Yes, I do know you can hear me.'

Ripley managed a weak smile. Maybe a lot of what the Major said was her aunt's guesswork and this time her imagination couldn't stretch as far as Joe and his whereabouts. One mystery solved.

Ripley tucked into her omelette as her dad came into the kitchen. 'Good morning,' he said brightly.

'Morning Richard, but I don't know anything good about it,' May said haughtily.

'Dad, please don't make us leave. Joe's gone and I don't want to leave here. I'm sorry for what happened.'

'We have to go, it's all sorted. Right, what's for breakfast?'

'I can cook you an omelette,' May offered.

'Could that stretch to omelette with bacon and mushrooms?' He smiled as though the world was his oyster and he didn't have a care in the world while he was breaking Ripley's and May's hearts. May nodded and began to crack eggs, imagining them to be her brother's thick skull.

Clarissa came to join them as Richard finished his breakfast. She was dressed up for something important.

'Why are you dressed like that? Where are you going?' Ripley asked.

'New beginnings. We have to make a good impression, it makes such a difference. You need to wear something decent. That nice blue dress I bought you in Canterbury would be alright.'

'I don't even know where we're going,' Ripley said, scowling. No way would she wear that dress. Her jeans and tee-shirt would have to do.

'Daddy's secured us a house in Epping Wood. Some business colleagues of his. A very exclusive area, so he tells me; isn't that right, Richard?'

Richard looked embarrassed as Ripley left the table and stormed out of the room. 'What's the matter with her?' Clarissa asked no one in particular.

'She's broken-hearted and you two can't see it when it's staring you in the face,' May said, and followed Ripley out of the room.

Ripley went upstairs and slowly began to pack her belongings. She'd leave her riding gear here for when she visited. Horse riding wouldn't be the same anywhere else.

Joe, where are you? I love you. She held his note to her chest after reading it again. You really did mean you wouldn't see me again.

May was sitting in her armchair staring out of the window when Ripley arrived downstairs half an hour later.

'I'm going to get a taxi to the clock tower every afternoon for a week, just to make sure he doesn't turn up for you.'

'Thank you, Aunt May. Deep down I don't think he's going to show, do you?'

'Never say never,' May said sternly. 'You never know in this world.'

'Never say never. That's going to be my life motto and I'll always think of you and Joe when I say it to myself.'

'Good girl. You have to stay positive and give off a healthy aura, then good things will come.' Ripley crossed the room and flung her arms around her aunt.

'You will be alright, won't you?'

'What, an old girl like me? I'll be right as rain. Now off you go dear, I can hear your mother hovering at the bottom of the stairs.'

'I love you, Aunt May.'

'I love you, Ripley.'

Ripley turned at the door. May was staring out of the window again, lost in her thoughts. Ripley couldn't see the stream of tears running down her cheeks.

Ripley looked through the back window as the car pulled out of the drive. Inside she was empty and broken. I love you, Aunt May; I love you, Joe.

Chapter 9

Ripley decided to give herself the best possible chance at her next private boarding school, by not admitting she had been to a state school. She hated the ploy, but needed to make some real friends who would help her rebuild life after Joe, and she'd learned the hard way at her old school how shallow people could be.

She had no idea how her bankrupt father could send her to private school again and she didn't care. The further away from her parents she was, the better. She rang May a couple of times each week and always had a laugh. May always had some story about the animals, the Major or some complaint about her helpers, which made Ripley yearn to be back there. Her aunt was probably giving her staff a hard time.

True to her word, Ripley stayed with May every holiday. Nothing was the same as it had been. The place seemed different now. Filou had died and only George was there to greet her now. She rode him every holiday, retracing the rides she used to take with Joe.

'So Joe never got in touch?' Ripley asked hopefully, the first time she returned to the house.

'You know the first thing I would have done was to tell you. No. I went for a week, every day at four, but nothing. I think the taxi driver thought I was mad, waiting for a man who never showed. I don't suppose I explained myself very well, he probably thought I had some form of dementia.'

Ripley always slept in her old room and rubbed her necklace; she felt close to Joe when she touched it. Each morning she would go to the window, remembering how excited she'd always felt to see him at work down at the stables feeding the horses. The new couple, the twits May called them, didn't open the stable until eight o'clock so it was always eerily silent and still. Ripley still held a candle for Joe and secretly yearned for him to turn up when she was at Cliff Top Manor.

Life at Cambridge University was different for Ripley. Most of the other students fell in and out of love, but for Ripley there was no one who interested her. She went out and joined in all the fun, but quickly brushed off any unwelcome attention.

There was a florist shop in the town and Ripley often stood staring into the window. The flowers reminded her of Joe and how lovingly he had tended the gardens at the manor. The shop was old-fashioned, with beautiful dark wood surrounding picture windows. Inside was light and airy with flowers adorning every space available. A dark oak desk, scattered with files and papers in disarray, stood in one corner. The disorder only added to the ambience and charm of the most beautiful shop in town. One morning the shop's owner came out, a rounded gentleman with red cheeks and a warm smile.

'Good morning. I often see you looking through the window. Is there anything I can help you with?'

'No, I like looking at the flowers. Your displays are always so beautiful.'

'Thank you. As it happens, I'm looking for a bit of help if you're interested.'

'I'm at the university, I don't know if the time I could be available would be much good to you.'

'My last apprentice studied there too. Have a think about it; it's always a bonus to have someone on board who's appreciative of beauty.'

'I would like to help. I don't need to think about it.'

'Great. Shall we say Saturday at eight?'

'See you Saturday. I'm Ripley Bradford.'

'Sorry, how rude of me. I'm Terry Cole.'

'Thanks Terry.' Ripley walked away with a spring in her step. A job in a florist's shop; she hadn't even asked about the money, what did it matter?

Four years later when Ripley was in her last year at university, May was taken ill. Ripley took her final exam and drove down to Crompton to take care of her. The shock of seeing her aunt so frail frightened Ripley.

'Aunt May, don't even think of leaving me. You're all I've got,' she half joked, trying to make light of a concerning situation.

'If I can stay I will, but the Major thinks my time is near. He says we'll have a jolly old time together.' Ripley could do no more than smile. Her aunt looked weak and tired; she shouldn't have to suffer.

Richard and Clarissa turned up for the funeral; there had been no sign of them in the weeks leading to May's death.

'We'll have to get the place on the market,' Richard said, immediately after the funeral, as they sat having a drink in a local pub.

Ripley was horrified; she still loved the old place. 'You can't sell it. You and May were born there.'

'I'm not ever going to live there, and we'll make a fortune. Developers are crying out for property in an area like that with so much land.'

Ripley began to cry tears of frustration. 'That's all you think about. Money, money, money! May held more love in her heart in a day than you'd know in a lifetime. You make me sick.' She stormed out of the pub and drove back to Cliff Top Manor, barely able to see the road for her tears. How could a brother and sister have turned out so differently? May had been right, they'd always been a world apart.

With her heart breaking, Ripley packed her things and left the old house for the last time. May had said Gran predicted Richard would sell to developers, they knew him so well. She drove to her flat in Cambridge, threw open the door and fell onto her bed, where she cried endless tears of self-pity. Another void in her life.

She had spent her final year at the university trying to decide which career path to follow, but as yet had no plan. The strange thing was, that she almost had too many options. Ripley toyed with the idea of continuing her studies with a PhD in science, but more studying didn't appeal to her.

On Saturday mornings she turned up for work at the florist's as usual.

'What are your plans, Ripley?' Terry Cole asked her. 'Do I have to start looking for a new helper?'

'I don't know what I'm going to do. I don't seem able to make any decisions and it's even worse since my aunt passed away.'

'You could do some more hours during the week if you like, until you sort something else out.'

'I'd like that, Terry. Thanks, but are you making the job for me, or do you really need help?'

'To be honest, I want to do fewer hours and I can't think of anyone I'd rather trust than you. I'd like to retire and sell the place, but my little flower haven is something special... I guess I'm not ready yet.'

Terry soon left Ripley to run the shop. Her happiest times were at work. She berated herself for ending up working in a floristry shop after all her education, but the shop was where she wanted to be. The regular customers gradually stopped asking where Terry was and almost expected Ripley to be in the shop alone. Early in the morning when she would be working on displays and arrangement orders, Ripley would see the same people walking past the shop. Most of them waved and a couple popped their head around the door to have a quick chat. The greetings always started the day off well and gave Ripley a warm feeling.

'The orders have almost doubled since you took over,' Terry told her on one of his rare visits. 'You've certainly got a flair with flowers.'

'I had a good teacher,' Ripley responded, meaning Terry, but also thinking back to Joe and the wonderful garden he tended.

'I was thinking of getting you some help, I know how hard it was on my own and you're doing so much more. To be honest I don't know what to do with the place. You've managed better than I ever thought and the more time off I have, the more I realise the shop has moved forward without me.'

'Sell it to me.'

'Sell it to you? You're joking, Daddy won't buy you a lowly florist shop.'

'I have my own money. A family fund for when I turn twenty-one is about to pay out. Nothing to do with Daddy!'

'Are you serious? You don't want to spend your life doing bouquets and wreaths.'

'Actually, I do. This is where I'm happiest.'

'Tell you what. You already know the sort of price I was going to ask. We'll both sleep on the idea for a week and then have a serious chat.'

'Sounds good to me,' Ripley said. She felt an enthusiasm she hadn't experienced since riding with Joe. The excitement of looking out of her window each morning came flooding back. There had been nothing to enthuse her again until now and the thought of owning the shop, made her heart lurch.

Could she really do this? The bank manager would be the first person to see. Ripley accepted the first appointment available, and took her first step towards a dream she hadn't realised she held before now.

Richard had worked for the firm, as he referred to them, for several years when a business opportunity came his way. Up until now he took the jobs as and when they were available, but he knew his status within the firm was lowly, keeping him humble and grateful. The firm had set him up in a house in Epping Wood and kept him in work at the casinos ever since. Now there was an opportunity to pay something back, to go in and invest some money and promote himself to a significant position.

Cliff Top Manor had been left empty and unkempt and Richard hadn't informed the solicitors that May had died. He had been advised his bankruptcy debts would have to be paid from the profits and he wasn't prepared to lose that amount of money while the debts hung over him; he only had a few years to wait until the debts were wiped off.

Ripley sat in her flat, going through the paperwork she had from the bank. She already knew the monthly takings and outgoings for the shop; she had easily worked out that the shop was within her reach, and with a flat above it she would be saving her rent. A week was too long to wait, but that had been the arrangement. A business woman shouldn't rush in like a fool. Her own business, she couldn't wait! The shrill tone of the phone returned her to earth.

'Hello.'

'Hello Ripley, how are you?' her dad said.

'Hi Dad, I'm fine, thanks.' Things hadn't been the same between them since they'd left Crompton after the funeral.

'I was thinking of coming to see you. How about Friday evening? We could go out for a meal.'

'Friday's alright with me. To what do I owe the honour of a visit?'

'Don't be like that, Ripley. I'd like to see you, nothing more. You've been so tied up with your studies the past few years we seem to have drifted a bit.'

The truth was that Ripley no longer held her dad in such high esteem. Since Joe went missing with no explanation, she suspected Richard of foul play, and that thought, for some reason, had never left her. Why would he have disappeared with no trace after Richard went to see him?

There had to be a connection and it had tainted the relationship with her dad forever.

Ripley was surprised on Friday evening when Richard showed up on his own.

'Didn't mum want to come?' she asked.

'I thought dinner for two would be cosy. Just you and me like we used to do sometimes, when we could get away.' Ripley smiled remembering how difficult her mother always made life for her and her dad. She had freed herself from the situation, obviously her father hadn't been so fortunate.

They sat in a small bistro waiting for their steaks to arrive. Ripley had decided not to tell her dad about the florist shop until the deal was finalised in a couple of months' time. She had the idea her news would be ridiculed.

'So what have you been up to, Dad?'

'Not a lot, this and that, you know how it is.' Ripley didn't but nodded anyway. 'What about you? What plans have you got now your studies are finished?'

'I've got something in the pipeline, but I'm not telling you until later.'

'Oh, little Miss Secretive. Here come the steaks; I'm starving.'

Ripley was relieved her dad didn't press the issue concerning her plans, due to the apt arrival of the steaks. They ate in relative silence apart from small-talk about how good the meal was and a holiday to France which Clarissa had planned.

Neither wanted dessert. The table had been cleared and a coffee sat in front of each of them along with a large brandy for Richard.

'Ripley, you have your inheritance due shortly and I have an investment opportunity for you. The returns would be better than you could get anywhere else and I'd make sure...'

'I've already decided what I want to do with the money.'

'Oh! What's that then?'

'I'm starting my own business.' She took a breath and cleared her throat. A florist's actually.'

'You're joking. A florist's? Flowers and the like? You'll never make any money. Now what I'm offering is a lifetime of income with no work involved. You'd just be reaping in the profits each month. You see...'

'No Dad. I'm buying a floristry shop. That's what I've decided to do.' She watched her dad's cheeks turn red. He loosened his tie.

'Ripley, you're being ridiculous. I didn't pay for you to be privately educated so you could open a flower shop. For once, do something sensible with what you've got.'

'Dad, I'm doing what I want to do. You won't persuade me otherwise.'

'Your grandparents worked hard to ensure the family would be looked after and you're going to throw it all away on a whim.'

'Don't try to make me feel guilty. It's not a whim and that's the end of the conversation.' She gulped as she finished her sentence. The shop was her dream and her grandparents had left the money for her to do with as she wished. Her father would not stop her by trying to inflict guilt on her. She had to be strong.

Richard fumed as he downed his brandy and paid the bill. A bloody florist shop. Maybe he needed to be more direct and tell Ripley the position he now faced.

'You see, I thought you wouldn't have made any plans and when this opportunity came along, I sort of... Well, I said I had the money to invest and to pull out now would put me in an awkward position, to say the least. I was only thinking of you and a good future for you, Ripley. The firm are the ones who helped out when our luck was down. They gave me the house at Epping Wood and loads of work which enabled you to go back to private education. I wanted to do this to sort of repay the debt by way of gratitude. Please would you at least consider it? I could show you all the paperwork and what you'd make each month.' He could hear himself almost begging. He should never had been so premature, boasting to the boss about his future investment and how he'd have no problem coming up with the money. Now Ripley was going to make him look like the fool, which deep down he knew he was. He should have asked her first. There was a time when she would have done anything to help him, but those times had long since disappeared for no reason which was apparent to him.

'No Dad. I'm sorry, but my mind is made up.'

'Just think about it. You wouldn't want me to be embarrassed would you?'

'No, but I can't give you that money. I've already given my word and I'm not letting anyone down.'

'Not letting anyone down? What about me, your own flesh and blood. After all I've done for you. You're beyond belief.' He pushed back his chair and headed for the restaurant door. They stood on the pavement for a moment in an awkward silence. Richard was tight-faced. 'Do you want a lift home?'

'No, I'll walk off dinner, thanks.'

'Give me a call if you come to your senses. Bye.' He stooped and kissed her cheek, almost reluctantly and barely making contact.

'Bye Dad.'

Ripley was relieved to be on her own as she went back to her flat. She turned into the main street, glancing into the shop windows as she walked. Her breathing felt erratic and she felt a bit wobbly at the knees. Her dad had been quite angry.

'Hello there,' a stranger said, making her jump.

'Sorry, hello,' Ripley answered. 'I was miles away.' He now looked familiar, but she couldn't place him.

'Alex Holman. You're in the flower shop at seven in the morning when I pass.'

'Oh right, yes of course. I knew your face, but couldn't quite place you.'

'I'm having a drink in The Eagle, if I can entice you to join me.'

'No thanks. I have to get home.'

'Is your boyfriend waiting for you?'

'No,' she chortled, 'but I do have to get back.'

'Perhaps another time then. See you Monday morning.'

'Will do. Bye.' She crossed the road and headed home. She used to go into the Eagle with her uni mates. What were they doing now? Most had gone back to their home-towns, or another place to begin their careers. A couple were still around, but no one she'd been really close to. Who was she really close to? There was no one who mattered to her now.

That was a sad place to be. She shook her head as she entered the flat and flicked off her shoes. She was happy with her lot; she didn't need anyone else.

On Monday morning, Ripley smiled and waved as usual when Alex passed the shop. Maybe she should have gone for a drink with him. She'd realised too late that she could have done with some company; her weekend had been quite lonely and unsettled.

She waited until mid-morning and then rang Terry.

'Hi Terry, are you ready for a chat?'

'Good morning. I'm always ready for a chat, Ripley. How about when you finish work tonight? I could stretch to Pizza Hut.'

'That sounds great. About six then, see you there.'

The lonely weekend had resulted in her constantly changing her mind about whether or not she should be helping her dad. The hairs on the back of her neck had risen when he said it was the same firm which had put him on his feet again after Cliff Top Manor. She wanted nothing to do with a firm that had enabled her dad to take her away from her Aunt May and Crompton. She knew she was being ridiculous. Her loyalty to her dad played on her mind. Should she try to help him? If she did, she couldn't afford the shop and in the past few days it had become her dream. The shop had been the only thing which had uplifted her spirits and now, with the anger she still held for her father, mixed with duty, love and loyalty, she knew she had to make a decision once and for all and stick to it.

At six o'clock, Terry was already at a table scanning the menu.

'Ripley.' He rose and kissed her cheek. 'Have you had a good day?' Ripley noted he looked happy and relaxed.

'Yes thanks. How about yours?'

'I haven't been able to put my mind to anything after your call. I knew you must have come to a decision and it threw me completely off course.'

'Do you mean you've changed your mind about selling?'

'No. The opposite. I've imagined a cruise with Saga, a trip to Australia and there's so much more. Now tell me you've changed your mind.'

'No, absolutely not. I've got the upstairs flat renovated and the kitchen out the back turned into a storage area...'

'You're as bad as me with all this planning ahead. Let's order and then get down to business.'

'Four-cheese, chorizo, ham and tomato,' Ripley said when the waiter took the order.

'My goodness, you must be hungry,' Terry chortled.

'I suddenly feel ravenous. I might even go for dessert later.'

The chatter was non-stop as Ripley and Terry went through the finer details of the shop sale. Neither of them had any surprises in store and the decisions made were amicable.

'I can't believe this is all working out so well. Thank you, Terry.'

'No, thank you. I couldn't be happier. I know the business is in good hands and I'm not asking you the price I would have taken from a stranger.'

'Terry, a business deal is just that; you can't let sentiment stand in the way of finance.'

'It's not sentiment. We've known each other a long time now. If I had a daughter, I'd have hoped she'd turn out as lovely as you. Your parents must be so proud of you.'

Ripley gulped. Oh no, don't be nice to me, I'm going to cry. 'I need the ladies,' she said, and rushed off.

Terry watched her. Now he'd really put his big foot in it and spoiled a wonderful evening. Whatever troubled that girl had hung over her for years. How could someone as easy-going as Ripley have any sort of trouble with her parents?

Ripley splashed her face with cold water and watched as the mascara ran down her cheek. What a wreck! Terry had certainly touched on a sore point. She had made a choice which was hers to make. How dare her dad try and spoil it for her? Hopefully Terry wouldn't ask her what the problem was. She wiped her eyes and cleaned her cheeks. Nothing could spoil what she had; no one could take it away from her. Her own business and flat.

Ripley confidently walked back across the restaurant to Terry. 'Sorry about that.' She sat down and took a sip of her wine. 'My dad thinks I'm wasting my education by wanting to be a florist and I suppose to a certain degree he's right.'

'Ripley, it's your choice. My parents thought I was gay when I said I was opening a florist's. I had terrible trouble with them for years. Parents can't rule your life, even though they like to think they can.'

'So you went ahead against their wishes?'

'Yes, and I have to say I never looked back. I loved the work. Well, to be honest it didn't seem like work, I loved it.'

'So how long was it before they stopped accusing you of being gay?'

'The day I told them they were right and I was happy. They looked at me, dad tried opening his mouth, but nothing came out.'

Ripley laughed. 'I had no idea. Not that it makes any difference. I think that's so funny. I would have loved to see their faces.'

'I have to say, the vision stayed with me for years. There's only so much you can take before you say enough is enough. I had my own life to lead and that's what I intended to do.'

'You're right. I'm buying the shop with my money and no one can stop me. Not by trying to send me on a guilt trip or anything else.'

'That's a girl. You go for what makes you happy. Life's for living Ripley and some things you have to put to one side and get over. If you don't, how can you ever be truly happy?'

'You're so right. I've made a big change and I have to let go of all the negative things which hold me back. Today is the beginning of the rest of my life and I intend to live it. Thanks Terry, you're a good friend.'

'No, I'm just an old fool who can see when people have a few skeletons in their cupboards which they need to be rid of.'

'Don't. My aunt had a ghost who used to visit her and give her advice. The rest of the family ridiculed her, but I was never sure.'

'I bet she was a happy soul though, wasn't she? In a world of her own, not caring what people thought?'

'Yes. You sound like you knew her. She was a lovely lady. I'm going to think of her when I deal with my dad in future;

she wouldn't have put up with his nonsense and in memory of her, nor will I.'

A calmness came over Ripley and she lifted her glass to Terry. 'To Aunt May, you and me and new beginnings.' Their glasses chinked and they took a drink, both about to start a new adventure.

Chapter 10

Within two months, Ripley had renamed the shop Flower Haven and moved into the flat above. She had considered renovating it before moving in, but finances dictated otherwise. A bright red sofa and a double bed were the sum total of her furniture. She convinced herself it would be much more fun to try and decorate while she lived there. What else would she do with her spare time after completing stock taking, ordering from suppliers, constantly changing the displays to give a fresh look each week and a hundred other tasks? Ripley loved her new life and the business thrived.

Ripley was out in the back room one morning, making up an order, when the shop bell sounded.

'I'll be with you in a moment,' she called out.

'No worries, there's so much to choose from it'll take me forever,' a friendly voice called back. Ripley tucked another bloom into place and hurried through. The woman had selected several flowers and lined them up on the counter, continuing to add to the pile.

'Good morning, sorry to have kept you waiting.'

'Not at all. I'm really enjoying myself. Now do you have a wide piece of yellow ribbon?'

'Yes, would you like me to tie them for you?'

'I'll do it. I used to work for a florist until I had the children. These are to cheer up my poor mum. She's not been well for a while.' Ripley cut off some ribbon from a large roll and watched while the flowers were expertly tied into a posy. The woman took the scissors from the counter and cut the ribbon tails into strands, deftly running the scissors along each one in turn to curl them.

'I can see you're used to this,' Ripley said.

'I do miss it.'

'I could do with an assistant if you're interested. I'm Ripley Bradford. I've only just taken over and I'm run off my feet.'

'Are you serious? I'd have to cut down the hours in the school holidays. My mum-in-law would have the children a couple of days a week. I'm Susie Pocket.'

'Perfect. When can you start?'

'I can't believe this. I only popped in on a whim and I've got a job. When do you want me? I do have to take the children to school and collect again.'

'Sounds perfect. Thank you. I started working here because I used to admire the window displays so often; sometimes things are meant to be. How about Monday morning? Drop the children off and come along then until the afternoon. I suppose we'll have to think about wages. Shall we talk about that on Monday?'

'Sounds good. Thank you.'

Ripley smiled as Susie left the shop carrying her posy. Susie Pocket; somehow the name suited her red hair and freckled, rounded cheeks. She was sure having Susie in the shop would be a bonus beyond the help she needed.

Ripley never looked back. There was always light-hearted banter with the customers and the atmosphere in the shop was always uplifted by Ripley's easy-going, friendly manner and Susie's frequent laughter.

'You've got an admirer,' Susie called through to the back room where Ripley was working one morning. She appeared in the doorway carrying a rose in a cellophane box.

'Ha! Ha! Where did you get that from?'

'A taxi delivered it. There's a card.'

Ripley took the box and opened it, releasing the small white envelope wedged inside.

'From an admirer.' She flipped the card over. 'Nothing to say where it came from. It might be for you. Maybe Kev's getting hopeful.'

Susie laughed. 'No, the driver said it was for the owner of the shop and that's you, no getting away with this one.'

'Do you think it's a customer?'

'We're going to have to scrutinise all of them and watch for the signs of love,' Susie said, enthusiastically.

'Signs of love! I don't think we'll go that far. It's probably some terrible, ugly old flirt, too worried about showing himself.' She walked to the draining board and picked up a slim vase, filled it with water and stood the rose on the window ledge. 'Don't you say anything, I don't want to encourage anyone.'

'You could do with a bit of fun, a nice man might be alright.' The bell sounded in the shop.

'Susie! Shop, now!' Ripley shook her head as Susie disappeared, laughing to herself. Ripley was far too busy to fit a man into her life and anyway she wasn't interested in anyone since Joe. First love had hit her hard and she wasn't prepared to repeat the heartache.

The roses arrived by taxi every Friday morning at around eleven o'clock for the next three weeks. On the fifth Friday after the first rose had arrived, Ripley was ready and waiting for the taxi driver with a barrage of questions. She learned nothing, except that the rose was left for collection at the reception area of a large office building on the outskirts of town. 'I don't know anyone who works over that side of town,' she told Susie as the driver left the shop. Susie turned out her bottom lip and shrugged her shoulders.

'It's nice to have a mystery admirer... Not that I ever have, but you have to admit it's exciting.' The rose mystery continued for six weeks and became a strange but expected occurrence, until one Friday when it didn't arrive.

'Oh well, he's obviously found someone else,' Ripley said, sounding a little disappointed. It had been intriguing trying to imagine who the stranger could be. She and Susie had scrutinised every man who came into the shop and the fascination had continuously captivated both women.

At three o'clock the shop doorbell drew Ripley's attention and she went through to see Alex standing in front of her.

'Hi, don't often see you these days. Have I missed you in the mornings?' she asked.

'No, I moved, so I don't walk this way to work now.'

'What can I do for you?'

'I'd like something special made up for someone I'd like to take out. I thought flowers were a safe option for making a good impression.'

'They certainly are. Do you have anything in mind?'

'No. You know what a lady likes, so you do something special for me. Will about thirty pounds give me an impressive display?'

'I should think any lady would be impressed. When do you want it?'

'Would tomorrow at three be alright? I'll come in and collect it.'

'Fine.' Ripley wrote out a ticket and handed it to him. 'See you tomorrow then.' She hurried back to the bouquet she had been working on and the bell went again.

The taxi driver, Bob, held up the familiar rose in a box.

'Bet you thought he'd gone off you. The receptionist forgot to book the taxi this morning, apparently it was a temp who was run off her feet.'

Ripley smiled. 'I still don't know who he is; he's being really elusive. Thanks.'

'See you, love. Have a good weekend.'

'And you.' Ripley looked at the rose and went through to the back to stand it in the vase she now left on the window ledge. She realised she was smiling to herself. This mystery man was getting to her.

The next morning was hectic with bouquets and table displays to make up for a wedding that afternoon. At one o'clock they stopped for tea. 'I'll deliver these and then do you want me back this afternoon?' Susie asked.

'No, there's only a couple of orders, I'll be fine. You get home with your family and have a good weekend.' Ripley sometimes found herself envious of Susie going home to her family. Since she'd bought the shop she'd seen very little of her parents, not that she minded that, but sometimes she felt lonely when she saw other people sharing their lives with loved ones.

At precisely three o'clock Alex turned up for his bouquet.

'If that doesn't woo her, nothing will,' Ripley chortled.

'I hope so,' Alex said. 'I'll be back to complain if it doesn't work.'

'No pressure then. Good luck.'

'Thanks. I need it with this one. Have you got one of those little cards to write on?'

'It's there tucked in the ribbon. Let me know how you get on.'

Alex laughed and left the shop. Ripley was thoughtful for a minute. Alex seemed nice; she hoped it worked out for him.

Half an hour before closing, Ripley was busying herself tidying the shop when the door opened and Bob the taxi driver walked in.

'Don't even ask. I'm sworn to secrecy on this one. Actually I'm not, I can tell you exactly where it came from.'

'So can I! I made this up an hour ago for someone I know. Are you sure he said to bring it here?'

'He said to make sure I delivered it immediately. What does the card say?'

Ripley slowly took the card from the envelope feeling as though she was intruding. 'Hope this impresses a special lady. Will pick you up at eight o'clock for dinner. Alex Holman.'

'So, are you going to dinner with him? You should really after all those roses he's sent.'

'How do you know it was him?'

'Stands out a mile. Going by that smile on your face, I'd say you're going.'

'I suppose it'd be rude not to.'

'You have a lovely time. Enjoy yourself.'

'Thanks Bob, I will.' Ripley stood in the middle of the shop still feeling as though there'd been a terrible mistake. Why hadn't Alex simply asked her out? Had he sent the roses? Was this bouquet meant for someone else? Had Bob got it wrong? She daren't unwrap the flowers in case Alex turned up for them again. Leaving the bouquet in a jug of water, Ripley locked the shop and went up to her flat. Now the big question was, should she get ready for dinner, or put her feet up and sit in front of the box with a glass of wine? She had no choice but to get ready and then feel like a fool when Alex didn't show up. She rested back in the bath and let the suds soothe away her worries. No one need ever know she had sat in front of the television on a Saturday evening like Billy-no-mates all dressed up with no place to go. What if Bob was right and Alex did turn up? Did she want to go out for dinner with him? She heaved a sigh and decided to let fate step in. She would get ready and if he showed up, she'd go to dinner with him. If not, she wouldn't tell a soul. Satisfied with her resolve she climbed out of the bath, dragged a towel over herself and went to look for something to wear.

Ripley sat nervously waiting, while peeking through the corner of the curtain at the road below. A dark car pulled up right outside the shop. Alex climbed out and looked up at the flat. Oh my God! Ripley realised she was shaking. The flowers were for her, the roses must have been from him. She switched off the light and then quickly turned it on again so she didn't look too keen; the bell hadn't rung yet and anyway she ought to leave a light on, she wasn't used to coming home in the dark. Her whole body felt hot as she waited for the bell. Finally she went to the window and peeped out from behind the curtain. The car had gone and so had Alex. She pulled back the curtain and pressed herself up against the window. He had really gone; the curtain fell back into position as she walked back to the sofa feeling deflated. If she'd gone downstairs when she'd turned off the light she'd be in the car and on her way to a restaurant at this very moment. She felt sickened by her own actions. That's it then! Why hadn't he pressed the bell? He must have changed his mind. Her heart raced and her hands trembled as her tongue constantly tried to reduce the dryness of her lips. She flicked off her shoes, un-clipped her hair and switched on the television. At least that would take her mind off the bizarre day she'd had. She wanted to ring Susie and tell her what had happened, but she really didn't like to intrude on her family time.

The bell rang causing her to jump. She grabbed her shoes and raced down the stairs.

'Alex, you went.'

'I know. I'd only just walked away from the car when the police drove past and said I had to move it. I ended up in a car park by the river.'

'Oh right.'

'You look beautiful. Shall we go?'

'Yes, I'll grab my bag from upstairs.' She raced upstairs, picked up her bag, took a quick look in the mirror and gasped. Her hair, which had looked so great, was now straggled around her shoulders as though it hadn't been brushed for a week. She quickly found her clasp and gathered it up at the back of her head and hurried back down to Alex. She suddenly felt rude not inviting him in.

'Sorry, leaving you on the doorstep like that.'

'That's fine. It's either a meal in town or back to the car park.'

'A meal in town sounds good.' Ripley could feel her heart racing as they walked the short distance to the middle of town.

'So did you like the flowers? I had a spectacular florist I know make them up specially.'

'They were lovely, thank you. Why didn't you ask me instead of going to all that trouble?'

'Last time I asked you said no. I thought you were obviously a girl who needed a bit of persuasion and I have to admit it seems to have worked.'

'So was it you who sent the roses each week as well?'

'Roses? Someone's been sending you roses? Not guilty on that score. There must be another admirer; I'll have to watch out for him.'

'Tell me the truth.'

'That is the truth. I know nothing,' he argued. Ripley was unconvinced, but it felt good to be going out for a meal on a Saturday night.

Ripley found her mind wandering to Joe throughout the meal, wondering what he would look like now and if he was even alive. It should have been him she was out with, not some stranger. Why couldn't she get over him?

At the end of the meal, Ripley insisted on paying half of the bill, knowing she wasn't going out with Alex again and feeling guilty about the amount of money he'd already wasted on her with the flowers.

'I never go out with a man if I don't pay my way,' she lied. 'I'm a business-woman and like to be treated as an equal,'

'If you feel that strongly about it I suppose I'll have to agree, but next time it's on me,' he said. Ripley didn't answer. Alex walked her to the door of her flat. She was grateful he didn't attempt to kiss her, or suggest coming in. She had enjoyed the evening, and being friends would have been okay, but men usually wanted more than that and Ripley still had only one man on her mind.

Monday morning the shop was rife with Susie's outbursts.

'Oh no. You should have rung me. You went out with the phantom rose sender and I've been oblivious all weekend.'

'He said he wasn't the rose sender, but I don't know if I believed him.'

'I can't believe what he did with the flowers. How romantic. When are you seeing him again?'

'I'm not.'

'Why?'

'Because I don't want to.'

'Why?'

'Because I don't.'

'But you had a good time and you went out on a Saturday night for a meal, and you said you liked him.'

'Yes, but I don't want to see him again. It won't go anywhere and there's no point.'

'I hope you don't mind me asking, but are you gay?'

Ripley roared with laughter at Susie's serious face. 'No, I'm not gay, I just don't want to go out with Alex again. Now, can we talk about something else?'

'I don't know if I can.'

'You can.'

'I'll try. But can you give me one solid reason?'

'No I can't.'
'But...'
'End, Susie. Go and put the kettle on.'

Susie knew when she was beaten, but she wasn't giving up on this one too easily. There was something sad and strange about Ripley whenever love or families were spoken about. Her eyes held a sadness and there were often times when Ripley seemed to be a million miles away.

Susie filled the kettle and started to put the coffee in the mugs. Then she saw the bouquet standing on the draining board. It wasn't any old bouquet, this one was special. Poor man.

That evening, Ripley gave Susie the bouquet to take home.

'I couldn't.'

'Yes you could because I don't want them in my flat and they're too beautiful to wither and die here in the back room still in their cellophane and ribbons.

On Wednesday, Alex came into the shop as Ripley was closing.

'How about dinner on Saturday?'
'I can't. I've already made arrangements.'
'Another time perhaps?'
'Perhaps.'
'I'll give you a call, I've got the shop number.'
'Okay, if you like.'
'See you soon, I hope.'
'Bye Alex.'

Ripley locked the door after he left and took the back door up to the flat. She felt mean, but it would also be mean to string him along when she was in love with someone else.

How could she ever have the same feelings for anyone, as those she'd held for Joe for so long? As she climbed the steps to the flat something dawned on her like a bolt from nowhere. If Joe was still alive, he'd have surely built a new life for himself and he could love someone else by now; when he had loved her she had been a mere school girl. Why would he have waited for her and not got in touch after all these years? To be honest the past couple of years he wouldn't have found her, but up until May had died, he could have easily got in touch.

Maybe it was time to start facing up to the truth. If he was dead, there would be no contact and if he were alive he had no intention of getting in touch. There could be no alternatives. Either way, Joe was gone forever and she had to start believing that and move on, or be a miserable lonely woman forever. It had been nice to dress up and go out on Saturday. Night after night she sat alone in her flat; life was passing her by. She brought the back of her hand up to her cheek and wiped away a tear and then wiped the other cheek. The tears fell faster than she could wipe them and she gave in to the storm which had been approaching for years. Her heart broke once again with the realisation of the truth.

Chapter 11

A single rose arrived on Friday morning.

'How did the date go?' Bob asked. 'He must still be keen, he's still sending these.'

Ripley took the box. 'It went well, thanks.'

'Have a good weekend, pet.'

'Thanks Bob. And you.' Ripley raised her eyebrows as she put the rose in fresh water.

'He's not going to give up,' Susie chortled. 'Why don't you go out with him on Saturday? There's never much on the box on Saturdays; what have you got to lose?'

Ripley shrugged her shoulders and drew in her lips. 'Shall I make coffee?'

'You haven't been right since the weekend. What are you thinking about in that pretty little head?'

Ripley filled the kettle and silently willed Susie to leave her alone. She'd been close to tears all week and although nothing had actually changed, she felt as though her eyes had been opened to the truth which she had to accept. Had it really taken her so long to realise? No, she'd known all along, since he hadn't turned up at the clock tower, but she'd never stopped herself holding on to a dream which would never materialise. She looked down the order book.

'Can you work for a couple of hours this afternoon? I know it's short notice...'

Susie smiled. 'Of course I can. Anything to help the course of true love run smoothly.'

'You're right. I definitely need some love in my life. There's only one arrangement in the book.'

A few hours later, Ripley threw open the door of the shop, making a grand entrance with a small black dog on a lead and her hands full of bulging bags.

'Hello, who are you?' Susie said, looking straight at the dog.

'We're not sure yet, we need to give that one some thought,' Ripley answered.

'So is this the man for you?'

'Hardly. I thought I'd give you something to think about, it's a girl.'

Susie patted the dog's head. 'You are a sweetie. Where did you get her?'

'The rescue centre. I told them to find me one that was small, quiet, polite, and deserved a good home and this little one was brought out. I couldn't bring myself to go and look at them all. I was lucky they had a young lad on work experience so he was allowed to choose her for me.'

'So had you thought about a dog before today?'

'No. I don't know why I'd never considered a dog; someone to talk to in the evenings. Today it felt right.' Ripley felt at a low ebb and wanted something to love and take care of. She knew a dog would return her love and at this time she needed love to fill the gaping hole deep inside her. Would she ever be able to move on and be happy? Joe had hung around in her mind forever, but the time had come to focus on something else and she had taken the first step. 'So now all we need is a name, little one,' she said, stroking the dog lovingly.

'Would you like to come to us for dinner tomorrow night? The kids can meet the new addition and maybe they'll come up with a name. Kev's trying his hand at a curry after watching Gordon Ramsey in India. Can't promise we'll be able to eat it.' She chuckled at her own humour.

'Thanks, that'd be really nice.' Life was looking up.

Ripley arrived at Susie's house the following evening laden with chocolate and sweets for the children and two bottles of wine.

'Come in, welcome,' Susie said. A small girl hiding behind Susie's legs peeped up at Ripley with large brown eyes. The dog licked her leg forcing a smile. 'She likes you, Holly. Say hello to Ripley.' Susie closed the door.

'Hello, Ripley.'

'Hello, Holly. What a pretty name for a pretty girl.'

'She was born on Christmas eve,' Susie said. Another girl appeared. She must be the ten-year-old; she was the image of her mum.

'I was born on holiday at the seaside. I'm Ocean.'

Ripley smiled. 'Ocean, I'm really pleased to meet you.'

'Let Ripley in. Ocean, take the dog in the garden for a minute, let her have a sniff around.' The girls and the dog raced off. 'We'll stay away from the kitchen for the time being; Kev's getting a bit fraught.'

Ripley laughed and sat on a large comfy sofa. 'Fraught?'

'Yes, he does that when he's stressed. What can I get you to drink? There's wine, juice, beer, and coke.'

'Oh, I brought wine with me. There you go.' Ripley handed over the bag she'd been clutching. 'There's some treats for the girls as well.'

'We'll save those until dinner's finished. Thanks. So wine, is it?'

'Lovely. White please.' Susie left the room and Ripley cast her gaze over to some shelves in the alcove, where several pictures sat showing the girls at various ages. She walked over to take a closer look. There were Susie and Kev on their wedding day, here were new born babies and over there small children blowing out cake candles and playing on the beach. Ripley sighed. Happy little family.

'There you go then,' Susie said, handing her a glass. 'Cheers.'

'Cheers.'

The door opened with a bang and the dog appeared followed by two panting children.

'We couldn't catch her,' Ocean said.

'She ran away,' Holly said, laughing.

'We thought of a name. How about May? You got her in May and it's a little name for a little dog. She already knows it. May. May.' Sure enough the dog ran to Ocean's flicking fingers.

'May,' Holly said, and the dog responded by dashing to her outstretched hand.

'Looks like you have a name,' Susie chortled. 'Sorry, they take after me naming everything related to when and where. They named the cat River. Guess where we found him?'

'The thing is my aunt was called May. I think she'd turn in her grave if I named the dog after her.'

'Did she like animals?'

'Yes, but...'

'Oh she won't mind a bit. She'll be glad she's still a part of your life. Did you get on?'

Ripley gulped at the question and had to clear her throat before her voice became clear. 'Yes, she was lovely.'

'May,' Susie called and the dog turned and ran to her.

'I think it's the tone you're all using. Listen, I'll show you what I mean,' Ripley used a high pitched voice. 'Fred.' The dog sniffed at the carpet in the corner of the room and took no notice. 'Fred! Mmm, I'm being ignored. May.' The dog turned and ran to Ripley who took a deep breath, knowing she'd been outvoted. 'Okay, May. I have to admit it suits you. May it is. Aunt May, if you're listening, I had no choice.'

A man who must have been about six foot three walked into the room wiping his brow. 'Sorry, I'm Kev. I was goaded into preparing the meal tonight. I've been tied to the stove for hours.' Ripley took an instant liking to him. His cheeks were red, as was his nose.

'Pleased to meet you. It smells delicious.'

'Goaded my foot. You volunteered after thinking you could do better than Gordon Ramsey. That remains to be seen, but I have to admit, if it tastes as good as it smells, you might be goaded into cooking duties more often,' Susie said, and giggled.

Kev frowned at the prospect. 'Well, it's already on the table. Be gentle with me, my love.'

Susie laughed. 'Right. Here we go! After you, Ripley.'

The centre of the table was an array of dishes of all sizes with chutney and finely chopped onions and salads. A large dish of still sizzling curry took prime position in the middle and two different rice dishes made up the display. A basket at one end contained poppadum, while one at the other end housed naan bread.

'This looks lovely, Kev,' Susie said, sounding shocked. 'I'm really impressed.'

'There's so much. It does look wonderful,' Ripley said.

'Don't be fooled. These two put it away like they've got hollow legs,' Kev said, motioning towards the girls. 'Sit down, Ripley, anywhere you like.'

'I want to sit next to Ripley,' Ocean said.

'So do I,' Holly chipped in.

'So do I,' Susie whined.

'And me,' Kev moaned, with his bottom lip turned out. They all laughed and Ripley sat down with a girl grabbing a chair either side of her. The dog crawled under the table and sat on her foot.

Ripley realised something within her had lifted. She definitely needed to get out more often. All work and no play wasn't any sort of life, even if it was what she loved. She could try to find some dog training classes, although May did seem quite obedient already. May. It sounded weird, but its familiarity gave a nice warm feeling within her.

The room was filled with chinking spoons hitting china as they delved into the bowls and filled their plates.

'Gordon Ramsey the second,' Susie declared. 'This is delicious. Guess you have yourself a Saturday job, Kev.'

'Can Ripley come next time Daddy cooks?' Ocean asked.

'She certainly can, if she eats up all her dinner and has seconds,' Kev chortled.

'I think I could manage that. This is lovely, thanks,' Ripley said, a feel-good feeling washing over her.

The following Saturday Bob walked into the shop carrying a bouquet Susie had delivered earlier.

'He's at it again. This one's determined to get you, isn't he?'

Ripley raised her eyebrows, tore the card from its staple and ripped open the envelope. 'Dinner tonight at eight. Will pick you up. Alex. I have to hand it to him he doesn't give up.'

'You will go, won't you?' Susie said, coming in from the back.

'It'd be rude not to, I suppose,' Ripley said with a grin at her friend.

'That's it, you go for it. Have a good time,' Bob said. 'See you next week with the rose delivery.'

'Thanks Bob,'

'What about May? I've never left her alone yet. She might think she's been abandoned again.'

'I'll take her home,' Susie piped up immediately. 'She can have a sleep-over with the girls. You can collect her in the morning.'

'If you're sure.'

'Of course I am. She'll be spoilt rotten.'

Alex rang the bell at eight. Ripley picked up her bag, and casually went down to the door. Tonight she felt relaxed and looked forward to a night out with good company.

Her week had taken a turn for the better. She'd taken May for walks along the riverside and to the park. It seemed other dog owners kept to regular times and routes. Ripley had already become familiar with a couple of other walkers before work began, and had time to stop and chat with others in the evenings. It was unclear who enjoyed the walks more. Ripley loved getting out in the fresh air and getting to know a few other like-minded people who loved their pets.

She opened the door. 'Hello Alex. Thanks for the flowers.'

'You're welcome. Tonight I've booked somewhere a bit special. Shall we go, my lady?' He held out his arm and Ripley slipped hers into it. He squeezed his elbow and held it for a moment as though securing her, before releasing the hold and leading her along the pavement towards the town.

'How's your week been?' he asked.

'Fantastic actually. I got a dog from the rescue centre.'

'A dog? Why ever would you want a dog?'

'I fancied one. It was on an impulse and she's lovely.'

'Nice. What did you do last Saturday?'

'I went to dinner with Susie and her family. She helps out in the shop.'

'Oh, right. It must have been her I ordered the flowers with.'

'You shouldn't keep doing that. I have enough flowers around me all the time. It's a lovely thought though.'

'I think you need to understand that if I want to send you flowers, that's exactly what I'm going to do.'

Ripley sensed a tone she'd never heard him use before. 'Sorry, I didn't mean to offend you.'

'You haven't.' He motioned her to the right. 'Here we are, down this way.' They turned into a side street and Alex stopped outside a dimly lit, double-fronted, old-fashioned restaurant with leaded windows. If snow had been falling the restaurant could have been straight from the front of a Christmas card. Ripley imagined a log fire would have been burning and little lanterns on the tables. 'The food in here is unbelievable.'

Alex opened the door and Ripley's eyes were drawn to one far corner where a patterned screen stood on the hearth. 'This is so quaint. I bet it's cosy in the winter,' she said. A woman in a black skirt and white blouse showed them to a table.

Alex pulled out a chair for Ripley.

'What can I get you to drink?' the woman asked.

'A pint of bitter for me and white wine, is it, Ripley?'

'Yes, thanks.' Ripley looked around. Two other diners tucked into prawn cocktails in stemmed glasses. She would order one for herself. 'How did you find a place like this? It's really tucked away.'

'It was recommended and I imagine that's how everyone knows about it. You'd never find it. I thoroughly recommend the honey-roasted ribs.'

'That sounds delicious.' The woman returned with the drinks and went to hand them a menu.

'We don't need that. Two honey-roasted ribs,' Alex ordered.

'And a prawn cocktail to start,' Ripley said.

'You won't want a starter. The ribs are almost too much for me.' He turned back to the waitress. 'Just the ribs, please.' Ripley felt her cheeks redden. How dare he!

'Cheers, here's to good food and wonderful company,' Alex said, raising his glass.

'Cheers,' Ripley said, still feeling miffed about the prawn cocktail.

The ribs arrived and Ripley felt secretly pleased she hadn't insisted on the prawn cocktail, but she still resented his interference. The plates were oval and the ribs filled them. Side dishes of mange tout and cauliflower cheese were put on the table.

'You won't taste ribs like this anywhere else.'

'They look yummy. Roast potatoes as well. We'll never eat all this.'

'And you wanted a starter. I do know what I'm talking about.' Ripley nodded in agreement and began her meal.

Her trousers felt tight by the time the meal was finished. Now she understood what elasticated waistbands were for. The button dug into her stomach as they walked back to the flat. Tonight she would invite Alex in for a drink. She had some beer and wine in the fridge.

They arrived outside her door. 'Thank you for a lovely evening, Ripley.'

'Would you like to come up for a drink?'

'On a second date? I'm not that cheap,' he said and bending forward he kissed her gently on the cheek. 'Good night.'

'Good night,' she said. Was he being serious? He turned and walked away. Ripley stood for a moment, expecting him to turn around laughing at his joke, but he didn't. He kept walking and didn't look back. Ripley put her key in the lock and let herself into the flat. Did that mean he thought she was cheap for asking and that was his way of getting the message across?

She kept her shoes on, half expecting the joke to be on her when the doorbell rang any moment. She went to the corner of the curtain and peeped out. The street was deserted. Oh well, she'd have a glass of wine on her own. She sat on the sofa and thought through her evening. Alex was almost controlling, but he was so polite and friendly he couldn't be directly faulted. He had been right when he told the waitress they couldn't manage dessert. Ripley hadn't even been asked, but again he was right, she couldn't have managed it. Next time she'd look at the menu and choose something lighter; she loved dessert.

The flat was quiet without May. It might be a good idea to leave May for an hour now and again while Ripley was down in the shop. She had to get used to being left sometimes. Until now, May had been really easy and Ripley saw no need for the classes she had considered. The walking, and the people she met were enough. She curled up in bed and felt at peace. Alex was nice. In the morning she'd collect May and take her for an extra-long walk.

On Monday, Bob walked into the shop carrying a shiny silver bag. 'For madam,' he said, holding it out.

'For me?' Ripley asked. She peered into the bag and saw a silver box. 'From Alex?'

'None other. Do you know you're my most exciting delivery? I never know what's going to happen next.'

Ripley laughed. 'Believe me, nor do I.'

'Come on then, open it,' Susie prompted. Ripley took the box, stood it on the counter and lifted the lid. A handmade selection of chocolates sat in delicately arranged tissue paper.

'Enjoy,' Bob said. 'Have a good day, ladies.'

'Bye, Bob,' Ripley said.

'See you soon, Bob,' Susie quipped. 'Look at those. I bet they taste good.'

'We'd better try one and see. You choose first.'

'No, they're your chocolates. I couldn't possibly. Oh, okay then,' Susie said, dipping her hand in and retrieving a round milk chocolate with an almond on top. Ripley chose a nutty cluster. There was silence as the women savoured every moment, leaning on their elbows with their hands supporting their chins. Both mouths moved in exaggerated sucking motions as they enjoyed the luxurious taste churning around their tongues.

'Go on, you first this time,' Susie said, running her tongue over her lips.

'Mmm.' Ripley scrutinised the box, chose a heart-shaped dark chocolate and pushed the box towards Susie.

'I shouldn't.'

'It'd be rude not to.'

'You're right,' Susie said, popping another into her mouth.

'Keep hold of this one, Ripley. Flowers and chocolates; he knows how to treat a woman properly.'

'I wonder if the bouquets will stop, or if the rose and chocolates will replace them. I won't have any complaints. Have another.'

'I can't. They're really rich... Maybe later.'

'Later then. Come on, we have orders to do.'

Susie always made up the bouquet for Bob to return an hour after it was delivered. Ripley had to admit she worried if the delivery was ever late, arriving back.

'How long is he going to keep this up for? Why doesn't he call and ask me out?'

'He's out to impress and he's certainly doing that,' Susie said. 'I wonder if he has a plan.'

'What sort of plan?'

'Like you say, how long will he keep this up and what will follow?'

Three months later nothing had changed. Bob arrived three times a week with a rose, chocolates and a bouquet with a time Alex would be picking her up for a date.

'It's about time he changed his tactics; a girl could get bored with the same old things week after week,' Susie chortled one morning after the chocolates arrived.

'I suppose I could pull him up on his consistency. But there again it would be a shame if he changed the chocolates. I don't think we can risk it.'

'No, you're right. Too much to lose. What's that?'

'Oh God, no!' Ripley took hold of the small box sitting amongst the chocolates and lifted it up. She looked at Susie. 'It can't be.'

'It could. Open the thing, I can't wait.'

Ripley pulled the tiny ribbon and opened the box. A diamond solitaire sat proudly on a silk cushion. 'Oh, look at this. Oh my God! I can't.'

'Ripley, it's the most beautiful ring I've ever seen. Must have cost a fortune. Not that money matters, of course.'

Ripley stared into the box. 'I'm not ready for this.'

'When will you be ready? When's the right time for anything? You've been happier these past months than I've ever known you.'

'I just don't know. I wasn't expecting this.'

'I have to say, he does like to give surprises and this must be the best one of all. Try it on.'

'I can't.'

'Yes you can.'

Ripley took a breath, lifted the ring from the box and held it to her finger. 'No, I'm not putting on the ring. If he wants me he'll have to go down on one knee and ask me properly. It's a real cop-out sending it by taxi.'

Susie roared with laughter. 'That's it. You go for it. Ripley, you're a lovely girl, he's a lucky man.'

'I haven't said yes yet. This way I have a bit of time to play with.'

'You are so funny. You will say yes though, I mean, when he asks you properly?'

'Possibly. I'll have to see.'

Chapter 12

The following morning Ripley woke with an uneasy feeling and then her heart skipped a beat as she remembered the ring. Her breathing quickened. She liked Alex and enjoyed their time together, but did she love him? He hadn't captured her heart with excitement as Joe had. She had never felt that jolt rivet her whole body when she saw him. Would anyone make her feel like that again? Does that feeling only happen once in a lifetime? She supposed other people didn't go about jolting and jumping when they'd had several lovers. Joe had been her only lover, so there could be no comparison, and she'd been so young at the time; much too young to understand her true emotions. Joe had infatuated her and she'd never got over the way he made her feel. His lifestyle had influenced her, making other men seem ordinary.

She sat up. How could she ever be happy if she tried to compare Alex to Joe? They were a world apart; she had to move on. Susie was right; the past few months had been her happiest for years. Throwing back the quilt, she reached for May's head and stroked her.

'Come on, I'll let you out; we're going to be late opening if we sit here contemplating all morning.' She hadn't been in contact with Alex since the ring arrived; she'd wait until he got in touch, and hopefully by then she'd have made a decision. She stopped short as she neared the door to the garden, causing May to look up at her. She shouldn't be feeling like this; she should be elated at the prospect of getting engaged to Alex. All she felt was undecided and anxious. May whined and scratched the door.

'Sorry May, there you go.' She unlocked the door, watched for a moment as May scampered down the steps, and then hurried through to the bathroom. She sat on the loo and stared at her reflection in the cabinet mirror. Her eyes looked troubled and her lips were tight and straight. She could always say no. Just because Alex wanted to get engaged, didn't mean she had to agree. An involuntary sigh made her consult her watch. Where had the morning gone? Ripley had never been this late opening the shop; she had to snap out of her present state of mind or she'd never get anything done today.

'Good morning,' Susie said an hour later, bustling into the shop, laden with bags. 'I stopped off and got a few bridal magazines and some lunch to save going out later.'

'Okay. Thanks.'

'You don't sound very enthusiastic. I thought you'd be on cloud nine by this morning. You did say yes, didn't you?'

'I haven't spoken to him.'

'Oh, I see. I'll put these out the back then. I suppose as usual I've jumped in with my two big feet.'

'Susie. Does Kev make your heart sort of jolt when you see him?'

'Depends what he's done wrong,' she chortled.

'I'm being serious. I look forward to seeing Alex, but I don't get all overcome with excitement; my heart doesn't race.'

'That kind of love is for the films. I suppose back at the start I did get excited, but it's been different for you. Alex isn't forthcoming with the emotional stuff, as far as I can tell. He's more your sort of cool-dude type and I suppose you give back what you get. Your relationship is sort of structured by the way he is; always sending gifts and being the perfect gentleman, so much so that he's almost controlling.'

'Is it enough? I don't really know if I love him, or if he loves me. You're right, I go along with his scheme...'

'It's not a bad scheme. He must love you. He kept at it until he captured you.'

'Captured! That's what worries me.'

'Bad choice of words. You were a lonely little soul before he came along. You have been happy since he came into your life and that must be worth something.'

'You don't fancy popping to the cake shop? I missed breakfast.'

'So have we made a decision?'

'Yes.'

'Whoopee! Yes, or no?'

'A Chelsea bun, please.' Ripley laughed at Susie's shocked expression.

Susie shook her head and left for the cake shop. For a young girl, Ripley was a bit deep. Or was she? She obviously wanted the earth to move and stars swimming around her head. Usually she was so level-headed. She'd be a fool to let Alex go; men didn't like being turned down. His courtship skills had been a bit strange, but then all men had their little ways. There was none queerer than folk. Ripley was a bit of a loner; who would she invite to her wedding? She rarely talked about her family. Susie realised for the first time how little she knew about the young girl she had become so fond of. Yes, she was deep. There must be some story behind it all.

Ripley bit into her Chelsea bun and looked thoughtful. 'I'm going to say yes.'

'Really? That's wonderful. Congrats, you had me worried for a moment there.'

'I had myself worried. He still needs to ask me properly though.' She took another bite and licked the sugar from her lips. 'I'll call him tonight.'

At lunchtime, Bob walked in carrying a small package. 'Different again. This man certainly knows how to woo. I see where I went wrong now.'

Ripley laughed. 'Yesterday's chocolates had an engagement ring hidden amongst them.' She took the package and pulled one corner open. 'I'll have to get the scissors.'

'So, you now have a fiancé?' Bob said. 'This is better than watching one of those serialisations on the box. Next instalment, same time, same place... What programme was that?'

Susie laughed. 'Oh Bob, she's much too young to remember... That was years ago, whatever it was. Come on Ripley, open the thing.'

'Theatre tickets for tonight. In London! The Bodyguard at the Adelphi. Pick you up at five, Alex xx. I'll have to close early.'

'The Bodyguard. How romantic is that!' Susie said with a tinge of envy.

'Have a great time and congratulations on your engagement. Maybe see you tomorrow for the next instalment,' Bob said as he pulled open the shop door.

'See you, Bob.' Ripley turned to Susie. 'He's a bit spontaneous. I never have much notice.'

'Ah! But you never know what the day might bring. How wonderful is that? A bit of spontaneity wouldn't go amiss in my life. Kev, can be very predictable. I do hope Alex doesn't lose these little charming ways once he marries you.'

'He seems pretty consistent at the moment. Watch this space.'

Alex drove his BMW fast and furiously, but always in control. He already knew where the best parking was available and deftly found time for a quick snack and drink before the show began.

They sat on opposite sides of the table in a brasserie. Alex picked up his glass. 'To the best girl in the world.'

Ripley raised her glass. 'To the best boyfriend.'

'You aren't wearing the ring. Do I have something to worry about?'

'No, I thought I might ask for a proper proposal.'

Alex looked around at the other clients. 'What, here?' He raised his eyebrows.

'No, wherever you like.'

'Where's the ring?'

'In my handbag.'

'I'd better have it back then. I'll decide when the time is right.'

Ripley handed him the ring box and tried to read his expression. His poker-face gave nothing away. When would the right time be? She suddenly felt uncomfortable. He might never ask her. A lump came to her throat. She must be mad. She'd gone from not wanting to get engaged this morning, to now worrying he might never ask her.

The Bodyguard brought on the most powerful emotions Ripley had ever experienced. The strong performances brought a lurch in her stomach and the songs made her cry. Alex took her hand and tucked in into his arm.

'How was the show? Did you say yes? I want to know everything,' Susie blurted out the second she walked in the shop door the following morning.

'The show was the most awe-inspiring thing I've ever seen. It was beautiful, the dancing, the acting, oh, and the songs, I cried and sniffled through the whole lot of them hardly able to see the stage.'

'And?'

'And what?'

'Did you tell him you wanted to marry him? Come on Ripley, tell all!'

'There's nothing to tell. I said I'd like a proper proposal and he took the ring back.'

Susie creased up with laughter. 'You should have known he'd do something like that. He likes to be in control. Now he's going to have to plan some special way to ask you. You could have just said yes and let him put the ring on your finger.'

'I know. I'd got quite enthusiastic about it by last night and now I feel deflated.'

'No, don't feel like that. Look forward to whatever he's going to come up with. It's bound to be some wonderful place he'll arrange.'

'And I suppose it'll give me more time to get used to the idea.'

'I thought you'd decided it was what you wanted.'

'What's in the order book? We'd better get on,' Ripley said authoritatively.

'You always change the subject when I hit a raw note. You're a funny one, Ripley.' No answer was forthcoming; Ripley already had her head in the order book.

A month later, Ripley had been out with Alex each Saturday and several other times, but there was never a mention of the engagement. The roses, chocolates and flowers still arrived and he was as attentive as usual, but nothing more.

One morning the chocolates arrived with a note. *Ripley, you need a passport. Please get one at your earliest convenience, Alex.*

'He's taking you abroad to propose. I'll look after the shop. I wonder where you're going,' Susie said excitedly.

Ripley grinned. 'Do you think he'll tell me the destination beforehand? I'll need to know what to pack. A surprise holiday, I can't believe how lucky I am.'

'I told you he was a good one. If I was you, I'd start getting a few things together. Knowing Alex, you might only get an afternoon's notice.'

Ripley clenched her hands together and let out a small squeal. 'I'll have to pack an extra bag, just in case. Do you know what time the shopping centre closes?' She couldn't contain her grin. 'Susie, can you believe this?'

'Yes, and you'd better get a passport form and start filling it in. You'll need to get a professional person to authenticate it for you.'

'He's so strange the way he never asks me anything. He could have said this on Saturday evening.'

'He likes to surprise you. You wait, when you're married you'll get notes in the cornflakes.' Susie giggled. 'Or a little message when you pull back the bed covers. *I want you tonight.*'

Ripley mocked shock. 'Susie, you're terrible.' Both women broke into rapturous laughter.

Ripley bought herself a large suitcase and began a shopping mission. She bought mainly clothes for warm weather in the hope that Alex had thought through his plan carefully. She also added a couple of warm tops to be on the safe side. Her passport arrived and her case was almost overflowing. At least she'd be ready now; he wouldn't catch her out.

Each Monday, Ripley checked the chocolate box for a note telling her when the holiday would begin. He knew how to keep a girl waiting. She imagined some romantic setting, just the two of them miles from anywhere. Perhaps a beach with white sands as far as the eye could see, or a cottage hidden away in the countryside with horses. Oh God, she must stop reverting everything back to her time with Joe. Alex was sure to have chosen something special for her, he always did.

Bob arrived unexpectedly on a Friday. 'A parcel for my lady. Could this be the one we've been waiting for?'

'Oh Bob, I hope so. I can't bear the suspense much longer. It's been nearly three months since I gave him the ring back.' A rectangle box held a necklace of ruby stones, housed in white-gold leaves on a delicate chain. 'This is beautiful. There's a note tucked underneath. Be ready for a two-week holiday tomorrow at six. Alex. Good job I've already organised the shop and May. No indication where we're going. I'd better ring Susie and let her know.'

'You enjoy yourself sweetheart. See you in a fortnight.'

'Thanks Bob. I will.'

Alex pulled up at precisely six o'clock the following evening and heaved Ripley's suitcase down the stairs. 'What have you packed in here?'

'I had to pack for all types of weather. No one told me where I'm going.'

He smiled. 'I thought you liked surprises.'

'I do.' She bent forward and kissed his cheek as he lowered her suitcase on top of his own in the boot of the car. He turned and put his arm on her shoulder.

'Let's not make a public display. We'd better get going.'

Ripley would never understand him. A public display; she'd only given him a peck on the cheek. She'd never invited him in for a drink after an evening out since the night he implied she was easy. He'd never touched her more than a kiss goodnight in the darkness of the night, or holding her hand. Squeezing her arm when it was slipped through his own was the closest he'd come to showing he had feelings for her. Maybe things would change when she wore his ring; they were going on a two-week holiday, and they would hardly be having separate rooms.

Alex pulled into a hotel by Heathrow airport. He pressed a button to release the boot and a uniformed man came with a trolley to take the cases. Another took the car to be parked. A doorman half bowed as he opened the large glass door and ushered them into the plush carpeted foyer. Alex spoke to the young woman behind the huge wooden reception desk.

'Good evening. I have two double rooms booked in the name of Holman.'

Two rooms! They weren't sharing. Ripley suddenly felt out of her depth. She didn't understand him at all and she was about to be engaged to him. Oh no! What if he thought she was a virgin? It had been so long it had probably resealed by now anyway. She gulped.

The woman handed him two keys. 'Welcome, Mr Holman. I have all your details. The doorman will escort you with your luggage. I have an alarm call booked for seven o'clock. Is that correct?'

'Yes thank you, and I have a table booked in the restaurant for nine tonight.'

'Yes you do,' she said, consulting the screen of her computer. 'Enjoy your stay.'

The footman led the way to the lift and the three of them stepped in. The journey to the second floor was silent apart from the gentle hum of the lift. A bell sounded and the doors opened. They followed the attendant into one suite and then a second. Alex tipped the man and they were left alone.

'This is more like an apartment than a hotel room.'

'Only the best for my girl. I'll knock for you at eight fifteen and we'll have a drink in the bar before dinner.'

'Okay. So we're leaving here in the morning?'

'Yes, we'll have breakfast at the airport. I've got a pass for the lounge.'

Ripley sat on the edge of the double bed with her feet swinging in mid-air and looked around. She knew Alex was financially secure, but these suites must cost a fortune. He'd told her he held a managerial position in an investment company. The offices were the same ones Bob collected the rose from every Friday. If this was an overnight stay, Ripley couldn't imagine where they were going the following day, but it would obviously be somewhere luxurious. She unzipped her case and fished out a black cocktail dress; day one and the first venue catered for. She was doing well so far.

The following morning she awoke to the sound of the telephone. She answered sleepily; she shouldn't have drunk so much wine the night before, she wasn't used to it.

'Hello.'

'This is reception with your seven o'clock alarm call.'

'Right. Thank you.' She put the phone back on the cradle and fell back on her pillow.

She awoke to the sound of an impatient banging on the door. 'Ripley, are you ready? We have to go,' Alex said, sounding disgruntled.

'Okay. Sorry, I must have fallen back to sleep.'

She heard an exhale of breath and leapt out of bed. 'I'll wait for you downstairs and for God's sake, hurry up.'

'Yes, I won't be long. Sorry.'

She rushed through to the bathroom. No time for a shower. She stared at her reflection; she looked as bad as she felt. She splashed water on her face and hurried through to find some clothes. She rammed the cocktail dress and shoes from the previous night into the case. Make-up! She rushed back to the bathroom. Good job! She'd have left her small toiletries bag behind.

Alex was pacing the foyer. 'This is not good, Ripley.' She felt like a scolded school child.

'I said I was sorry. I didn't fall back to sleep on purpose; I had a bit too much wine last night.'

'We'll have to keep an eye on that if it's a problem.'

'It isn't a problem. I'm not used to it.' She followed him out to the waiting car. 'My case is in the room.'

'No, it's in the car. Now get in, we're late enough already.'

Ripley sat in the passenger seat feeling cross. She had a headache, in fact her head was spinning and she felt sick. What she didn't need was a telling off. They arrived at the airport, Alex parked the car and a shuttle bus took them to the terminal.

Alex consulted the screens. 'This way,' he said, pushing the trolley towards a check-in desk.

'Good morning sir, madam. Mauritius today, is it?'

'Yes, that's right.'

Mauritius. Ripley's heart skipped a beat. Romance at its very best. White beaches and sunshine. Bliss.

Chapter 13

The doors of the plane swung open and a gush of hot air hit them. 'It feels as though they've got the hot air fans blowing straight at us,' Ripley said, squinting in the sunshine as she stepped off the plane.

'This is summer starting. The temperatures tend to stay around thirty degrees at this time of year, so we'll be alright for sunshine.'

'I wish I'd known you'd booked for Mauritius. I could have been excited for weeks instead of wondering.'

'Don't worry, there's a few surprises in store which will be more than enough excitement.'

Ripley felt a gush of happiness. 'Are we staying near the beach?'

'All will be revealed in time. You'll have to contain yourself a little longer.'

A man carrying a board with *Holman* written in large black pen stood waiting as they walked through arrivals.

'Welcome to Mauritius. I am Paulan and I will drive you to your hotel. I will take the trolley. I trust you had a pleasant flight.' He spoke slowly and precisely.

'Thank you,' Alex said. 'The flight went remarkably quickly.'

Ripley watched in silence as they drove through the small towns. A lot of women were in saris, while others were in knee-length cotton dresses. Two women walked along balancing large baskets of fruit on their heads. Dogs ran around freely and the place bustled with activity. Men with sun-scorched faces stood at stalls selling bananas. The shops were mainly old, with rotting wood above the doors displaying names. London Store, Sugar's Food, and Stop Here were a few she noticed. Small kiosks offered ready-cooked food, and a few men stood eating what looked like rolled pancakes. In stark contrast to what Ripley had imagined, the place looked poor, as did most of the people.

The Paradise Hotel boasted a beach position, with the suites having a private balcony and access to the beach. Ripley stood once again at the reception desk to be advised she had her own suite. The panic of not being a virgin struck her for the second time in as many days. Alex surely couldn't be virgin; he was thirty-two.

'Alex, this is wonderful,' she said as she walked out onto the balcony and looked at the golden sands and shimmering sea. 'What's that line out there? It looks like the waves are breaking.'

'That's the coral reef. It goes around the whole island apart from a couple of breaks. We'll be snorkelling out there. You don't dive, do you?'

'I've never tried it. This is so amazing. Thank you, Alex. I do like the way you surprise me with such lovely things.'

'Good. I'm glad you appreciate my efforts. Dinner is at seven. I've booked a table on the beach. Have a bit of a rest and I'll come for you at six fifteen.'

'I'll be ready. What is the food like here?'

'A variety of fish like you'll never have tasted before and all kinds of meat and curries. In fact, the island is so diverse you'll never be short of choice.'

Ripley watched as the man she would soon become engaged to and yet still a stranger, went to his own suite.

She smiled to herself, went onto the balcony and down to the beach. The water was cool and refreshing as she paddled while walking. She stood and looked at the sea which glistened in the setting sun. She looked down and saw tiny fish darting and swimming around the rocks only a few inches in front of her. Panic drove through her. The sun was setting; how long had she been here? Alex would go mad if she was late again. She rushed back along the beach, finding it difficult to walk at any sort of speed with the sand slowing her down.

At last the hotel was in view. Alex was standing on his balcony, the one next to hers, and he watched as she hurried up the path to her room.

'Ripley, you went out and left your door open. Anyone could have gone in.'

'I thought I'd have a quick look at the beach. I didn't realise I'd walked so far. What time is it?'

'Five past six. You have ten minutes.' He turned and went into his room.

'*Five past six, you have ten minutes,*' Ripley mimicked quietly, and then berated herself for being so childish. He was right once again; it had been foolish to go out and leave her room unlocked, but why did he always make her feel like a naughty school girl?

The water in the shower cascaded down her body and she felt refreshed. Would he ask her tonight? A small shudder ran through her. She chose a cream-coloured, halter-neck dress, brushed her hair and tied it back, leaving a few strands falling down. The last lashes were being coated with mascara when a knock sounded on the door.

She looked at her watch; he was quarter of an hour late. Unforgivable by his standards, but much needed.

'You look divine,' he said, as he held out his arm for her. 'Shall we?'

'Thank you. I'm looking forward to sampling this wonderful cuisine.'

'I have some business in Port Louis tomorrow. I need you to sign some papers, as a witness. Afterwards I'll take you to a café where you'll taste some local food, very different to what they serve up in the hotels.'

'Have you been here before?'

'Yes. I've taken a couple of holidays here. The perfect place for relaxation but not a lot else.'

After a drink in the bar, they followed a waiter onto the beach. Nightfall was as beautiful as the day had been, accompanied by the sound of the lapping sea and a few lights in the distance.

'What are those lights all the way out there?'

Alex followed the direction of her finger. 'Fishermen. They'll be out around the reef while the tide is high.'

A lone table, with candles flickering in the slight breeze, stood on the beach.

'This is wonderful. Listen to the roar of the sea out on the reef, I never noticed it earlier,' Ripley said. 'This is the most romantic place I've ever had dinner.' It had to be tonight he would ask her.

'I'm glad you like it.' The waiter pulled out Ripley's chair and laid the napkin across her lap. The lights from the hotel gave a warm glow in the darkness.

Alex suggested they tried the lobster. 'I don't know if I'll like it. I've never tried it,' Ripley said.

'If you don't we'll order something else.'

'We could end up with several meals. I do want to branch out and try new things. What's the point of being here and not trying anything?'

Ripley learned how to eat lobster and was relieved there were no other diners around to see the mess she made of it. Alex laughed at her efforts and then proceeded to show her how to eat it properly. The fresh fruit salad dessert was an easy option in comparison.

They sat enjoying the tranquillity, listening to the waves continually breaking out on the distant reef. Alex arose and walked around the table, where he dropped to one knee.

'Ripley, will you do me the honour of marrying me?'

'Alex, I'd love to.'

He brought the ring box out of his pocket, pulled the ribbon undone and opened the box. Two rings sat together on it.

'Two rings?'

'Yes, the second ring is the wedding ring, for a later date.' He took the solitaire from the box and took her hand. He gently pushed the ring into place and looked up into her eyes and kissed her lips tenderly.

'I love you, Ripley.'

'I love you, Alex.' A slight uncomfortable feeling ran through her as she spoke. She shook her head as though to clear the thought.

'What is it?'

'I can't believe all of this. This place, dinner on the beach and now this.' She looked down at her hand, stretched out her fingers and admired her ring.

Romantic music floated through from the hotel. Alex moved his chair and sat next to Ripley, facing the sea. He took her hand and squeezed it. 'You've made me the happiest man in the world. We've got our whole lives ahead of us.'

'I feel as though I'm in a dream and I don't want to wake from it.'

'You don't have to. This dream will go on forever.'

An hour later, Alex walked her to the door of her suite and bent to kiss her lips, pulling her close. 'Good night, sleep well. We'll have breakfast at nine and then head off for Port Louis.'

'Good night, Alex. Thank you for the most wonderful evening of my life.' She looked at him earnestly.

'Are you okay?' he asked. She nodded.

Ripley stood with her back against the door for a few moments after she shut it. Now she was worried. He was obviously waiting until they were married. Should she tell him? No, she couldn't. Would he be able to tell? How could she enter into a marriage with a lie? Alex was making her feel guilty about something which had been so beautiful. She didn't have to go along with his principles and if the clocks went back she wouldn't have changed a thing. If he asked, she'd tell the truth and if not, she'd hold on to her secret and wonderful memories forever.

The lift staggered to a halt on the second floor of an office block and they waited on a bench in a small room.

'What exactly have I got to sign?' Ripley asked.

'It's some documents I need you to witness. Boring stuff, but I have to get it sorted today. You only have to watch me sign and then your signature goes underneath to confirm you saw me sign.'

Alex left Ripley and went to find out what was happening with the papers he had to sign. He came back a moment later.

'The papers are ready, come through.' Ripley followed him into another office and stood next to him as he signed two papers. He pointed to a box underneath and Ripley signed to confirm his signature on both forms. They went back to the waiting area and a few minutes later a man handed Alex an envelope.

'Thank you for your help,' Alex said as he ushered Ripley back towards the lift. 'Lunchtime.'

They climbed back into the taxi and Alex asked to be taken to another village on the coast. 'This taxi is the same one which brought us here,' Ripley whispered. 'Did he wait all that time?'

'Yes, it's what they do here. At the end of the day it'll cost about ten pounds, if that.'

They drove along a beautiful coastal road where the sea lapped the rocks and then they travelled inland for about a mile up a mountain road. The taxi came to a halt outside a small, green, untidy building.

The driver went in and reappeared a few moments later with three polythene boxes of food which he positioned on the front seat before pulling off. Ripley gave Alex a questioning look, lowering her forehead into a frown.

'Don't do that,' Alex laughed. 'We're going to the beach to do some snorkelling.'

'I saw some fish the other day.'

'Not like the ones you're going to see today.'

They drove along a dirt track and the car stopped in the middle of nowhere. They climbed out and the driver opened the boot which was full of snorkels, masks, flippers, towels and costumes.

'You bought me a bikini?'

Alex laughed at the tone of her voice. 'How did I manage that?'

They followed the dirt path and arrived onto a beach which seemed to stretch forever in both directions. The driver disappeared and Alex spread two towels on the golden sand. He handed Ripley a box which she opened dubiously and peered in.

'What is it?'

'Biryani, cooked like no other. Here, have a plastic fork.'

Ripley tucked in. She laughed aloud. 'This is a world apart from the hotel and dinner on the beach last night. I love it.'

'I told you, this is a diverse little country. I'm so glad you like the things I do. This sort of event is so important and people just don't think these kinds of experiences matter. We'll sunbathe for a while and then explore the sea.'

Ripley sank back on her towel and closed her eyes. This was bliss.

'Are you happy?' Alex whispered.

'Extremely.' She opened her eyes against the bright sun and looked left and right along the beach. 'There are no people on this beach.'

'There is a hotel a bit further on. Sometimes a couple of people venture along for a walk, but not often.'

A while later they put on the snorkels and masks and carried the flippers down to the water's edge. 'Don't try to walk forwards in the flippers, it doesn't work,' Alex advised.

Ripley had trouble pulling hers on, they were so tight. She walked a couple of steps back into the clear water and let herself down. She turned onto her front. Now she had to put her face in the water and breathe through the snorkel. At first she spluttered and panicked, then she gained confidence and managed to stay down for a moment. There was a yellow fish with large fins swimming past. A green, blue, yellow and red fish glided in front of her. A whole school of shimmering blue fish swam past and Ripley suddenly realised she was floating and using the snorkel.

They snorkelled between the corals, watching the fish searching for food. Ripley had never seen anything so beautiful. After two hours they walked ashore and relaxed on their towels before collecting their belongings and heading back to the taxi.

'What a wonderful holiday.'

'It's only just begun. There's so much to see and do, but not things you'd expect.'

'Like what?'

'A crocodile park, you can stroke lions...'

'I don't think I'll do that.'

'I've done it before and lived to tell the tale.'

Ripley touched her stomach as it rumbled. 'I'm really hungry.'

'Snorkelling does have that effect. I thought I'd let you choose what we eat tonight.'

'You're going to let me choose? That's kind of you, Alex.'

'I thought you'd appreciate it,' he said, totally missing the sarcasm in her voice. 'You should go for something with a bit of spice.'

'I thought I was choosing.'

They climbed into the taxi and were soon back at the hotel. 'I'll collect you at six thirty for dinner.'

'Okay, see you then.'

Ripley was getting used to having her own space and had to admit she enjoyed it. She spread out on a sunbed on the balcony and opened her book.

She jolted awake some time later. Oh no! What time was it? Ten minutes to get ready; this was becoming a habit.

The next day was spent on the beach at the hotel. Again there were only a few people about, apart from a waiter appearing now and again to bring fresh drinks.

After dinner that evening, Alex hovered for a moment at her door. Oh God! He was going to spend the night with her. She looked at him expectantly.

'I have some plans for tomorrow. I won't meet you for breakfast, I'll be in touch at some point to let you know when I'll see you.'

'Right.' She was taken aback. Where was he going? 'Can't I come with you?'

'No.'

'Right. I'll wait to hear from you then.'

'I love you, Ripley.'

'I love you, Alex, but I don't always understand why you want to be secretive.'

'Good night, Ripley.'

'Good night, Alex.'

She went into her suite with her heart thumping. Was he meeting someone he'd met last time he was in Mauritius? Why was he always so strange? The past few days had been so wonderful and now she felt uneasy, but she had no idea what about, exactly.

She woke and took a moment to remember she would spend the day alone. She glanced at her watch. Eight o'clock. She could afford another half an hour in bed. The phone rang barely two minutes later. Alex must have changed his mind.

'Miss Bradford, this is reception. There is a parcel for you. Would it be convenient to deliver it now?'

'Yes, okay.' She pulled back the covers and sat on the edge of the bed. Another one of Alex's surprises no doubt. She wrapped herself in a robe, hurried through to the bathroom, cleaned her teeth and ran the brush through her hair just before there was a knock on her door.

A woman in a grey, skirt-suit, with glasses perched on the end of her nose, stood before Ripley, looking prim. 'Good morning, Miss Bradford. Would it be alright to call you Ripley?'

'Yes, of course.'

'I'm Selena and I am here to take care of all your needs for the day. If there's anything, no matter how small, I'm here to please. Might I come in?' She handed Ripley a box.

Ripley stared at her for a moment. The last thing she needed was this woman hanging around her all day. *Alex, what the hell have you done this for? You just spoiled my day.* 'Yes, sorry, come in.'

'Carefully now,' Selena said, looking down the passage way outside the door. 'You might want to stand back a bit.'

Ripley did as she was told. A man walked in carrying several bags and placed them on the table. A trolley was wheeled in with breakfast.

'Breakfast. In here?'

'On the balcony with buck's fizz. Then we can get on and pamper you.'

'Pamper me?'

'Hair, nails, make-up, all the usual, plus anything special you require.'

'Such as?'

'A massage, a pedicure; anything you fancy.'

So he had booked her in for a day of pampering. Ripley wouldn't have chosen to spend her day having beauty treatments, but it made a change from the norm. She might even enjoy it.

She was half-way through her breakfast before she remembered the box. She went into the suite where Selina was busy laying out tubes, tubs, towels, make-up and lotions, on the table. She picked up the box and returned to her breakfast of fruit and various croissants and pancakes. There were a few side dishes containing vegetable curry. For breakfast? She gingerly took a pancake, added some curry and rolled it. Wow! This was good.

The shiny silver box caught her imagination. A piece of jewellery? A voucher to walk with lions? She shuddered and picked up the box. Something moved inside. A shake told her the item was more solid than jewellery. She lifted the lid and stared. A remote control fob sat pinned to a small silk cushion. BMW. He couldn't have bought her a car, could he? She shook her head, replaced the lid and rolled herself another pancake.

'I think I'll go for a walk before we start all this,' Ripley said, motioning towards the potions and lotion now filling the whole table.

'Okay, see you in a while. No rush, take your time,' Selena answered brightly.

Ripley sauntered along the beach. She would have been a lot happier to spend her day like this. Her mind flitted to the fob. Alex was somehow mysterious, she couldn't work him out and just when she thought she was beginning to understand him, he threw another spanner in the works. Always nice spanners of course, but nonetheless bizarre. In his own way he seemed quite eccentric, or was the word she was looking for *peculiar*?

Some of the shells were beautiful; she hadn't noticed them before now. After picking up a collection, she made her way slowly back to the hotel, raising her dress to her knees and wading through the water.

An entourage arrived one after the other to deliver the various treatments. Ripley started with a massage, something she'd never tried before. She had to admit she was enjoying herself being pampered. She could have fallen back to sleep and stayed comatose for the rest of the day, but Selena had other ideas. Toe and finger nails painted, Ripley chose to have her dark locks curled and then gathered back from her face. She was finding her hair unmanageable hanging around her face in the heat. Selena flitted in and out, opening and closing the door to the suite, and Ripley couldn't see what was happening.

'Right, it's all coming together,' Selena said, sounding important. 'The make-up girl's on her way up now.'

A few moments later a young girl introduced herself as Pinkie. 'What would you like? Do you like a lot of make-up, or a more natural look?'

'Definitely natural, and browns suit me best.' Ripley closed her eyes as Pinkie started applying creams. Maybe Alex was taking her somewhere special tonight. She wouldn't have minded another meal for two on the beach; last night had been wonderful.

'Put it there.' Selena could be heard ordering someone. 'Careful. Yes, those can go over there. Where's the... Oh, okay, I see it.'

Ripley felt like sleeping for the second time that day. Surely all this fussing would soon be over, there wasn't a lot else they could do to her and she was starving. It seemed like hours since breakfast.

'Have a look. I can change it if you don't like it,' Pinkie said, holding up a mirror. Ripley stared at her reflection.

'I look so... Like I stepped out of a magazine, but I can't actually see any make-up... Yes, I do like it.'

Pinkie started packing up the make-up and Ripley stood. She'd tell Selena she'd had enough and she was relieved of any further duties. She gasped when her gaze took in the room.

'Oh my God, no! What the hell is that? What's going on?'

'Are you okay, Ripley? It's your dress. We can make any adjustments you need...'

'My dress! Just like that! A wedding dress arrives and I know nothing about it.'

'Mr Holden said he'd chosen the dress. Take a closer look, it's beautiful.'

'It might be beautiful... Is that what all this has been about? Has he planned a wedding?' Ripley was close to tears. Selena nodded.

'He said it would be the most wonderful surprise of all,' she said in a lowered voice. The room had come to a standstill. There was silence until Ripley burst into tears.

'Pinkie, set your stuff out again while I have a word with Ripley,' Selena said, taking control of the situation. 'Come through to the bedroom, Ripley, and we'll sort it out, whatever the problem is. This can be an emotional time, don't you worry, I've seen it all before.'

'So you've had other brides who don't know it's their wedding day?' Ripley shouted.

'Well, to be honest, no...'

'No! I thought not! How dare you agree to manipulate me into having all this... this... I don't even know what to say to you.' She felt outraged. She ran through to the bedroom, threw herself onto the bed and cried. How dare he? How dare they? She wouldn't go through with it; not now and not ever! Her heart raced with frustration and anger. She sunk her face into the pillow and sobbed.

Chapter 14

Ripley sat on the edge of the bed and caught sight of herself in the mirror. Gone was the beauty who had looked back at her only a short time ago. Now her eyes were puffed and her cheeks red and streaked. There was a gentle tapping on the door and Selena half whispered, 'Ripley, please can I come in?'

'Yes,' Ripley said, feeling remorseful over her outburst. Selena's head appeared around the door as though she half expected something to be thrown at her. 'Come in. I'm sorry I took it out on you. The shock of it all was too much.'

Selena walked into the room. 'How do you feel now?'

'Calmer, but I don't know if I can go through with it.'

'Shall I leave you to think it through?' She raised her eyebrows and cocked her head to one side, looking like a puppy waiting for a ball to be thrown. Ripley nodded and once again she was alone.

She reached for her handbag, still on the chair since the previous day. A quick rummage produced her phone. She pressed the shop number and waited until the ringing tone sounded. Pick up Suz, please, for once, pick up.

'Hello, Flower Haven...'

'Susie, I don't know what to do.' The tears fell once again and she sniffled into the phone as she reached for the umpteenth tissue.

'Ripley, is that you? Don't cry. Whatever's happened?'

'I got engaged and it was on the beach and it was so nice and now I've had my hair and make-up and everything else and I didn't know and then there was a wedding dress and I didn't even look at it and now I don't know what to do. How dare he do this and this woman she knew all along and they manipulated me and...'

'Hold on. Stop crying and slow down. So you got engaged; has Alex got another woman? Whose is the wedding dress? Sorry, it's a bad line, I couldn't get half of what you said.'

'It's my dress.'

'Right. So you choose a wedding dress...'

'No, he did. He planned the whole thing behind my back.' Ripley took a deep breath. 'I know I'm not making sense. You know what he's like. He bought the dress and organised for me to have a day of pampering, but it's my wedding day and no one told me.' She burst into another flood of tears.

'Okay. So the wedding was one of his surprises. Ripley, you know what he's like; he thought you'd love it, he's probably spent the past few months planning it all for you. Is it so bad? Where are you?'

'Mauritius.'

'You lucky thing. A wedding in Mauritius, most girls would love a surprise like that. You're just a bit shocked by the whole thing and feeling overwhelmed, but when you really think about the trouble he must have gone to, you are so lucky. He really loves you, Ripley, and yes, he is controlling and that's something you'll have to learn to live with, if you love him. He thought he was giving you the best he could.'

'I know. As usual, you're right. So you think I should go through with it?'

'Sweetheart, it has to be your decision. Just sit down quietly and give it some thought. I'm sure you'll make the right choice. And you need to remember how long it took him to give back the engagement ring; a wedding could be years down the line.' Ripley giggled. 'That's the spirit. And if you do go through with it, let me know, or I'll be worrying for the next fortnight.'

'Thanks, Susie. I already know. Today is my wedding day and I intend to enjoy it.'

'Congratulations and lots of love. Have a wonderful time.'

'We will. Thanks, Suz, you really saved the day.'

'Rubbish! I just managed to pull you out of panic mode. And on your wedding day a bit of panic means you're normal. Take care, I'll be thinking of you.'

'Bye Susie.' Ripley switched off the phone and flung it back into her bag. She took a deep breath and went to the bedroom door and flung it open.

'Right. I'm ready to go. Let's have a look at the dress.'

'Have your make-up touched up and try it on. The hairdresser will come and fix the straggly bits.'

'Have I got a veil?'

'Yes.'

'I might need to try it on seeing as the hairdresser's coming back.'

Ripley felt good. Susie was a lovely friend, what would she ever do without her? Today was her wedding day. She sat down and Pinkie brushed her cheeks with powder and looked at her eyes.

'Nothing a quick touch-up won't put right,' she said confidently.

At five o'clock, Ripley walked out of her suite onto the beach in a winter-white, full-length dress fitted at the top, with tiny diamonds swirling down the bodice. The walkway had been decorated with floral displays either side of the path. On the beach, Alex stood waiting with a vicar and two other people. No, don't cry now. She felt like a princess who was the star of the ball going to meet her prince. She slowly walked towards him; he turned and tears welled in his eyes.

'You look beautiful.' He kissed her cheek and took her hand.

The vicar smiled and began the service. Ripley followed as best she could, but most of it went unnoticed, as she watched the waves breaking on the coral and the sun, now descending, casting pink patterns in the sky.

'I now pronounce you man and wife,' the vicar concluded. 'You may kiss the bride.' Alex looked into her eyes which were glazed over. He gently lifted her chin and kissed her.

With the formalities over, the bride and groom walked along the beach hand in hand. 'This was quite a big thing to surprise me with. How did you arrange all the paperwork?'

'I have my ways. You signed the papers on Monday.'

'You're joking! I didn't have a clue. The dress is out of this world. You have extremely good taste.'

'Nothing but the best. Did you like your wedding present?'

'Wedding present?'

'The silver box, don't tell me...'

'Oh, I wasn't sure what it was.'

'The controller fob for a convertible BMW. It's waiting for collection when we get back.'

'Oh Alex, I don't know what to say. Thank you doesn't seem enough.'

'Say you'll never leave me.'

'I won't.'

'Say it.'

'I won't ever leave you.' What a strange request to make on their wedding day.

Alex smiled.

The same table on the beach had been laid for them. Champagne flutes now took the place of wine glasses and a large, metal bucket housed the bottle. A waiter fussed around and poured.

'Alex, earlier I wished I was going to be eating here again tonight. I couldn't have hoped for anywhere better than this.'

'I'm afraid I took the liberty of ordering the food in advance.'

'I'm sure it's going to be good.'

Ripley watched as rolled leaves were placed on her plate. 'This looks intriguing, what is it?'

'Fish in banana leaves.'

'Do we eat the leaves?'

'No, you unroll them.' Dishes began to arrive on the table, full of vegetables, meats and sauces. 'I ordered a variety for you to sample.'

They made their way through the food and managed to drink three bottles of champagne, as a quartet in the corner of the terraced area continued to play romantic melodies in the background.

'Would you care to dance with your husband?'

'I would, but don't let me fall, I've had a bit too much champagne,' Ripley slurred slightly. 'Sorry.'

'You don't have to be sorry. You've made me the happiest man on earth.'

They danced, or moved might be a better description, for three songs before Ripley began to feel giddy.

'I think we'll get you back to the suite.' Alex put his arm around her and supported her back along the beach to their rooms. He took her up the path to his suite and helped her onto the bed.

He slowly and meticulously undid her dress, and removed her shoes. He unfastened her bra and slid her panties down before stroking her young skin and removing his own clothing. He ran his fingers up and down her body and then gently lowered himself on top of her. She groaned as he entered.

Ripley felt dazed. She could feel the urgency of his movements.

'Oh Joe, that is so good. Joe, I love you.'

The sudden blow across her face brought her around with a jolt and she yelped in pain bringing her hand up to her cheek.

'You bitch! You fucking bitch! Get out. Get out now!' She pulled herself up from the bed and nearly fell over. 'Get out you whore.' He pulled her arm and dragged her out onto the terrace before pushing her roughly down the path of his suite and up to the door of her rooms.

'Don't, you're hurting me,' she said, as her feet barely touched the ground. He flung the door open and pushed her in. She fell onto the floor in a heap, crying. What happened?

Why was he doing this to her now? She heard the door slam.

She crawled to the bathroom and put her head over the toilet, where the remains of her meal congealed at the bottom of the pan. She stood at the sink and splashed her face with cold water. What the hell happened? She went through and crashed out on the bed, too drunk and too exhausted to understand.

Dawn broke and the sun streamed in through the windows. She looked around in a daze, her head thumping. Where was Alex? Something had happened, something she couldn't quite remember. She was naked apart from her wedding veil which was still clipped to her hair. She loosened the clip and pulled it free letting the veil drop to the floor. Something wasn't right. They married, ate, danced and then what? Maybe Alex was cross she'd had too much to drink. The top of her arm was sore. No, not just sore; it felt bruised. She went through to the shower and let the warm water run down her. She needed something for her pounding headache. The phone rang before she was close to done. She leaped out of the shower and grabbed a towel.

'Hello?'

'I'll be coming to your room in five minutes, we need to talk.' The line went dead. Oh God, he sounded furious. Ripley pulled on a dress and went to look in the bathroom mirror. She resembled Dracula, with black make-up under her eyes and smudged down her cheeks. She quickly wiped them clean, reapplied fresh mascara and then noticed her hands were shaking.

She opened the door to Alex, who barged into her, putting his hand around her throat, forcing her back into the room. 'Who the fuck is Joe?'

She shook her head. 'I don't know.'

'So why were you calling me Joe, when we were making love?'

Ripley gulped. 'I don't know. You're hurting me.'

'If you're lying to me...'

'I'm not. I don't know anyone called Joe.'

He released his hold, went over to the window and stood with his back to her. 'Don't do this to me, Ripley. Get ready and we'll go for breakfast.'

Ripley went through to the bathroom and closed the door, relieved to have a moment to herself. Her whole body was shaking. *Come on, pull yourself together.* How could she have called him Joe? She tried to control herself by taking a few deep breaths. She had to go and face him. Her hand went sub-consciously to her throat. She took a last look in the mirror and went to face her husband.

'Okay, I'm ready,' she said, forcing a smile and sounding brighter than she felt.

'Ripley, tell me now, do we have a problem?'

She cleared her throat. 'No, no we don't.'

'This is the last time we'll talk about this. Time for breakfast.'

Ripley struggled through breakfast, trying to hide the sickness she felt inside. She'd been too frightened to tell the truth and now she had to live with her mistake. In future she'd have to be careful how much alcohol she consumed.

'This morning we're going out on a boat to do some snorkelling and then swimming with dolphins. A champagne lunch on a larger vessel will follow and a trip around the island.'

'Swimming with dolphins; I've always wanted to do that.'

The atmosphere between them was strained. Ripley knew Alex was still seething inside. His stony eyes were a giveaway and as well as the fact he'd tried to make conversation by telling her where they were going instead of giving her another surprise. Another sure sign of his grievance was his flat tone, which Ripley had never heard before.

All this was of her own making. She should know how much she could drink before causing a problem; poor Alex had every reason to be angry. One day into her marriage and she'd already messed up, and now she had to work at getting back on track. She never wanted to see the angry side of Alex again.

Was Joe going to haunt her for the rest of her life? She'd already let him step into her marriage and cause trouble. She couldn't let what had gone spoil her future. *Get a grip, Ripley, and let go.* How many times did she have to tell herself? She shook her head.

'What are you thinking? You're shaking your head.'

'Nothing, I hoped the water out near the reef wasn't going to be too cold.' Another lie and a further step into deceitfulness. All she could hope for was that time would surely solve her problem and last night's mistake would eventually leave her in peace.

Chapter 15

When they returned to the hotel, the atmosphere that had threatened to spoil their honeymoon had lifted. Ripley could tell Alex wasn't completely over what had happened, but he was a lot brighter, and now at least they were laughing again.

Swimming with the dolphins had been everything Ripley had dreamed it would be and she found the relaxation and freedom uplifting. The dolphins almost came within touching distance and some mothers with their young swam confidently past as Ripley watched in awe. The boatman was obviously experienced and told them when to get into the water as a new school appeared. Ripley had tried to keep up with the group, but found they quickly swam past.

That evening they ate in the hotel dining room and Ripley chose to drink only water. She wondered if the table on the beach had been booked and then cancelled, but she wasn't brave enough to ask. They sat in the bar and watched some Sega dancing, the most popular form of dance and music in Mauritius, so they were informed by the leader of the group, who played the animal skin drum. The traditional costumes were a blaze of colour and Ripley was mesmerised.

'Come and join us,' the dancers called out to the audience, and several people stepped forward. A man in red trousers and a green flowery shirt took Ripley's hand and pulled her onto the dance floor. She looked back at Alex, who was telling a girl in costume to leave him alone.

The dance was easy to follow and Ripley soon lost herself to the rhythm, looking over to Alex now and again to encourage him to join her. Was he deliberately looking the other way? Eventually she gave up and went back to join him at the table.

'Oh, you've finished cavorting about, have you? I'm tired.'

She ignored his tone and hoped he hadn't reverted back to the mood he'd been in earlier. 'Yes, I'm tired too; too much trying to keep up with the dolphins.'

He took her hand and led her to his suite in silence. Once inside, her hand was dropped. She had an uncomfortable feeling. Alex went to his bed and sat back on the pillows. 'Undress.'

Ripley looked at him and could see it was a demand not a request. Her first instinct was to ignore him, or remonstrate about his rudeness, but something told her she was already on dodgy ground. She gave him a blank stare and bent to take off her shoes. She flung them under a chair and proceeded to relieve herself of the rest of her clothes.

'Slowly. And make it like you mean it,' he said drily, his hands resting behind his head. Ripley stood in her underwear, not prepared to go any further. She felt uncomfortable and foolish.

'If you want the rest off, you're going to have to do it yourself,' she said bravely, and walked over to the bed.

Alex said nothing but started undoing her bra. This wasn't how it was supposed to be. They should be embracing each other and enjoying themselves. All she felt was a distance and coolness between them. He lowered himself onto her and began fondling her breasts, working his way down to her thighs before entering her, rather abruptly.

She stared at the ceiling; she had to stay in complete control, she daren't make another mistake in a moment of pleasure. She wasn't sure that pleasure was the right word to use for something which felt so awkward and gave no enjoyment. Alex began breathing faster, groaned and collapsed onto her.

'Did you enjoy yourself? I didn't hear you making much noise.'

'I tried keeping quiet, we are in a hotel.'

'Yes, I suppose so. But did you have a good time?'

'Yes, great thanks,' she said. Would she ever stop lying to him? Telling lies frightened her; it was something she didn't like doing and wasn't good at.

The rest of the honeymoon passed with tranquil days on the beaches, snorkelling, exploring the island and eating far too much food, but Ripley dreaded the nights. Alex liked her to parade around the bedroom in underwear he had bought her. Suspenders, leatherwear and lace were his favourites. The dressing up made her feel embarrassed; she wasn't good at flaunting herself and the situation was worsened by her lack of enthusiasm for lovemaking. She could never relax and enjoy herself for fear of saying the wrong name. The more she tried to make a conscious effort not to say *Joe,* the more the name seemed to be in the forefront of her mind, teasing and tormenting her. Alex appeared to have forgiven her faux pas, but it was Ripley who could not get over her mistake.

During the flight home, Alex brought up the subject of parents.

'I suppose we now have the fun bit to look forward to: breaking the news that we've done our mothers out of a wedding and a time to be the star attraction.'

Ripley laughed. 'They must be quite similar. My mum would have been in her glory as *mother of the bride*. She'll never forgive us.'

'We'll have to brave it and face the music. I suppose we need to pay them a visit to make the introductions. That should be interesting.'

'Why? What's your mother like?'

'You'll find out soon enough. We'll do mine first, and get it over with.'

Ripley stared out of the window at the fluffy clouds below and let her mind wander. She should be feeling elated, but she didn't. Nothing felt right. She knew Alex was controlling, but the last two weeks had shown her how little she knew of the man she'd married. She had been informed Alex had bought a house which they were to move into straight away. He'd hired someone to buy the fixtures and fittings, and furnish it ready for their return. Ripley would have liked to have seen the house they were to share and chosen some of the furnishings. It appeared Alex was richer than he'd previously divulged, but it was his money to spend how he wished, and actually she found the shop a full-time job, so maybe she should be grateful he took care of other issues. What would her mother say? She shook her head. None of it really mattered now.

On Sunday evening they pulled up outside a modern, detached house set in gardens behind a high brick wall, with automatic gates. Alex swept into the drive and Ripley stared up at her new home unimpressed. Why couldn't she snap out of her present frame of mind? It felt as though nothing would ever be right again.

The house boasted large open spaces, under-floor heating and a wide, wooden staircase. The furnishings were expensive, but bland. Cream-coloured walls, cream sofas, cream dining chairs with a light wooden table, cream-based curtains with pale blue and brown stripes. The floorboards were a pale wood, as were the kitchen units.

Alex opened one of the kitchen cupboards which was full of white mugs. Another housed white crockery. 'Lovely. What do you think? All ready to move into.'

Ripley opened the double-door fridge freezer, surprised to find it already stacked with an assortment of food. 'All ready, down to the last detail,' she said.

Upstairs were four bedrooms all with king-size beds, made up with quilts, flowery in pastel shades. She opened a wardrobe door half expecting new clothes to already be there, hanging and ready to wear, but it was empty.

'I knew you'd like it. There's still some finishing touches needed. I'll get the cases from the car,' Alex said, and disappeared downstairs.

Ripley opened the door to the en suite in the master bedroom. All white, but the tiles had blue grout which surprised her. *Colour, whatever possessed him?* She opened another door leading off the room. A walk in dressing room with a full length mirror, things were looking up. One of the walls had a large picture window, while another had doors leading out to a terraced area. She walked outside and gasped. To one side were woods and a lake and to the other, stables.

Alex came out behind her and wrapped his arms around her middle. 'Beautiful isn't it?'

'Stunning. Are you planning on getting horses?'

'No, not planning to. I've ordered a Chinese meal. Do you want a quick shower before it arrives?'

Ripley stood in the shower and let the water wash away her troubles. The grounds were fantastic, surely Alex must want to get horses at some point. Why else would he have built stables? May would love it here. She dried off with a towel, and went downstairs to find Alex. He had already set the table with wine glasses, plates and cutlery. The Chinese containers were in the middle of the table on mats.

'I thought we'd help ourselves. How was your shower?'

'Great. I think I'm going to like it here.'

'Only think? You're going to love it. Tuck in, cheers.' He raised his glass of red wine. Ripley smiled as their glasses chinked together.

Susie shrieked as she entered the shop on Monday morning, seeing Ripley already re-arranging the displays. 'Give us a hug.' She rushed over and smothered Ripley in a bear hug. 'Married! We should have guessed he'd have something out of the ordinary planned, and you never rang me back.' She released her hold and picked up Ripley's hand, looking at the rings. 'So now you need to tell me all about it and then I'll tell you about the shop stuff.'

'It's lovely to see you and so good to be back. Sorry about the phone call, you were right as usual. Overwhelmed was an understatement...'

'You'd had a shock...'

'Yes, shock is probably the right word. I'll put the kettle on and then we'll get down to the gossip. The shop looks good, you've done a great job, thanks.'

'I was in my element. I loved every moment of it,' Susie said. Ripley went through to the kitchen smiling to herself. Life was good.

Susie sipped her coffee and almost choked. 'A new BMW and a horse? My God, is he a millionaire?'

'Shh! I don't know, I think so. Apparently he does manage the company, but he owns it as well. He wouldn't approve of me talking about him like this.' She gave a small shudder. 'I think he must be a millionaire, you should see the house. Anyway, I knew about the car, he sent the fob on the morning of the wedding. But the horse!'

'Go on.'

'I am. After dinner he took me out to the garage and there is this silver convertible. I drove it here this morning...'

'Oh my God, you have to take me out in it. Did you realise he was rich? You never said anything.'

'Not really. I knew he spent a fortune on flowers, but no... Anyway, so he closed the garage door and we walked around the back to the stables and he opened the top door and a white stallion poked his head through. Oh Suz, you should see him, he's beautiful.'

'I didn't even know you liked horses.'

'My aunt kept them, so I rode when I stayed with her. I never dreamed of having one of my own.'

'You've landed on your feet, Ripley.'

'Maybe. Let's have a look at the orders.'

'You haven't told me about the wedding yet.'

'Not much to tell. Lovely dress, pretty bouquet, candle-lit dinner for two on the beach and then...'

'La, la, la, too much information.' Susie covered her ears in mock disapproval. Ripley was pleased to change the subject.

'Snorkelling is out of this world, and swimming with the dolphins... I'll bring all the pictures in later this week when Alex has sorted them out.'

'There you go.' Susie handed her a silver bag. 'A wedding gift.'

Ripley took it and then reached into her own bag. 'Thank you. I've brought you something from Mauritius. I'm sure I put it in here.' She searched for a further moment before handing a small package to Susie.

Ripley watched while she carefully undid the wrapping paper as though her life depended on it. 'A necklace, it's beautiful. What's it made from? Look at the colour.'

'Coral from the reef. I'm sure they aren't supposed to be damaging it, but they have to feed their families somehow. You always admired my shell necklace, so I thought you'd like it.'

'Thank you. I'll treasure it.'

'I hope you'll wear it.'

'I will. Where's your necklace? I've never seen you without it.'

'Thought it was time I moved on.' Ripley hadn't wanted to stop wearing the shell necklace Joe had given her, but felt she should.

Susie tapped the wedding gift bag. 'Open yours.'

Ripley read the small card. *'To my dear friend Ripley on the occasion of her marriage. Lots of love, Susie xxx.'* She undid the silver bow and pulled the paper free. 'A photo frame. Thank you, I love it! And look at all the little flowers around the edge.'

'That's why I chose it. I loved the colours and the way it all sort of entwines.'

'Alex has chosen all creams for the house. This is going to brighten the place up.'

'And there's a little something else.' Susie handed Ripley a velvet, padded book, edged with gold trim. 'It's a memories book. My mum gave me one when I married Kev. You can fill it with all sorts. Tickets, pictures, scribbles of your thoughts, anything you like. Mine's so special to me.'

'I'm sure this one will be to me. Thank you' Ripley embraced Susie for a moment before she felt her eyes welling and broke away. 'Do we have any orders for today?'

'No. Some for tomorrow though, and there's a funeral on Friday. I've done the ordering. It's great to have you back...'

'It's great to be back...'

'You're kidding me. Work or Mauritius? I know what I'd choose even though I do love my job.'

Ripley smiled a little falsely. Mauritius had been beautiful, but had she been there with the right person? The million-dollar question. Her mind seemed to flit back and forth and now she wasn't sure of her feelings or anything else. Time. She needed to give it time. Obviously she needed time to adjust; these things couldn't be rushed. She had a man who loved her, but she couldn't be certain of her own mind.

On Friday evening the newlyweds drove to Holman House in Hampshire, the home of Alex's parents. Ripley drew a breath when she saw the size and grandeur of the house.

'You said it was a little place in Hampshire; I think that may have been an understatement.'

Alex laughed. 'I thought it best not to worry you, some people are phased by all this, but I grew up with it.' He stopped the car at the bottom of the concrete stairs leading to the front door. Ripley climbed out and looked around at the impressive gardens. Alex ran up the stairs, two at a time, pulled on a handle and a bell clanged inside the house. Ripley slowly followed him up, wondering what the evening would bring.

A balding, short man in a black jacket opened the door and smiled. 'Mr Alex. Wonderful to see you, sir.' They stepped into a tiled atrium with a stained-glass, raised pyramid over the highly polished, wooden staircase leading to the first floor.

'Good to see you, Bartram. I'd like to introduce you to Ripley.'

'How do you do, madam?' Bartram said, and bowed his head slightly.

'Very well, thank you.'

'Where are my parents?'

'I believe they are waiting to receive you in the drawing room, sir.'

'Come on, Ripley. Let's get this over with. Bartram, take care of the car, there's a good chap.'

Ripley was aware that Alex had changed his voice to accommodate his authority and standing. She immediately made the connection with her mother's telephone voice. It brought a smile to her face that she quickly curbed.

Alex took her hand and led her into a large, bright room. Stately portraits adorned the walls. A man stood with his back to them and a tall, slim, blond-haired woman, balancing a cigarette holder between her fingers, stood up.

'Alex, you're late. Wonderful to see you,' then as an afterthought, 'and your little friend, of course.' She crossed the room and kissed the air next to his cheek and then looked Ripley up and down.

'Good evening, Mother. Good evening, Father. Lord Anthony and Lady Angela, I would like to introduce Ripley, who gave me the honour of becoming my wife two weeks ago.'

'Your wife? Don't make such jokes Alex, you'll embarrass us all.'

The man, who until now had faced the window, turned and eyed Alex suspiciously. 'Alex.' He nodded his head as he spoke. 'Ripley. An unusual name, my dear. Enchanted, I'm sure.' He turned back to look out of the large, double window doors.

'We married in Mauritius. Decided to forgo all the pomp of a traditional wedding and opted for some private time.'

Alex's mother covered her mouth with her hand. 'Alex, you've married her? This, this...'

'Ripley. Yes, I married her.'

'How could you do this? Didn't you consider the consequences?' She faced Ripley and took a step towards her, casting her eyes up and down as though Ripley were something disgusting standing before her.

Ripley gulped. 'I'm pleased to meet you.'

'Pleased. I'm sure you are. Are you pregnant?'

'Mother!'

Ripley shook her head. 'No.'

Lord Anthony walked over to the fireplace and pressed a button. Within a few moments a maid appeared. 'Sarah, inform chef tonight is a special occasion and arrange for champagne and the works.'

'Very good, sir.'

Lady Angela fell back into a winged armchair and patted her nose with a white lace handkerchief, as though trying to extinguish a bad smell.

Alex took Ripley's hand and led her to a window seat adjacent to where his father had returned to peer out into the grounds with the light now fading. 'The gardens look spectacular, Father.'

'Yes. I brought in a young chap from the village to help Simms, and he seems to be doing a grand job.'

Lady Angela exaggerated a sniff. 'I've arranged for Miranda to come for a ride with you in the morning.'

'Why have you done that, Mother?'

'You two go back a long way, I thought…'

'I know what you thought. You can jolly well cancel her.' He turned to Ripley. 'Shall we have a wander around the grounds before dinner?'

Subtle lighting in trees and a full moon shone down, casting shadows and added a romantic ambience to their walk.

'Sorry about Mother. She can be so tactless at times.'

'She doesn't like me. Who's Miranda?'

'Miranda is the daughter of one of mother's friends. They own an estate a couple of miles away. Mother invites her every time I come to visit in the hope the two of us will hit it off. I think I've thwarted her plans. Miranda was never my type anyway.'

Ripley smiled. 'And what is your type?'

'Someone like you who doesn't have their nose up their own backside.'

'So nice I have endearing qualities. I'll take that as a compliment.'

A bell sounded in the distance. 'Dinner. Now don't let Mother get to you, we're out of here tomorrow afternoon.'

'I don't know it's going to be much better with my parents.' They hurried back to the house and found Alex's parents already seated at either end of an enormous table which looked as though it had been laid for royalty. Alex pulled out a chair for Ripley and then walked around the table to take a seat opposite her.

'So Ripley, you must be a special lady to have captured Alex. We were beginning to think no one would take him and we'd be lumbered forever.' Lord Anthony smiled at his own joke.

'I captured her, Father. Made me do all the running as well.'

'That's what I like to hear. Alex needs a challenge to keep him on his toes.'

'I hope you made a pre-nuptial agreement,' Lady Angela said, giving her son a sour look.

'I'd give her everything I had, Mother, if it would make her happy,' Alex retorted. Lady Angela gave a disapproving huff and began to eat her soup.

Lord Anthony wiped his mouth. 'So how was Mauritius? Still hot, humid and corrupt?'

'Funny you should ask. We spent most of the time lost in our own world and didn't really notice a lot else. Ripley loved the dolphins.'

'And the snorkelling,' Ripley added.

Lord Anthony beamed. 'You two should get along fine. Always a bonus to have a partner who shares the same interests.'

Lady Angela dabbed her lips with her napkin. 'You wouldn't have expected me to go in the sea. Filthy habit. All those dirty people using it as a… Well, it's quite disgusting.'

In bed later that evening Alex and Ripley relaxed, but were unable to sleep.

'Your father's really nice,' Ripley whispered.

'Yes, shame Mother can't come down a peg or two. You managed her well.'

'When I told her my father was a financial consultant, I thought she was going to explode.'

'She'll be nagging me to make some sort of late pre-nup.'

'I don't mind, if it's what you want.'

'I don't want that at all. I tend to go the other way and dig my heels in when mother oversteps the mark and tries interfering in my business. I'd have thought she'd know the way I am by now.'

Ripley smiled. She couldn't imagine anyone telling Alex what he should do. 'My parents are very different to yours, but our mothers do have a few similar traits, I'm afraid.'

'Ripley, all I want is you. We had to make these visits, but believe me, that's where it ends.' Ripley was relieved to hear it. She didn't need to be explaining anything from her past. The less said the better.

A knock on the bedroom door awoke them both the following morning.

'Yes,' Alex said sleepily.

'Miranda will be here in half an hour, so if you want breakfast...'

'Mother, I asked you to cancel her.'

'Well I didn't. It would have been rude.'

Alex heaved a deep breath. 'Okay.' His mother's footsteps could be heard walking away. 'Damn woman. You watch her jaw drop when she sees you in riding gear too.'

'I didn't bring mine.'

'I did.' Alex smiled slyly. 'I know my mother too well.'

Ripley had to avert her eyes when Lady Angela realised three of them would be riding. 'Oh, the girl will have to ride Ned. He's the slowest. You and Miranda will want to head off, no doubt.'

'No Mother. Ripley is an accomplished rider, she'll take Serb. Morning Miranda. May I introduce my wife, Ripley?'

Miranda gave a small gasp. 'Wife! Congratulations,' she said flatly and then turned to Ripley. 'I'm sure you'll find ways to deal with his little indiscretions eventually, like I had to.'

'I already have. Nice to meet you. I thought Alex might have mentioned you.'

Alex cleared his throat. 'Let's go.' He winked at Ripley, smiled in approval, and led the way out to the stables.

In a funny way, the trip to Alex's parents had cleared the air and Ripley now felt closer to her husband. She understood why he had to be controlling; it was probably a trait passed down from his mother along with a need to establish himself as his own man in the world of the upper classes.

They left Holman House and the trip to Ripley's parents' home passed quickly, with lively banter and discussions revolving around the comments made by Angela and Miranda.

'I don't think you'd have stood a chance with those two if you had married Miranda,' Ripley said, smiling at the thought of Alex trying to control two of the most precocious women she'd ever known. Her own mother was tame by comparison.

'Perish the thought! Thank God Mother made me dig my heels in about that one. She probably saved me from a fate worse than death.'

The trip to Alex's parents passed quickly and they headed off to face the music with Ripley's family.

'Your family home,' Alex said, as they pulled up outside Ripley's parent's house.

'Not really. I've only been here once myself. And don't forget we're only here until tomorrow afternoon and then we're free again.'

'It'll be fine. They can't be that bad.'

'No, I'm being unfair, they are okay, especially when I don't see them too often.'

The front door flew open and Richard stood with his arms open ready to embrace Ripley. 'My girl. Lovely to see you. You're looking great. Come in.'

'This is Alex. Alex, Richard.'

'Come in. Pleased to meet you.' They shook hands, Richard cupping Alex's hand in between both of his. Ripley kissed her dad and for once, of late, it felt good to see him.

'Hi Mum, this is Alex.'

'Hello darling.' Clarissa turned to look at Alex and her mouth fell open. 'Alex, pleased to meet you.' Clarissa hadn't missed the designer clothes, nor the Cartier watch he wore. 'Come through and I'll pour some drinks.'

'New sofa since I was last here,' Ripley commented.

Her mother exaggerated the voice usually kept for answering the telephone 'Something to tide us over until we move again. Now, what would you all like to drink?'

Alex and Richard chatted away like old friends, while Clarissa sat on the edge of her seat drawling at Alex, trying to edge her way into the conversation. Ripley could stand the small talk no longer.

'I have something to tell you. In fact, we do. We got married a couple of weeks ago.' Silence loomed for a moment.

Clarissa's face tightened. 'Without us! Why? Why would you hurt us by doing that?'

'Clarissa, because they wanted to get married without all the fuss, I expect. Congratulations, both of you. Welcome to the Bradford family, Alex.'

'Thank you. Your daughter has made me the proudest man in the world. She's very special.'

'You don't have to tell me that; I know she's wonderful. As it happens I have a bottle of champagne which should be reasonably chilled by now. Clarissa, would you get the flutes?'

They left the room and Ripley raised her eyebrows at Alex. 'Mum's going to be hard work.'

'Can't be as bad as mine. I'll get her around.'

'I think she likes you. Good luck, it's a stage further than I got with your mother.'

Clarissa placed the flutes on the coffee table and Richard popped the cork. 'Here's to Alex and Ripley, may all your troubles be little ones.'

'Dad! That's not even funny.'

Richard laughed. 'Sorry... Seriously, we hope you will both be very happy in your new life together.' They raised their glasses and chinked them. Clarissa tried to raise a smile that fooled no one.

Richard smiled. 'Come on then, tell us all about it. Where, how, we want to hear it all, don't we sweetheart?' Clarissa re-filled her glass at double the rate of anyone else's, and by the time they left in a taxi to go out for dinner that evening, she was already tipsy.

Richard had booked a table at a plush restaurant on the other side of town. By the main course, Clarissa had allowed the drink to loosen her mouth.

'We could have come to Mauritius and shared your day. I can sort of understand not wanting a big do, but not to want your own parents...'

'Mum...It wasn't like that...'

'I take full responsibility. Ripley didn't know herself until we arrived there.'

Richard tried reasoning with his wife. 'Darling, we already know what happened. It's gone, the moment is past. Can't you be happy for them and welcome Alex into the family graciously?'

'Oh there's nothing wrong with Alex and I do welcome you.' She picked up her glass and wobbled it in the air towards Alex. 'For a moment we thought we weren't going to be able to prise her away from that awful gardener. What was his name?'

'Clarissa, that's enough.'

'Joe. Yes, Joe, that was it...'

'Mum, leave it. You're getting embarrassing.' Ripley began to feel hot and flustered.

'I'm getting embarrassing? It would have been embarrassing if you'd have ended up with a lowly land worker, I can tell you.'

Richard cleared his throat and glared at his wife. 'So Alex, how many men do you employ?'

'About thirty,' he replied curtly. His change of tone didn't go unnoticed by Ripley.

She sneaked a look at Alex's face and saw anger written in his eyes. Her heart raced. Clarissa had a big, drunken mouth. There wasn't a chance Alex hadn't made the connection with the name. She always hated lying, but Alex hadn't given her an option and now she'd been caught out. He would go mad; she had to tell the truth and hope for the best. Why did everything have to be so complicated?

Chapter 16

'So, you don't know anyone called Joe? You're a liar.' His fist went into her stomach and she fell to the floor. 'You fucking bitch. I knew. I fucking knew you were lying, but I wanted to believe you. I loved you and you lied to me as though I mean nothing.' They were back at her parents' house, up in the bedroom.

'It happened years ago. I didn't want to talk about it. We've all got skeletons.' She had stayed on the floor curled up to protect herself from any more blows he might be about to deliver. Maybe she should scream out and alert her dad. No, this was all her fault and it would cause a rift and make matters worse.

'No, we have not all got skeletons. I have never sunk so low as to lie to you and I expect the same regard from you, but it seems you are not of similar calibre. I hate you, Ripley, for your lies, for your weak morals and for marrying me under false pretences. I'm going to bed and don't bother joining me.'

He undressed and the lights went out. She waited a while and then found her way across the room to an armchair. He couldn't mean what he said. For God's sake, how pathetic was he? So what, she had a previous lover? He'd never asked her before they married. She should have braved up to him and told the truth the day after the wedding. She felt sickened; everything had been going so well and they'd only been married a few weeks to have had such an awful argument.

Dawn broke with a welcome start to a new day and Ripley, after staying awake all night, crept downstairs for a drink. Clarissa was already in the kitchen.

'You're up early,' Ripley said, as she went to the coffee pot and reached up to the shelf for a mug.

'We argued when we went to bed and then I haven't really slept. Richard thinks I should apologise.'

'You said some pretty thoughtless stuff.'

'Well, I was upset.'

'That's no excuse.'

'Let's forget it.'

Ripley took a sip of her coffee and shook her head. Her mother was selfish and twisted. She'd almost admitted to telling Alex about Joe deliberately because she was miffed about the wedding. What a bitch! Ripley took her coffee through to the lounge and sat looking out of the window. Her stomach felt bruised where Alex had thumped her. She put her coffee on the table and covered her face with her hands. How could he hate her? Maybe the heat of the moment made him say such an awful thing. Sex before marriage wasn't a crime, or anything to be ashamed of, and yet somehow he'd managed to turn it into something dirty. He must have strange convictions about sex; shame he hadn't let her into the secret before they became too involved. If she were honest with herself, the signs had all been clear: his refusal to kiss her properly on their first few dates, his dislike of showing any emotions in public, and his refusal to have sex before marriage. At the time she'd accepted his attitude as strange but quaint. Now she realised the problem ran much deeper.

The lounge door opened and Alex stepped into the room and closed the door.

'I want to head off early. I don't need to be around you or your family. I'll drop you off at the flat.'

'You can't mean we're finished because of something I did before I even knew you.'

'How can I trust you when you lied to me? A marriage should be about love and trust, both of which you obviously know nothing about. Do you want a lift, or will you make your way back later?'

'I'll come with you. Alex, you made it difficult for me to tell you the truth. Hitting me is not acceptable. How can you expect me to be honest when I'm frightened of the consequences?'

'I'll get my stuff and meet you in the car.'

'I have to say goodbye.'

Alex sat in the car and revved the engine in frustration. He looked at the clock and tapped his fingers against his knee. One more minute then he was out of here. He tooted the horn and revved the engine again. The door to the house remained closed. He drove out of the road and headed towards home.

Ripley gathered her belongings together and went along the landing to her parents' bedroom. She gingerly knocked on the door.

'Come in,' Richard said, covering his nakedness with the sheet. 'Good morning. How are you?'

'Okay. We're heading back home.'

'Oh dear. This is to do with what Clarissa said, isn't it?'

Ripley's tears fell uncontrollably down her cheeks. She nodded. 'It's complicated,'

'These things often are. He'll come around, he loves you. I could kill her. Come here and give your old dad a hug.' As she rose from the hug she saw the car pull out of the road and felt her anger rise. How dare he leave her here? Sunday service on public transport, great. She raced down the stairs and threw open the front door. He was already out of sight. She stood with her back to the door and cried.

'Hey, what's all this?' Richard said as he walked down the stairs.

'He's gone without me. I'll have to go home by train.'

'Bastard. I'll drive you home, pet. Come on, no more tears. You'll be laughing about this in a couple of days.'

Ripley wasn't convinced Alex would be that easy. The journey home with her dad took her back to the old days when they were close.

'Look at this!' Richard said, as they pulled up outside the shop. 'Flower Haven. You've done well.'

'I've got one employee and I have to say I love my work.'

'That's the most you can hope for. All those people who do what they have to, only to put food on the table. Not a good place to be.'

'How's work going for you?'

'Brilliant. As it happened the deal never went through when I needed that money, so I never lost face and everyone was happy.'

'I'll make us a drink.'

'No, let's go out for lunch, just you and me. I've missed you Ripley.'

'I've missed you too.'

Ripley sat alone in her flat that evening trying to run through all the possible scenarios of her present predicament. What outcome did she want? She should be hoping he'd ring her and forgive her lies, but that wasn't what she wanted. He should apologise for being so controlling and forcing her to lie. He should be on bended knee begging for forgiveness for hitting her. She couldn't remember the night of the wedding but had a feeling he'd been rough with her then as well. No way would she run back to him. She had no regrets from the past and he was not going to make her apologise.

'Are you going to tell me what's going on, or do I have to guess?' Susie said, half-way through Thursday morning.
    'There's not a lot to tell,' Ripley fibbed.
    'Well I know you've been living back upstairs in the flat since your visit to the parents.'
    Ripley bit into her bottom lip in a bid to hold back her tears. 'We fell out. I lied and he found out. It was all so stupid.' The tears flowed as Ripley told her story and blurted out her feelings including the ones she'd held on to for Joe, over the past years.
    Susie listened and passed the tissue box at frequent intervals.
    'He's a bully. A man who has to revert to using his fists on a woman, isn't a man at all. You've done nothing wrong. I've still got things I'd never share with Kev, and I daresay he's got stuff he'd not tell me. It's like a need-to-know thing, and where relationships are concerned, it's better not to

know everything sometimes. You're a normal, loving girl, Ripley. You should have no regrets.'

'I don't know what to do.'

'Do nothing. How do you feel about him?'

'I don't know. I've made such a mess of it all.'

'No you haven't. Maybe this is just a blip. Given time you'll know what you want, and whether or not that involves Alex.'

'Thanks Susie, you always have a way of making me feel better. I'm popping to the cake shop, you put the kettle on.'

Susie absentmindedly filled the kettle. Her mind had drifted away to Ripley and her young lover. She'd held a candle all those years. How could someone vanish off the face of the earth so easily? Maybe Ripley's love wasn't reciprocated and he was glad to disappear once her father gave the marching orders. Whatever the reason, Susie's heart went out to her young friend. A pang of guilt washed over her. Why had she been so persuasive when Ripley got involved with Alex? She didn't like to say so, but once a man is violent towards his wife, there's not a lot of hope for the future. Ripley would be as well to get out now and move on. The water gushed over the side of the sink, soaking her clothes and flooding onto the floor. *Damn!*

Two weeks later, Alex turned up at the flat. Ripley gingerly opened the door, half expecting trouble.

'We need to talk,' Alex said, somewhat formally.

'Come in.' Ripley closed the door and realised she was shaking, as she followed him up the stairs. She still wasn't sure of the outcome she expected or wanted for their marriage.

They sat at opposite sides of the living room facing one another.

'I've decided to forgive you. I can't ever forget what you did to me, but we're married and we have vows to fulfil.'

'I don't know what I want any more Alex. You thumped me and I find that unforgivable.'

'So you drive me to an anger I can't control, and then you can't forgive the consequences? So you want a divorce four weeks into our marriage?'

'I don't know what I want. You frightened me.'

'You are an impossible woman. I came around here with all good intentions. You know where I am.' Without a glance in her direction he stood and walked away, letting himself out of the downstairs door.

Ripley trembled. She went to the kitchen and poured herself a glass of white wine, returned to the living room and slumped onto the sofa. He was hard work. Why hadn't she realised that before she married him?

Ripley stared at the distinctive line staring back at her. She shut her eyes for a moment and tried to make sense of the latest disaster. There had to be a mistake; this couldn't be happening to her, not now. She ripped the second tester out of its packet and ran the tap to make her want to pee again. She knew she didn't really need a second test; the morning sickness had set in with a vengeance.

Six weeks into a marriage which had already fallen apart, and she was pregnant. She sat on the lid of the toilet and put her head in her hands. How could she have the baby knowing Alex's violent temper could kick off at any time?

She'd be tied to him forever and if he frightened her, what would life be like for a child?

Ripley kept her secret for a week before Susie sussed out the situation. 'So are you going to tell me, or do I have to keep pretending I don't know?' Ripley dropped her eyes to the floor and shuffled her feet nervously.

'How do you know?'

'You've been having morning sickness for a start, and I can tell. Call it a woman's intuition. How do you feel?'

'Terrible. I can't stop being sick...'

'I mean about the pregnancy.'

'Oh. I have no idea. The more I try to decide how I feel and what I want to do, the more confused I am.'

Susie sighed. 'I don't envy you. How about trying to be practical? I find that strategy usually sorts out a few problems.'

'I don't understand.'

'Well, for a start, do you want Alex involved? If you might want to be a family, you need to move back in with him and start getting to know each other and build some bridges. If you're considering not having the baby, you need to go and talk to someone for a bit of guidance. Counselling would help. If you want to bring the baby up alone, you need to find out about childcare, or consider if you want to give up the shop.'

'Oh my God! I thought you were making things easier for me.'

'I am. You need to get some perspectives on your choices and hopefully you'll know what you want to do.'

'My main issue is with Alex. Once he knows I'm pregnant I won't stand a chance of making my own decisions.'

'So don't tell him yet.'
'More lies.'
'No, think of it as self-preservation. You have to put yourself and the baby first.'

Ripley thought through Susie's advice and went along to a private clinic to talk to someone about having an abortion. She knew it would be the last thing she wanted to do, but Susie was right, she needed all the facts. The meeting didn't help with making any decisions and Ripley came away armed with a few leaflets and a headful of uncertainties.

Next, she rang Alex. 'I'm moving back in with you at the end of the week, Friday. We've both been at fault...'

'Now hold on a moment...'

'No, Alex. Either we make a pact to start again, or we finish our marriage once and for all.'

Alex cleared his throat. 'No more lies?'

'No, and no more violence.'

'I'll see you Friday then.'

'See you Friday.' She put down the phone with her hand shaking. She'd stood up to him; she'd taken the first step towards her goal of finding out if they could live together. It felt as though she was embarking on a mission instead of joining her husband to try to make their marriage work. Did she want it to work? God only knew, but at least she was on her way to find out. She rubbed her tummy. *Don't worry little one. I won't let anything bad ever happen to you.* A couple of tears fell onto her cheek and rolled down. She'd been in such turmoil over Alex she hadn't given much thought to the child she carried. What sort of mother was she? Surely not a bad one already.

Sorry little fella. I'll look after you. Her thoughts sparked some maternal feelings she hadn't realised she harboured. She did care about her baby, it was only the surrounding issues which were a problem. She knew she wanted her child. She patted her stomach and felt a love deep down inside.

Two weeks after moving back with Alex, all seemed quiet and they'd even shared some fun. Ripley felt relaxed and took regular, gentle exercise on her horse, Shimmer. He would amble through the woods on a now well-trodden path, allowing her mind to wander to the future. Important decisions shouldn't ever be rushed, but time was running out. Alex needed to know about the pregnancy soon. He had kept to the pact, and the past hadn't been raised, allowing them both a chance to settle down to the task of living together as man and wife. Although they hadn't been back together long, Ripley felt she no longer had good reason to hold back her secret any longer.

Alex stood at the stable door as she turned into the yard. 'You need a horse so we can ride together,' Ripley called out, above the bellowing of the wind.

Alex took one rein in his left hand and looked up at her with a vengeance. 'You fucking murdering bitch! You killed our child…'

'No! No, you've got it wrong.'

'Got it wrong? Like I always do!' He reached up his hand and dragged her down from the horse. Shimmer reared up in fright and his front legs came down on her. Ripley yelled out in pain as Shimmer broke free from Alex's grasp and raced off towards the woods. Alex kicked out at Ripley, left her crying in agony and ran off after the horse.

Ripley struggled up and doubled over. Clutching her stomach, she made her way to the house. She felt in her pocket for her phone and went to the bathroom and locked the door. Blood was seeping through her jodhpurs from between her legs. She called Susie.

'Ripley. Talk to me. What's happened? Ripley.'

'I think I'm losing the baby. Alex pulled me off Shimmer.'

'Okay. Are you lying down? I'll call an ambulance. What's the address?' Ripley told her. 'Alright, I'm coming over.'

The last thing Ripley heard was Alex beating his fist on the bathroom door.

Chapter 17

'Dad!' Panic ran through her.

'Shh. It's alright. You're safe.' Tears welled in his eyes. He had her hand held tightly in his own. 'You're going to be fine. You need to rest.'

She cast her eyes around and realised she was in hospital. 'My baby?'

Richard looked above her head towards the wall. 'I'm sorry love. There won't be a baby now.' He bent forwards and held her in his arms while they both sobbed; Richard cried for his daughter and she wept for her baby.

A doctor entered the room. 'Ripley, pleased to meet you at long last. You gave us all a bit of a fright there.'

She wiped her eyes with the back of her hand. 'How long have I been here?'

'Two days. You had severe concussion, along with other complications. How are you feeling?'

'Sore. Everywhere.'

'You were injured quite badly; a fall from a horse can be dangerous. Good job you were wearing your helmet.'

'I fell? How? I don't remember anything.'

'Can't help you with that one. You might find your memory returns shortly, but for now, rest is the order of the day. Ripley, did you know you were pregnant?'

'Yes, and Dad told me already.'

'I'm afraid the fall ruptured your womb and your fallopian tubes were a mess. Sorry to be the bearer of bad news, but you might be infertile.'

She heaved a deep sigh and stared out of the window at the clouds floating past. Never say never, Aunt May had told her, and she was going to hold on to that thought forever.

Susie burst through the door carrying a bunch of flowers and a box of chocolates. 'You've woken. Thank God.' She looked up to the ceiling and made the shape of a cross on her chest.

'Dad, this is Susie. She works in the shop with me and she's the best friend ever.'

'Well, I'll go and grab a coffee so you two can chat. Back soon.' He blew a kiss and headed out the door.

'Do you remember what happened?'

'No. The doctor said I fell from Shimmer.'

'Like hell you did. You rang me and I called the ambulance. You said Alex pulled you off the horse.'

'Why would he have done that? The doctor thinks I might not be able to have children. Oh God! I can remember sitting in the bathroom.'

'You were outside the stable on the floor when I got there. You were in no fit state to have got to the bathroom.'

'Oh.'

'You look tired. I'll pop in the restaurant and tell your dad you're having a rest. See you tomorrow. Take care, lots of love and don't worry about the shop, it's in good hands.'

Ripley closed her eyes and then opened them with a jump as Alex pounded into her with his fists and feet. She looked around, relieved to see no one. The memories came flooding back like a rude awakening.

Richard opened the door slowly and popped his head in. 'You are awake. I looked in on you about half an hour ago but you were sleeping.'

'Dad, Alex did this.'

'What are you talking about? You had a nasty bump on the head and you're probably in shock. The mind...'

'No Dad. I don't know why, but Alex pulled me off the horse and I ran up to the bathroom and rang Susie. He bashed on the door shouting... then I don't remember what happened. He did this, I know he did...'

'Don't get upset. I won't ever let him hurt you again.'

'I won't be safe when you've gone. You don't know what he's like.'

'Has he hit you before?'

Ripley nodded. 'I'm frightened.'

'Don't be. Now listen. I need to talk to you. Your Aunt May left Cliff Top Manor to you. It's all a bit complicated, but our parents left it to her. I assumed it would come to me when she died, but in her wisdom, she left it to you. Probably for the best. Anyway, I only found out this week after my bankruptcy was lifted...'

'Why hadn't the solicitor told you?'

'Because I told him not to open her will. Once he did that, we'd have legally had to declare it. I won't bore you with the details. We thought we were doing the right thing and as it turns out, the old place was never mine and is never going to be.'

Ripley looked at her dad's face and couldn't help letting out a small giggle. 'Dad, what are you like?'

'I suggest, when you get out of hospital, you head off to Crompton and do a bit of convalescing by the sea... I'll take you and maybe stay a few days. Your mum's on her way here. She was away in France with a friend when all this happened and I didn't think it fair to worry her.'

Ripley gave him a knowing look. 'No point worrying her and her rushing back. You did right. Alex won't be able to find me in Crompton.'

'I told you, don't worry about him.'

'I love you, Dad.'

'I love you, my special girl.'

Ripley felt her heart lift as they pulled into the driveway at Cliff Top Manor. It felt like she'd come home. She pulled the white dust-sheets away from the furniture and almost choked with the dust that filled the air.

'You're supposed to lift them carefully to stop the dust going everywhere,' Richard said between coughs and a few sneezes.

'I can't bear to see it all covered like this. May would hate it.'

Richard smiled. 'You really did love her. I didn't appreciate that at the time, I'm sorry. I probably broke both your hearts.'

Ripley nodded.

'Grab the end of this one and we'll fold it,' Ripley said, trying to lighten the atmosphere. Too much regret; it was time to move on.

They walked into each room in turn. 'Mum's kitchen. Did she ever cook anything in it?'

'I doubt it. I can't recall her cooking anything since I married her.'

'May's sitting room. I wish she was still here.'

'To taunt me. God, she could be cantankerous and without even trying. It came naturally to her. She could never get your name right. Damn woman. I don't know what your mother expected me to do about it, but it was always my fault.'

Ripley laughed. 'She knew my name. She called me Ritly to get at you and mum.'

'I knew it! I damn well knew it!' He looked at Ripley's face and broke into laughter himself.

They climbed the stairs. Ripley opened her bedroom door and went straight to the window and looked down at the stables, which were deathly quiet and still.

'I know I made some mistakes and someday I hope you'll forgive me,' Richard said as he entered the room behind her.

Ripley kept her face to the stables. 'I already have. You did what you thought was for the best at the time.' She turned and faced him. 'Dad, you didn't hurt Joe? He left, right?'

'He left,' Richard said convincingly. Ripley nodded. Somehow the answer had hurt her more than she realised it would. She gulped and with tears welling she turned back to the window and continued to stare down at the grounds.

'I think I knew that all along really.'

'How about going out to dinner? I know a nice little restaurant.'

'Pinkies?'

'None other.'

An hour later Richard pulled up outside the restaurant. Pinkies had closed down. The once colourful pink diner was now no more than a deserted, shabby building; Ripley felt as though another piece of her past had abandoned her. The only good thing about coming back to Crompton was the distance between herself and Alex. Richard stayed for four days. They walked along the beach, ate out most evenings and Ripley made an amazing recovery from her traumatic experience. The loss of her baby tormented her, but she'd managed to convince herself that having Alex's child would have been a mistake for them all.

They returned from lunch on the afternoon Richard planned to leave Cliff Top Manor.

'Police. What do they want?' Richard said, not expecting an answer as he was already half out of the car. 'You wait in the car.'

Ripley watched as the policeman talked to Richard in a low voice. Richard slowly walked back to the car and climbed in the driver's seat. He pressed the buzzer and the gates creaked open. He started the car and turned to look at Ripley.

'Alex was found dead...'

'Dead! Oh God, he hasn't committed suicide, has he? I sent a horrible message saying he'd killed his own child.'

Richard soothed her shoulder. 'No, he was found in his car in the early hours of this morning in some remote lane with a bullet through his head...'

Ripley gasped. 'Murdered?' Richard nodded and followed the police car into the grounds of the house.

'The police need to question us both. They went to your shop and your helper...'

'Susie.'

'Yes. She told them where you were. Might be best not to mention what he did. Stick to the story that you fell from the horse.'

'Why?'

'Because it will open a can of worms and cause all sorts of suspicions and questions. Easier to say you came here for a few days to recuperate from the fall.'

Ripley felt uneasy as she answered the questions, but her dad had been right. The police seemed happy with the answers, and soon went on their way. 'Poor Alex. Who would do such a thing?'

'Don't go upsetting yourself now. He obviously had another side to his character and upset someone. Look at what he did to you; people like that are rotten through and through.'

Ripley felt shaken and somewhat saddened. 'I'm going to bed. I've got a headache coming on.'

'I won't leave today, we'll see how you are tomorrow.'

'Thanks, Dad.'

Richard sat in the lounge swilling a large brandy around his glass. The bastard had deserved it. Thought he'd got away with hurting his girl.

I hope you rot in hell.

Part 2

Chapter 18

Joe grabbed what he could, stuffed it into a rucksack and made his way out of Cliff Top Manor for the last time. He daren't see Ripley again, he couldn't bear to see her heart break, and anyway what could he tell her? He staggered down the pathway and stumbled along the beach blinded by his tears, the rain lashing down on him with a vengeance. The rucksack he'd hurriedly packed, weighed him down, getting heavier as it soaked up the torrents of water falling on him. He tripped on the rocks in the darkness and eventually fell onto his knees, sobbing tears of self-pity, knowing life would never return to what it had been and also aware he'd lost Ripley forever. The wash of the incoming tide eventually covered his feet and began working its way up his legs. If he couldn't have her, life wasn't worth living. He'd lost everything dear to him: his home, the horses, and most of all Ripley. The money in his pocket was more than he'd ever envisaged having, but it meant nothing in his broken world. *A new start,* Richard had said. Joe didn't want a new start; he only wanted what he already had. His mind drifted away with the sound of the tide coming in fast and furious. His whole body shook with the cold and shock, at what had happened to his peaceful domain.

'Oh, nice of you to join us.' The gruff voice belonged to a well-rounded, unshaven man with thinning grey hair. Joe looked around, his vision slightly blurred. 'You were lucky I found you. What were you doing on the beach on a night like that?'

Joe slowly recalled the events of the previous evening and groaned aloud. He wasn't happy with his rescuer. 'I might ask you the same question.'

'My old mum died and I downed a bottle of rum and fell asleep along the beach sometime in the afternoon, I guess. Now, what's your excuse?'

'I got kicked out of home. I didn't want rescuing.'

'A young lad like you can't be thinking like that. Nothing is that bad. Give it a day or two and all will be well.'

'Not this time. I can't ever go back.'

'Did you do something bad?'

'I fell in love with the wrong girl, I guess.'

'I see. Love does not begin and end the way we seem to think it does. *Tis better to have loved and lost than never to have loved at all.* That was Alfred Lord Tennyson. He died about a hundred odd years ago.' Joe looked blankly at his rescuer.

'Where am I?'

'You're on board the Princess Grace in Whiteleaf harbour. We transport various cargo all around the world. I carried you all the way back here. It sobered me up, I can tell you.'

'I need to go.' Joe's hand went down to his trouser pocket. He was naked apart from his underpants.

'Don't worry, your money's drying up there along with your clothes. A tidy sum for a lad to be carrying around.'

'I didn't steal it. It was given to me to make sure I disappeared for good.'

'A pay-off. And will the young lady be proud of you for selling your soul?'

'It isn't like that, and I don't want to talk about it.' Joe pulled back the sheet and sat up, banging his head on the top bunk.

'There's not a lot of room in these little cabins. What are you like at cooking, son?'

'Not bad.'

'The ship leaves port in two days. Don't suppose you have a passport?'

'No.'

'Time enough to travel to London and get yourself one. We need a kitchen hand. It's not a bad life on board. No women to tempt you or lead you astray. It'd give you a bit of time to sort yourself out. You'll need to go and get the forms from the post office, get a couple of photos done and then the captain will authorise them.'

Joe was thoughtful for a moment. He couldn't risk being near to Ripley for fear of weakening. At least out at sea he wouldn't be tempted.

'What about the captain? Hadn't we better clear it with him first?'

'Already asked him while you were sleeping. I'll take you up to the canteen and you can grab a bite to eat before you set off.'

Joe pulled on his clothes and followed Bill though the narrow corridors. He couldn't eat a thing, although his stomach was rumbling.

Within the hour, he'd set off for the station to catch a train to London. The journey gave Joe nearly two hours' thinking time. How could he have been so weak that he even thought about giving up on life? What about Ripley? She'd hate him forever when he didn't show up at the clock tower like he promised. She'd forget him sooner than he'd forget her. Would his heart ever stop aching for her? Love wasn't supposed to hurt like this. Everyone was supposed to live happily ever after. Someone up there was looking out for him and had sent Bill to find him. Money in his pocket and a new start. He'd been given a second chance. He'd never felt so low, but something inside spurred him on.

Joe returned to the ship the next day, after securing himself a passport. The ship bustled with men hurrying to prepare for leaving port. 'I'll show you around the galley,' Bill said, and led the way. 'We prepare three meals a day for seventeen crew members. We make our own bread and generally work thirty-five days on and then have thirty-five days off, but it's pretty flexible. Your duties will be washing up, general cleaning of the meat room and fridges, along with the storeroom. You'll help with the ordering of provisions at the end of each month and hopefully we'll get a chance to sample some of your cooking. It sounds a lot, but if you keep on top of it, it's a doddle.'

'I'm used to hard work. I did days or split shifts at the restaurant and then tended to the horses, grounds and other animals, when I had time off, '

'So you'll be used to early starts then? That's always a bonus. You'll do fine here, laddie. Try and put the past behind you. Don't cry because it's over, smile because it happened. Can't quite recall who said that, but I'll let you know if I think of it later.' Joe smiled. He liked Bill.

Joe shared a cabin with a Chinese man named Chen.

'My name means I am great. I am pleased to meet you. Do you want the top bunk? My legs don't reach down easily.'

'Fine. I'll take the top then. How long have you worked here?'

Chen rubbed his chin and looked upwards. 'Five years.'

'Your English is good.'

'I was born in England. I ran away from a big, large lady. Escape to the sea, my friend said. How about you?'

Joe felt a smile rise inside as he imagined the tiny Chen with a big, large lady. 'No big, large lady for me. Only a slim, beautiful one.'

'And you've left her alone?'

'I can't talk about it. I hurt too much on the inside.'

Chen nodded and changed the subject. 'I work in the galley too. I will be your friend. If you want some help, you only have to ask me.'

'Thanks Chen, I will.'

Joe found more than enough to keep him busy at work and in his free time he often sat alone on his bunk and wrote letters to Ripley. He poured out his emotions and love for her, but never intended to send them. How could he when their love was forbidden?

Most of the crew were friendly and meal-times were always filled with noise of banter and ridicule. One man made Joe feel uneasy. Sparky was one of the louder, more confident men and his jokes always seemed to hit a raw nerve and rubbed Joe up the wrong way.

'A pretty boy with muscle. Bet you've had a few girls screaming, eh?'

'No. I respect women.'

'Oooh! He's been scorned,' Sparky sneered.

Chen tried to help. 'Joe had a beautiful, slim girl. Joe wasn't scorned.'

'Bet she needed a real man, not some young whippersnapper. A real man would have shown her a good time.'

Joe stood and left the table, his meal unfinished. He slung his food in the bin and the plate into the sink and began to tidy up around the galley.

Bill joined him a few minutes later, putting the stack of plates he was carrying into the sink. 'You don't want to let people like that get to you. You have to get used to a bit of banter on board; they don't mean any harm.'

'I know, but I'm not in the mood for it.'

'You can't spend your whole life mourning for something that's gone. Tis better to have loved and lost, than never to have loved at all. Alfred, Lord Tennyson. My old mum had a multitude of sayings. One for every occasion she reckoned. I don't know that many.' Joe found himself feeling somewhat relieved as that was the second time he'd heard that one.

A week later Sparky sat down to his meal sporting a grin. He waited until everyone was seated around the table. He looked at his food, and then, in a loud attention-seeking voice, he spoke.

'I don't know how I get through each day without you. I will never stop loving you. You mean the world to me and always will.'

The other crew members started mocking his loving comments, aimed towards his plate of food.

'You're going soft in the head.'

'Tell he hasn't had a port stop for a while.'

Sparky continued. 'I miss you every day. I can still feel the touch of your soft skin against me...'

Joe leapt up, sending his food flying, and launched himself across the table on top of Sparky, who fell backwards onto the floor with Joe on top and pummelling down on him with his fists. Joe could feel himself being dragged off Sparky, his fists and feet still lashing out.

'Calm yourself, lad. What's happened?' Bill said, as two men held Joe in a tight embrace. Joe dribbled as he spoke.

'He's been in my private stuff and read my letters.'

'No lad. Sparky wouldn't do that.'

Sparky pulled himself up from the floor, his mouth bleeding and his head gashed from the fall. 'You'll pay for this you little shit. Think because you have a bit of muscle behind you, you can lash into people when you feel like it?'

'You've been in my private stuff and read my letters.'

Sparky wiped his mouth with the back of his hand and spat blood onto the floor. 'Like hell I have. You want to be careful of making wild accusations; could get you into a lot of bother.'

'See lad? You were mistaken. Best you apologise and let that be an end to it.'

Joe looked at all the expectant, accusing faces around him. He'd attacked a long-standing member of the crew and no one believed his reason. 'Sorry. I might have got it wrong,' he said reluctantly.

Sparky nodded and sat back on the bench, most of his meal spread out across the table. When the fuss has died down, Joe caught his oppressor's eye and knew he wasn't off the hook. Sparky held a cold look of hatred in his eyes.

Joe regretted attacking Sparky. Not because Sparky didn't deserve it, but for the constant hassle which came Joe's way after the brawl. At every moment he could, Sparky whispered another line or phrase Joe had used in his letters. He was always careful to make sure no one else was in earshot and Joe felt constant frustration and resentment. Joe drew farther away from the rest of the crew and often confined himself to a quiet area of the ship where he was out of reach of the spiteful taunts.

During these quiet moments Joe would find his mind drifting back to Cliff Top Manor and his childhood years when he had been trouble free. Would he ever be free of the misery which now tormented his every waking hour? Sparky's taunts brought back painful memories of how he had walked away from Ripley and how her heart must have broken the same as his own.

Joe had to find another job, one which would take him away from his tormentor forever, but for now until the ship docked at the next port, he was captive and vulnerable. He had found a stack of empty storage crates up on the top deck and he sat around the back of them, often in the dark, with the crates giving him sanctuary.

Sometimes the other crew members would pass by, unaware of his presence, chatting or discussing some issue either on board or in the world news. Joe would sit and ponder on the snippets he heard often envious of the companionship the men shared.

A storm had been brewing most of the day. Joe wrapped himself up in wet-weather gear and headed up to the top deck for his hideaway. He heard the familiar voice of Sparky and his heart skipped a beat.

'I love it out here on a night like this. The rain burning your face and the wind almost knocking you off your feet.'

'I'll take your word for it. I'm heading back down,' another voice said.

'I'll stay on up here for a while and then come down to warm up with some rum.'

Joe froze. He daren't move as he could see the familiar outline of Sparky only a few feet away standing at the railing and looking out to sea. Sparky kept raising his face up into the wind and rain, which was now getting heavier. Joe could feel the rain and the splash of the waves soaking into his clothing; he began to shiver with the cold and his nerves.

The waves crashed into the side of the ship and Joe wished he had stayed safely in his cabin. A large wave lashed onto the deck and as the deluge of water plunged back into the sea, Sparky was dragged off his feet. A muffled cry could be heard through the storm and Joe raised his head to see what was happening. Sparky was nowhere to be seen. Joe scrambled free of the crates and ran to the side of the ship. The light from the ship gave a silhouette of Sparky's head and a hand reaching out in desperation.

For a split second Joe stared, then ran for the lifebelt that hung on the railings a little further along the deck. He slipped a couple of times and slowed himself down before unleashing the safety belt and throwing it with all his might in the direction of Sparky.

Sparky grabbed out at the ring and hung on with both arms as Joe pulled him towards the ship. Joe began shouting for help, but the rest of the crew were inside, or out of earshot. He secured his end of the rope to the railing and ran for help.

Several men heaved Sparky up onto the ship and he crashed onto the deck trying to catch his breath. Joe kept to the back of the group as Sparky caught his breath in between coughing up spurts of water. He looked up at the small gathering and came to a stop when his eyes met with Joe's.

'Thanks lad. I thought I was a goner there for a moment. I owe you my life.' He held out his hand and Joe stepped forward to shake. 'You could have walked away... I'm sorry, that was a brave thing you did there for me. You could've been washed over...'

'Let's get you inside before you catch your death,' Bill said. 'A spot of rum will warm us all. Joe, you go and start pouring.' As Joe made his way down to the galley he had a sneaky suspicion Bill was ensuring Joe would be present around the table for once.

The atmosphere was light and jovial with Sparky continuously raising his tankard to Joe while shaking his head in disbelief at his brush with death. Joe had mixed feelings. He didn't trust Sparky and wouldn't ever forget the way he had tormented him for the past weeks, but it was somewhat of a relief that his ordeal might be over and Sparky might relent, at least for a while.

Chapter 19

The ship docked in Guatemala and most of the crew were going ashore. Since the rescue a week previously, Sparky had tried befriending Joe. He popped his head around Joe's cabin door.

'You coming ashore? I'd like to buy you a drink.'

'No. I've got some stuff to do here.'

'Bollocks! You spend too much time on your own. Come with us, you'll have a laugh.'

Joe took a deep breath. He lived each day as though he needed to make it through to the night and cross another day off the calendar. Life had no purpose apart from work and sleep.

'Okay, I'll come.'

'Good. Meet you on deck in ten minutes. Don't forget your passport.' Sparky headed off and Joe felt a surge of excitement wash over him. He hadn't left the ship before now; it would be good to visit somewhere new.

The group went through customs and walked up a rough, cobbled street towards the town. A restaurant bar in a shabby back street was their first stop.

'They do a good lunch in here,' Bill said. 'Thursday is the traditional day for tamales; you won't get better.'

'Tamales?' Joe frowned as he spoke.

'It's made from dough and usually with pork or chicken. A bit like a pie, sort of.'

Sparky ordered the beer and three drinks later the tamales arrived. Joe had never been so relieved to see food;

the beer had gone straight to his head, he wasn't used to drinking much. After lunch several men went off to some other establishments in town to find women who were up for a bit of fun for a small fee.

'I'll take you somewhere special,' Sparky said. 'The girls are a bit younger.'

Joe scoffed. 'I don't want young girls. I'll stay here; stop in for me on the way back to the ship.'

'You'll be missing a good time.'

'I don't want a good time.'

'Right. If you're sure, I'll be back in about an hour or so.'

Joe ordered another drink and settled down to people watch. Two grubby-looking men, with unkempt hair stood at the bar drinking spirits from a bottle sitting on the bar between them. Joe wondered how the barman would know what to charge; perhaps it was sold by the bottle. The men topped up their glasses without exchanging a word. Another man, sat reading a newspaper with a dead cigarette end hanging from the side of his mouth. He'd had the same amount of beer in the bottom of his glass since Joe had arrived.

A girl of around Joe's age arrived behind the bar and the barman went off through the curtain at the back. She wiped down the bar and looked over in Joe's direction before lifting the end of the bar and walking over to him.

'Can I get you another?'

Joe felt as though he'd had enough already but wasn't comfortable sitting with an empty bottle in front of him. 'Thanks,' he said, as he nodded.

'You off the ship?'

'Yes, been let out for the afternoon.' She walked off in the direction of the bar, her dark, shiny hair hanging almost to her shapely bottom. Joe averted his gaze for a moment but soon looked over at her again. She was heading back clutching an opened bottle.

'There you go,' she said, placing the bottle on the table. 'I'm Claudette.'

'Joe. Not very busy this afternoon.'

'There's another ship been docked, so it might liven up soon.' She smiled as she spoke, her eyes like black shining coals. 'How come you're alone?'

'My mates have gone for a wander around the town.'

She laughed and threw her head back. 'It's the first time I've heard it called that.'

'I was trying to be polite,' Joe chortled.

'No need around these parts. Tell you what, there's a nice bit of cake in the kitchen; I'll go and cut you a slice. My mum wanted to know what the foreigners thought of it.'

Joe smiled as the down-to-earth Claudette disappeared through the curtain, obviously to the private quarters. He suddenly realised how long it had been since he'd spoken to a woman. His mind immediately went to Ripley and his heart gave an involuntary jerk.

'There you go; the best in town.' The door to the bar swung open and a lively crowd of men, who had clearly already had plenty to drink, entered the bar.

'Thanks, looks good,' Joe said, and felt a little peeved that the new arrivals would take the attention of Claudette, whom he wouldn't have minded getting to know a little better. He watched her well rounded but taut bottom, as it moved seductively from side to side when she walked. He took a deep breath and picked up the cake. It smelled of coconut and something else he couldn't place. He took a bite and wasn't disappointed. Moist and flavoursome with a good spongy texture not dissimilar the cake his own mum used to make. He felt his eyes well up and hung his head down, looking at the cake while trying to gain control. The beer had certainly gone to his head.

The newcomers were a rowdy lot and kept making rude comments to Claudette. She seemed to take the innuendoes and suggestions in her stride, but Joe nonetheless felt embarrassed for her. She shouldn't have to put up with vulgar men like that, with their one-track minds.

'Hey, how about a bit over the counter?' one man said as he grabbed himself between the legs and roughly shook his manhood.

'She wants a real man,' another drawled. He stood on the foot rest and hung over the bar, dragging Claudette towards him and forcing her head down.

Joe stood, raced across the room and launched himself onto the man's back. The chap fell backwards and out of nowhere Joe felt a fist land a blow on his cheek. He turned to see two other men coming for him, while the chap he'd knocked to the ground was pulling himself up rubbing the back of his head.

Sparky and the other men were suddenly amidst the crowd and chairs and bottles were being thrown with fists hitting whomever they could. Joe was thrown to the ground when a kick landed between his legs.

'Come on, let's get out of here,' Sparky said, dragging Joe to his feet. 'Follow me.'

Joe followed as the men from his ship threw a couple more punches and made their way out through the door. He looked back when he got to the door and saw Claudette standing behind the bar, her face capped in her hands as she looked at the devastation in the bar. Joe turned and walked back in. He was half-way across the floor when he heard footsteps behind.

The police were following him, brandishing guns. He held his hands up, suddenly feeling quite sober. The bar was wrecked and it was he who had started it. Would they shoot him? Claudette was now speaking in her own language to the police. The abusive men were pointing at Joe, who felt his arms yanked behind his body, and cuffs were placed around his wrists.

The police roughly yanked him by his arm out onto the street. He saw Sparky, Bill and the others at the other end of the road as he was thrown into the back of a van and driven away. He groaned in despair. Would anyone be able to get him out of this mess? The ship would leave this evening; there wasn't much time.

A while later Joe was roughly hauled from the van and led into a police station. The handcuffs were undone, his possessions placed in a bag and Joe sat in a cell with around twenty men. Three were sleeping, four were drunk and the rest stood, or sauntered around in a world of their own.

'What you done, lad?' Joe looked up to see an old, unshaven man with no teeth staring down at him.

'I got involved in a fight.'

'Don't worry, you'll be out in the morning...'

'The morning! My ship leaves tonight.'

'Oh. A bit of a problem then. They don't move too quickly in these parts, especially with foreigners.' Joe sunk further down on the bench and exhaled loudly.

Two guards opened the door and another man stepped into the cell; the door was quickly slammed shut and locked again.

Joe leapt up and ran towards the door. 'Excuse me. Excuse me. My ship leaves tonight. Do I have to pay a fine or something? I need to get out of here. I can pay.' Joe's voice fell on deaf ears as the guards continued to walk away and out of sight. Joe slammed himself down on the bench in frustration.

'You might as well relax, son. They'll not care if you were off to the moon.'

'What did you do?'

'I shot my neighbour. Only in the foot, mind. Interfering bugger. He deserved it.'

'So what will happen?'

'They'll lock me up for a while and then let me go, which is when I'll kill him.'

Joe wanted to be on his own. He looked around at the other inmates and wondered exactly how many of those were murderers. The old man had seemed so harmless. All the men were shabbily dressed and appeared poor. This place was a world away from anything Joe had experienced before. If ever he managed to get back to the ship, he'd never go ashore again.

At break of dawn the following morning, Joe was released. The wad of notes he had in his pocket had seriously dwindled. He tried to remonstrate with the police, but suddenly saw himself being thrown back in the cell, so he gave up. He should never have taken that much ashore in the first place, but he had few places to hide it on board and had thought it would be safer in his pocket.

He hurried through the deserted streets looking for a sign of the sea. At last, through the maze of dilapidated shacks, he spotted it. As he approached the harbour his worst nightmare was realised; the ship was nowhere to be seen. Now he was stranded in this awful country and didn't know where to turn. He sat on the harbour wall, allowing his feet to dangle over the edge. What a stupid, ridiculous situation. He'd have to try to phone the shipping company for advice. He didn't even have enough money for a flight out of here.

'They let you out then?'

Joe looked up and shielded his eyes from the early morning sun. 'Claudette, I'm so sorry. I'll pay for any damage. Well, I haven't actually got much money left and I didn't pay my bill. My ship left without me.' He felt close to tears.

'Are you handy with your hands?'

'Yes, very.'

'Come back with me and you can help to repair the damage. Thank you for trying to rescue me, but I didn't need saving. It's like that all the time. Once the men have a few beers inside them, they get brave.'

'I think that's what happened to me. I will come back and help with the repairs though.'

'I need to buy the fish. That's the boat landing now.'

Joe looked around to see an old blue, wooden boat being dragged up onto the beach on the other side of the quay. Joe had always thought he lived basically, but these people lived such simple lives; it was an eye-opener. Claudette made her way over to the fishing boat, and after some wrangling she strode back to Joe clutching a bag of fish.

They walked through the narrow streets, between the shacks and ended up back at the bar. 'I suppose I have a lot of explaining to do. Your father might not want me around.'

'No, he's okay. I already explained last night and he went to the station to try and get you released. Someone was there from your ship trying to get you out as well.'

'That was extremely decent of him.'

Claudette pushed open the door and Joe was amazed to see several people all seated at the bar eating breakfast and drinking coffee. Claudette's father looked up from filling the mugs and smiled.

'He doesn't speak English. Well, not much,' Claudette said, before babbling away in her own language to her father.

Joe looked around the room. In the far corner were a stack of broken chairs and a table with its leg missing. He walked to the bar and held out his hand to shake with Claudette's father.

'I'm so sorry. I will do all I can to repair the damage.'

Claudette translated. 'Pepe says he knows you were trying to protect me and he thanks you.' She turned back to her father when he spoke again. 'He also says that a hammer and nails are out the back.'

Joe smiled. 'Does he have a screwdriver and screws?'

'No he doesn't.'

'Okay. I'll go and get some. I saw a small shop on the way here.'

Joe walked along deep in thought. He'd make a start on the chairs before lunch time and then he'd have to find a payphone. The ship's company was the only hope he had of leaving this place. Then he'd have to find somewhere to stay with what little money he had left. He could see himself sleeping rough on the beach; not the safest place to be in these parts, he imagined, with everyone so poor.

He'd mended most of the chairs when Claudette brought him some lunch. 'My father says you can stay with us and work behind the bar until you sort something out.'

'Really? Phew, that's a weight off my mind. I thought I'd be down on the beach getting mugged and all sorts. Can you say thanks for me and tell him he won't regret it?'

'He says only one condition: no sticking up for me with the clientele.'

'Promise. I'm well-behaved when I don't drink.' Claudette smiled and went back to the bar.

At lunch Joe made the call and was told he'd have to wait a couple of weeks and then ring the company again when they would have sorted something out for him.

'Two weeks! All my belongings are on that ship. I only have the clothes I stand in and very little money.'

The company operative sounded sympathetic. 'There's nothing more I can do. We only dock our ships in Guatemala once a month. I do understand, but I'm afraid I can only authorise the next ship to pick you up and even then it won't be the Princess Grace.'

'Okay, I'll ring back in a couple of weeks' time. Thanks for your help.'

Joe walked slowly back to the bar. He should be grateful he had somewhere to stay and he was being fed. He didn't feel safe in this area. Men drove around in open Jeep-type vehicles with machine guns clearly in view and he felt that every time someone looked at him he was about to be mugged. He knew he was being unfair. Claudette and her family had taken him in when they didn't need another mouth to feed. They had already been running the bar without his help; he was excess to requirements. A month! A whole damn month. He felt sickened by the prospect.

Joe soon found lots of ways to be useful around the place. He relieved Claudette's mother, Maria, of the washing up and taught her how to make scones. He would always be the one up, and out of bed at the crack of dawn to collect the fish from the harbour. He slept on a large piece of foam under the stairs. Pepe had lent him some clothes and Claudette had donated a pink comb. He had spent a small amount on toiletries and took pleasure from the fact that the rest of the family seemed to share them.

One night Joe lay on his makeshift mattress, about to doze off, when he heard footsteps. He opened his eyes but could see nothing. A hand touched his face and he jumped.

'Shhh. You'll wake the whole house. Come to my room,' Claudette whispered.

'I can't.'

'Why not?'

'It's not right. Your parents have shown me respect and hospitality.'

'They won't know. I'm not going to tell them, are you?'

Joe took a deep breath. 'Go back to your room, Claudette. I'll see you in the morning.'

'Fine!' She stomped away so loudly Joe was sure she'd be heard. He rolled over to face the wall and tried to sleep.

After a restless night, Joe walked down to the harbour as usual to collect the fish. Claudette was sitting on the harbour wall.

'Good morning,' he said, trying to sound casual.

'What's so good about it? You pretend to be friendly and then you turn me down. Being treated so badly doesn't make a girl feel good and after all I've done for you. I persuaded my father to take you in and this is the thanks I get. You don't even like me.' Her exaggerated tone, trying to evoke sympathy, struck a raw note.

'I never asked you to persuade him. In fact I'll move straight out if that's the way you feel. And I do like you.'

'I knew you did. I don't want you to move out. You hurt my feelings.'

'I didn't mean to. I'm sorry.' He scuffed his shoes on the concrete floor, keeping his head down.

Claudette slipped down from the wall and moved herself closer. Her arm reached up to his face and she gently ran her finger down the contour of his cheek. He looked up and she bent forward, placing her lips on his. Their embrace felt like a bolt of lightning racing through Joe's veins. Claudette pulled back to let him catch his breath and then lurched forward for another go.

'I knew you wanted me. I suppose last night you were taken by surprise. Tonight we'll put things right. We will make love until the morning light.'

Joe didn't think of a quick enough answer before Claudette had her tongue down his throat again. When she came up for air the moment had passed; Joe knew where he would be headed for later that evening.

The day passed quickly with Joe, as usual, keeping busy. Somehow he didn't feel comfortable with the sleeping arrangements and it wasn't only Claudette's parents he was worried about. He had a pang of worry and uncertainty in the pit of his stomach that he couldn't quite place. He should be elated that a woman as beautiful and sexually attractive as Claudette wanted him, and yet he didn't feel comfortable.

There was nowhere to hide. Joe lay awake facing the wall and heard the familiar footsteps creeping towards him. His heart dropped.

'Joe, I thought you were coming to my room. I've been waiting for you.'

'Claudette, I can't.'

'Oh my God! Not this again,' she said. 'Why?'

'I don't know. It doesn't feel right.'

'But you said you liked me. So you lied?'

'No, I didn't.'

'Then come to my room and prove it.'

Joe needed a roof over his head for the next three-and-a-half weeks at least. 'I don't want to push you into anything.'

'You aren't pushing me; I'm begging you for it.' She bent down and licked his lips with little flicks of her tongue. Joe gulped and knew when he was beat. He threw back the covers and followed Claudette along the passageway to her room.

Claudette closed the door and pulled her shirt over her head revealing her nakedness. Her pert breasts boasted two erect nipples that showed her readiness. She confidently walked over to Joe and pulled at his pants before dropping to her knees. A few minutes later she looked up at him.

'Why isn't it working?'

'Because I don't feel right. I told you.'

'Okay. Run away, little boy. Tomorrow I will find a real man and you will have lost out forever.'

Joe pulled his pants back on and left the room feeling sick. He couldn't stay here now, and he had nowhere else to go. A dangerous beach was the only place to hide; this adventure could only get worse.

Chapter 20

Joe arrived back at the bar with the fish and placed them on the counter. Maria put his breakfast on the table and studied him closely.

'Claudette, a bad girl. You stay here.'
'You speak English?'
'Not so good.'
'No, it is good. I would like to stay here.'
'You stay. You much help. Claudette, she like the men.'

Joe nodded. Maria obviously knew her daughter well, but could he stay and have Claudette lusting after him all the time? He had little option but to try. There was nothing Claudette could do that would be worse than the beach.

'Thank you. You are very kind. I will stay and help you.' Maria's deep smile lines around her mouth and eyes found new depth as her face lit up.

'You are a good boy. Now eat.'

Joe picked up his cutlery and tucked in. How did Maria know Claudette had tried it on? What had she heard? He felt his cheeks redden at the thought.

Strangely, Claudette latched on to other punters who came into the bar and never bothered Joe again. Joe saw her eyes sparkle at the prospect of another man to prey on and the men always responded to her flirting. Joe realised that he wasn't like other men. He had to have feelings before he could be sexually attracted. The first kiss with Claudette had aroused something within him, but in reality it was short lived. Was there something wrong with him?

Joe was to meet a new ship the following day. The month had passed with little excitement apart from the stream of men whom Claudette enticed. Joe often wondered if she actually slept with them all, or if it was just a game of chase with no outcome.

When the time came, Maria cried when she said goodbye and Pepe firmly shook Joe's hand before disappearing through the curtain to the back. 'I'll walk down to the harbour with you,' Claudette said. 'Can't have no one waving you off, can we?'

'Thanks. I've enjoyed my time here,' he said, and he felt a bit of nostalgia creep in as he walked through the streets for the last time.

'I expect you'll dock here again sometime. I hope so anyway.'

'Maybe. I don't really know if the company will keep me on after all the trouble I've caused.'

'Joe, I want to thank you.'

'For what?'

'You've made me feel different about myself. I'm still having fun, but I'm so glad I didn't lose my virginity that night...'

'You're a virgin?'

'Yes, and desperate to lose it like all my friends have, but you taught me to have some self-respect and that's what I'm going to do.'

'But all those men?'

'It's a game. I need to know that I'm wanted; even if I don't see it through.'

'Love is so important and until you truly love someone, you don't really understand what it's all about.'

'Have you been in love?'

'Yes, and if I'm honest, that's why I couldn't do anything with you.'

'So where is she?'

'In England.'

'So when do you get to see her again?'

'Never. It's a long story; maybe if I come back I'll have time to tell you.'

'That's so sad. You're so lovely, I'm sure someone else will come along.'

'I don't think so. I've been in love for so long, and it still hurts.' Joe took a deep breath. 'That must be my ship over there. So good to have met you, Claudette. Tell your family thanks again. I don't know what I'd have done without you all.'

'You're like family, Joe. Don't forget us.'

Joe leaned over and kissed her cheek, then turned and walked away before she could see the tears in his eyes.

The new ship was much the same as the last one. He was to stay on board for two weeks and then meet up with the Princess Grace. Nothing had been mentioned about his dismissal, so Joe was keeping his fingers crossed.

Joe sat in a bar along the main road, opposite the harbour, in Acapulco. He had stayed in a guest house for two nights and now awaited the arrival of his original ship. At long last he spotted a shadow looming on the horizon. He looked at his watch and his heart skipped a beat. That must be it. He finished his coke and took a slow walk to the harbour where he sat on a wall overlooking the beach. Fishermen were emptying their catch into nets to be dragged onto the shore. The pelicans were having a feast.

Now he could read the writing along the side of the ship. He strained his eyes trying to spot movement on the deck. Until now he hadn't realised how fond he'd become of his shipmates and life on board, although he accepted it was probably just good to be back to normality.

He stood as the ship approached and saw an arm stretched up high in the air waving. The figure was too far away to make out who it was, but Joe waved back enthusiastically, almost jumping in the air. The pilot boats led the ship into the docking bay and Joe raced forward. Now he could clearly make out the men.

'Bill. Sparky. Good to see you.'

'Ahoy. Been a long time,' Bill shouted back.

'Too long.'

'Joe, you old trouble maker,' Sparky yelled, waving his fist in the air. Joe grinned, relief washing over him. 'You up for a jar or two?'

'Never again!' Joe had never been so sure.

The gang plank was eventually placed and Joe hurried aboard.

'That's not the same tee-shirt we left you in, is it?' Bill chortled.

'Fraid so. They stole most of my money at the police station. I've got loads to tell you.'

'You aren't serious about not coming for a few drinks with us? You know old Bert had a heart attack and got airlifted off to hospital. Died a couple of days later,' Bill said.

'Sorry to hear that. I'm surprised he didn't give himself an attack when he threw a chair over the head of one of those blokes in Guatemala. I mended every one of those chairs.'

'Come ashore with us. There's so much to catch up on,' Bill said pleadingly.

'No, I am seriously not going anywhere except my bunk. I assume I still have the same one?'

'Yes, they didn't replace you, so we've been short-handed since your little escapade.'

'Sorry. I'll see you later then. There's a few nice bars along the main drag.'

'We've got our little haunts in every port. See you later, we're out of here tomorrow.'

'Okay, see you later.'

Joe made his way to his cabin. He'd change his clothes and have a shower. He hadn't liked to take Pepe's clothes, although Pepe had insisted, and Joe knew he wouldn't be able to replace them. On board the other ship he'd had work issue clothes for the galley, so he'd been able to wash his clothes and dry them on the pipes leading from the boiler room.

Joe opened the cabin door. 'Chen! Good to see you.'

Chen held out his hand and then pulled Joe close in a hug. 'My friend, I was so worried about you.'

'No need, I survived thanks to the wonderful family who own the bar we smashed up.'

'Oh. We were bad.'

'Too much beer. I'm never doing that again.'

Chen laughed. 'Of course you will. In a few weeks you will forget.'

'No. Not this time. I've learned my lesson.'

Chen headed off to meet the others and Joe stripped off for a shower. He took a clean towel from his drawer and felt in the back for his money. It wasn't there. He frantically pulled the drawer out onto the bottom bunk and emptied it, kneeling over the contents, lifting the garments one by one like a mad man. No money. He stood and went to the cupboard. His second stash had gone. He stood on the top bunk and lifted one of the ceiling panels. He pushed his hand into the gap and felt around. Nothing. Chen wouldn't have stolen it. Joe's heart raced. All that money, thousands, gone. Who would have done such a thing? He wrapped his towel around his waist and went along to the shower room. He felt gutted. One of his so-called mates had done this.

'Joe, my man. Good to see you.'

'Hi Sparky. How are you?'

'I'm good. Hear you're not up to coming ashore for another fight then. You know the captain tried to get you out, but they wouldn't hear of it. Said you had a lesson to learn.'

'I certainly did. I'll see you later. I'm quite tired.'

'Have to say you don't look quite right. See you later then, mate.'

Joe stood in the shower, letting the water run over him. If only it could wash away his troubles. He tried running through everyone on board and establishing who the thief might be. No name was forthcoming. Who would have known about the money? No one except Bill and the idea that Bill had stolen it was ludicrous. Bill had given it back when he'd dried his clothes, after finding him on the beach that night. Joe turned off the shower and dried himself off before returning to his cabin. He searched each hiding place once more in a desperate bid to find his money, even though he knew it would be fruitless.

He climbed on to the top bunk and pulled the pillow under his neck. He'd been so glad to be back and now he was sick to the stomach. Did he need the money? If Richard Bradford hadn't been so generous, he wouldn't have had any money. It had got him a passport and a job; what more did he want? Easy come, easy go. The idea a thief was aboard bugged him more than losing the money. He'd have to report it.

Eventually Joe dozed off and it seemed like only moments later the bright light above his bed was turned on and he brought his hand up to shield his eyes.

'Oh, so sorry, I forgot,' Chen said, quickly switching it back off again.

'It's okay. You startled me, I must have dropped off.'

Joe could hear Chen rustling about with his clothes before climbing into the bottom bunk and falling asleep immediately, his breathing heavy and steady.

'Chen.'

'Oh! Yes.'

'Did anyone come into the cabin while I was away?'

'Bill. He said he needed to take some of your possessions to keep them safe.'

'Ah. Okay. Thanks Chen. Sorry to have woken you.' A broad smile fell across Joe's face and he fell back into a blissful slumber.

Joe stayed aboard the Princess Grace for a few years and rarely ventured ashore, except for provisions. On those occasions he would join the other men for a meal, but then always made his way back to the ship after only a couple of drinks. He had no need for women and was always happy with his own company.

One afternoon, after the ship had docked in Whiteleaf for the eighth time since Joe had come aboard, Chen rushed into the cabin. 'Joe, Bill says you have to meet him up on the top deck right now. Tis very important.'

'I don't go ashore in Whiteleaf, Bill knows that.'

'He says you must meet him on the top deck. Very important.'

Joe sighed. Why did they always have to go through the same old routine every time they docked? They all knew Joe had no interest in going ashore and yet they insisted on trying to persuade him at every port. 'Okay, I'll be up in a minute.'

'Very urgent you come now. Big surprise for you. No, not surprise, big shock!'

Joe laughed. 'Well in that case I'd better hurry. Lead the way.' Big surprise, big shock, Joe had heard it all before. There was no way he'd ever be persuaded to go ashore in Whiteleaf, there were far too many painful memories. He'd play the game and then go back to his cabin for a sleep. He liked times when the ship was quiet and he felt as though he had the place to himself. He even liked the noise of the crane as it lifted the cargo ashore. He often stood and watched as the crates were expertly manoeuvred into the exact position to be collected by the respective trucks.

Joe followed Chen up to the top deck and then froze at the sight before him.

Part 3

Chapter 21

Ripley returned to Cambridge several weeks later, knowing she couldn't leave Susie to run the shop single-handedly for much longer. Susie hadn't complained, and was undoubtedly loving her time in charge. That thought had finally been the factor which brought Ripley to her decision.

'Ripley!' Susie yelled in a high pitch as Ripley walked through the door of the shop. 'God, I've missed you.' She ran over, squeezed Ripley in a bear hug and began to cry. 'You've had such a bad time, what with Alex dying and all that other business...'

'Hello Susie. Actually I'm fine.' She wriggled free of the hug and dropped her bags to the floor. She looked around the shop and felt a twinge of remorse, but not enough to make her change her mind. 'It's good to be back Suz. Thanks so much for taking care of it all so well.'

'Ah, you know I love it.'

'I do and I do need to talk to you. But first things first. Kettle and coffee; I've bought cake for a celebration.'

'A celebration? What are we celebrating? What have you done now?'

'Nothing. Kettle and chat.' She turned the sign on the door to closed and pulled down the blind.

Susie filled the kettle and felt a shudder run through her. Ripley must want to shut up the shop and leave the area. The town held nothing but bad memories for her now. Susie would put on a brave face and encourage Ripley in whatever new plans she had. She'd miss this place; it'd grown to be a part of her life, but Ripley was her friend and she wanted the best for her.

'Here we are then, coffee for two. It must be serious if you've shut the shop early.'

'Only half an hour and yes, it is very important.'

Susie gulped and braced herself. 'Whatever you've decided I'll support you all the way, and I'd like you to know my days spent in this shop haven't been like a job, they've been a pleasure... An absolute pleasure.'

Ripley cried and nodded. 'I know, I've loved it too, but it's time to move on.'

'I already knew you were going to say you wanted to shut up shop...

'No.' Ripley wiped her nose and eyes on an already sodden tissue and tried to gain some control. 'I'm not shutting it; I want you to have it. I'm giving you the shop as a gift.'

Susie took a deep, quivering breath. 'You can't do that. I couldn't accept, it's too much.'

'Your decision. Either take it or shut it, whichever, but I hope you'll take it.'

'You can't afford to give it to me.'

'I can. As Alex's widow, I inherited everything. I offered his assets to his parents, but they wouldn't hear of it. They said that they were just happy Alex found someone to love who loved him. They knew what he was like and how controlling he could be. His mum even apologised for trying to interfere. Susie, say you'll take it.'

'What are you going to do?'

'I want to stay in Crompton; Cliff Top Manor is where I belong.'

Susie cast her eyes around the shop. 'I can't believe it. Are you really sure? And you know if ever you change your mind...'

'I won't. Is that a yes?'

Susie nodded and began to bawl. She grabbed a tissue from the box on the counter. 'Thank you. Thank you so much,' she almost whispered. 'Can you come for dinner tonight? Kev's doing a special.'

'I wouldn't miss it for the world.'

'When are you leaving?'

'Not for a little while. I've got all Alex's stuff to sort out and I have to change the deeds on this place. Don't forget there's the upstairs flat to rent out.'

'I don't know what to say. For once I'm speechless.'

'How about, *shall we get back to mine and slice the celebration cake?*'

'Let's go. Kev's going to be bowled over... We've had quite a tough time since they stopped his overtime...'

'I had no idea. Oh Susie, I'm going to miss you. You'll have to bring the family to Crompton, the kids will love it. I've got so many plans.'

'Try and stop us.' Susie looked around as though seeing the shop for the first time. 'I'm absolutely gobsmacked; is this really going to be mine?'

'It is yours! There's no going back now.'

Susie hugged Ripley tight and wiped her eyes again.

A short time later Ripley looked back as she pulled the door shut. The first stage of her plan had been put into action and she felt elated.

Three weeks later, May sat on the front seat of the car strapped in by her dog harness while Ripley drove to Crompton for her new start. Susie would be the only thing she missed about Cambridge. Her floristry shop had been good, but now she had new horizons to reach.

Ripley went back to the house she'd shared with Alex and began sorting out her things. On the bed was the book Susie had given her when she'd married Alex. She looked down at the page and read the appointment she'd made for the clinic when she'd been sorting out her options. So Alex read her diary. No big surprise, but it had answered a few questions.

Alex's assets were in the hands of the lawyers, but Ripley was already a rich woman. The amount of money he had stunned her. Aunt May had also left her a lot of money, which Ripley intended to pass on to her dad. Today felt like the beginning of the rest of her life.

She drove through Whiteleaf and stopped off to order horse feed and bedding. Shimmer was due to arrive later that day and Ripley had a romantic notion of riding along the beach with May trotting alongside. Her dreams and romantic ideas sometimes stretched out of control and she often found herself laughing at her ridiculous notions. Sometimes she dreamed of running a riding centre for deprived and handicapped children. Other days she would want to start an animal sanctuary and take in any needy waifs and strays. Old people, children and the homeless, the list was endless. She had to do something and make a difference. She had time and money; all she needed was a cause she could devote herself to.

'Stay there, May. I won't be long. I might even get you a treat if you wait quietly.' She pushed open the glass-panelled door and stopped dead as a poster caught her eye. She pulled out a scrap of paper from her bag, jotted down the telephone number, and continued into the shop to order the horse feed.

The day passed quickly with unpacking her car and getting her horse settled in his new stable.

'You are going to love it here. Maybe not as posh as the last place, but it has potential and I have a hoard of plans,' she said to Shimmer, whose head was over the stable door. She stroked his nose and gave him a swede. 'There you go. We'll soon be growing our own once I get the gardens cleared.' After shutting the stable door, she slowly walked back to the house with May at her heels. Life felt good. She was at peace; she was home at last.

After scrambled eggs on toast for dinner, she began to go through some of Aunt May's old papers. She must have kept every receipt since time began. There were books of payments, bank statements and booklets for every appliance in the house. There was a dark blue book with the first page titled *Richard*. The pages were filled with sums of money with the last one dated three days before Ripley and her family had left Cliff Top Manor all those years ago. Ripley knew the dates exactly. It had been the most devastating and awful time of her life, when she lost Joe forever. The book didn't make it clear if the money had been paid to her dad, or if it was from him. Ripley put it to one side; she'd ask him about it next time he visited. Most of the papers she binned. There was still a multitude to go through, but Ripley was getting bored.

She went through to the kitchen and put the kettle on. She'd give her dad a quick ring, she'd promised to let him know she'd got home safely. She rummaged in her bag for her phone and came across the bit of paper with the hastily scribbled number. Her dad could wait a bit longer; she'd ring this number first. How could she have forgotten?

'Are the donkeys still needing a home? Great...' She couldn't stop smiling as her dreams began to take shape.

Half an hour later she rang her dad.

'It's Ripley, sorry I forgot to ring earlier.'

'I knew you must be busy. Has Shimmer got there okay?'

'Yes, and I've got two new additions arriving tomorrow.'

'Oh God! What?'

'Donkeys. They needed a good home and I've got spare stables.'

Richard laughed. 'Why do you want donkeys?'

'They needed a home and I had one to give them.'

'You're going to end up like May if you're not careful. She took in everything going.'

'That's not such a bad thing. I loved the way she had this place.'

'I'll come down at the end of next week; probably stay the weekend. Take care and good luck with the donkeys.'

Ripley slept soundly until the early hours of the morning and awoke with a start to an elderly gentleman standing at the foot of her bed, and wearing an army uniform.

'Sorry, didn't mean to startle you,' he said casually. 'Thought I'd pop in and see how you were doing. I promised your Aunt May I would. I told her you'd be back.'

Ripley rubbed her eyes and stared at the man, as May began to growl. She instinctively knew who this man was. Could she be dreaming? She pinched her arm until it hurt; the pain was real enough.

'Is my Aunt May here?'

'No, she died at peace and therefore she passed through straight away, whereas I had so many issues, in fact I still do and that's why I'm here. I can't pass through until I'm at peace. You aren't at peace either; I'm going to try and help you. Maybe I was wrong not to have got involved years ago, but sometimes the time isn't right. You have to learn to trust me.'

'I do.'

'No, at the moment you're wondering if this is all a dream, or if you're going as mad as your old aunt. Today there will be a connection with Australia. I'll pop past again soon.'

'But...' Ripley looked around the room, he'd already disappeared. She felt eerily calm which was strange. How could she feel so tranquil after a visit from a ghost? Was she really awake? Had she dreamt the whole thing? Australia? What had he meant about not getting involved? She shook her head and pulled the quilt up to her chin.

She awoke at dawn and looked around the room expecting to see the Major standing in his army jacket, waiting for her to wake. 'I wish you could talk, May. Did we really get a visit last night?' She ruffled the dog's head and pulled back the covers, as usual making her first delight of the day gazing at the stables below.

Ripley spent the day realising her dream of riding Shimmer along the beach with May trotting alongside. Her mind constantly wandered back to the time she'd spent with Joe and a familiar yearning returned to the pit of her stomach. The recurring questions came to her mind, but as usual, no forthcoming answers. She had been so sure of his love and she knew the impact he'd made on her life would stay with her forever.

The horse box arrived in the afternoon, with Doris and Ethel on board. 'Welcome to your new home,' Ripley said, as she led Doris to the stable block, closely followed by Ethel and their previous owner, Kate.

'I can't thank you enough. They're really good girls, I'm going to miss them so much,' Kate said.

'Call in anytime you're back in the area.'

'I don't think I'll be back for years. I'm off to Australia with my husband's new job.' Ripley coughed back a choke.

'Are you okay?' Kate said, looking concerned.

'Yes thanks. Australia, how lovely.' She'd never really doubted Aunt May had her visitor, she'd even heard voices now and again, but for her to now be in touch with a ghost was so weird and unbelievable. She couldn't tell anyone; they'd think she was as mad as her aunt. She felt a bit crazy even thinking about it.

Kate headed off after a tearful goodbye to her pets, and Ripley went indoors to find some carrots. She'd let them acquaint themselves with their new stables and put them out to graze tomorrow.

Richard, as promised, came for a visit the following weekend. Ripley was determined not to tell him about her visitor. She found herself willing the Major to return; she had so many questions to ask, but he didn't, which made Ripley doubt herself. Maybe Kate had mentioned Australia on the phone, when they'd made the arrangements for the donkeys, and the visit from the Major had all been a dream. Something deep down longed for the visit to have been a reality, but Ripley berated herself for being so ridiculous.

'So tell me your plans for the old place. I know you won't be converting it like I would have done,' Richard said.

'I'm having it restored to its former glory. I've got three different builders coming next week to take a look and give me some prices. I found some lovely old photos of the place that will help.'

'That'll cost a packet. Don't go leaving yourself short.'

'I wanted to talk to you about the money.'

'I can't lend you much; your mother keeps booking us up for all these expensive holidays.'

Ripley laughed. 'I know; she was telling me last week. Mauritius, so I hear.'

'Only because you went and she felt she missed out on the holiday and the wedding. She hasn't stopped going on about it...'

'Dad, May's money. I want you to have it. Alex left me plenty and it's only right you have some inheritance from your family.'

'You don't need to do that.'

'I want to. Aunt May left quite a tidy sum. Look, there's the latest bank statement. I've already talked to the bank manager about transferring it. You'll even be able to pay off your bankruptcy debts.'

Richard took the statement and whistled. 'Cantankerous old biddy. All this for herself. Ripley, I can't take this from you.'

'Up to you. It'll sit in an account and gain interest until I die, when the government will get it, no doubt.'

'Okay, I see your point. Alex must have left you plenty if you can afford to give this much to me. Wow! For the first time in my life I'm a rich man. Thank you.'

'You're welcome, but it should have been yours anyway. It was family money.'

Ripley had to admit, sharing the money made her feel good.

Susie rang nearly every day to update Ripley on the shop.

'I don't need to know, it's your shop now.'

'I know. I still can't quite believe it though, and I want you to know I'll never let you down.'

'I never doubted that for a moment.' Ripley loved the calls. She was updated on local news and Susie's family. She often felt as though she was only around the corner. 'So when are you coming for a visit to lovely Crompton?'

'Weekend after next. I'm leaving Kerry in charge.'

'Kerry! You took on help! Well done, I was so worried at how you'd cope alone.'

'Yes, in the end I listened to my sensible head and realised it must have been the same for you when you took me on.'

'Weekend after next. Wonderful. The work on the house won't have started, so you'll have a before, and then next time you visit will be an after. I can't wait! I have two donkeys, chickens and a turkey now. The children will love it here.'

'I know we all will. I'll be in touch before then anyway. I have to get going, I can smell the cabbage boiling away.'

'Bye Suz. Have a good week.'

Life at Cliff Top Manor was fantastic. Susie and the family came to visit every six weeks, Richard was a frequent visitor and her mother popped in, when her heavy schedule allowed. Ripley had noted that her mum didn't seem to know the amount of money Ripley had given her father. Nothing much ever changed between those two; Clarissa soon would have had a multitude of things she needed doing to the house and places she wanted to visit. Her dad knew when to keep quiet.

Renovations on the house were nearly complete and Ripley had been in talks with a local group who helped disadvantaged children. The plan was for small groups to spend some time on the farm riding the donkeys, getting to know the animals in the petting pen, which Ripley still needed to organise, and playing on swings hanging from the oak trees. A tree house set in one of the oak trees was her latest idea. A local firm had given quotes and offered a generous discount to help a good cause. Ripley felt as animated as she had when she'd taken over the flower shop, but this was so much more rewarding.

Every third Saturday, a group of three or four children and their helpers, would arrive for a day at the farm. Ripley provided lunch, snacks and drinks and revelled in these wonderfully rewarding times when the children were able to interact with the animals and the specially created play areas. By four o'clock when she waved the mini-bus off, she was always exhausted but fulfilled.

Life was as perfect as it could be; at this time in her life there was nothing else she needed nor wanted, and then the Major returned for a visit.

Chapter 22

Ripley stood over the stove, stirring the bacon and cheese pasta she had prepared for dinner that evening. She brought the wooden spoon up to her mouth and tasted the sauce; it needed a bit more seasoning. She added salt and pepper and tasted again. As the spoon went to her mouth, a voice behind her made her jump.

'May would have liked what you've done to the old place.' The spoon dropped to the floor with a clatter, splattering the sauce everywhere.

'Sorry, didn't mean to startle you. I thought if I arrived during your waking hours you might take me seriously.'

'I do take you seriously. I used to hear you talking to Aunt May. It's a bit strange, that's all.'

'I've toyed for weeks with what I'm about to tell you. Then I thought to myself, let her decide for herself.'

'About what?' Ripley said, as though talking to a ghost as one prepared dinner was the most natural thing in the world. She had picked up a cloth and begun to wipe the sauce splashes from the floor and units.

'Joe will be on a ship called the Princess Grace; it docks at Whiteleaf tomorrow afternoon.'

Ripley stopped wiping the cupboard and looked up at the Major. He had already left. 'No, please come back. He didn't want to know me, he left. Do you know if he would want to see me? Please come back.' She stood up, looked around the kitchen and waited. The pan on the stove sizzled and popped, as it gently simmered away. *Princess Grace tomorrow afternoon.* What if Joe shunned her? He wouldn't, he was too polite and well mannered. Could she stand to see the look in his eyes which told her he'd left because he wanted to? Her mouth felt dry. She switched off the pasta and went through to May's old sitting room, the one room in the house that hadn't been touched during the renovations. Her heart pounded and her breathing quickened. Could she turn down what was probably her only chance of seeing him again? Her mind whirled out of control at the possible scenarios she might face. Eventually she rang Susie.

'Go for it. You've thought about him all these years; you can't miss the opportunity you've been handed. A ghost, do you mean like a dream?'

'Sort of. I'll explain more when I see you. So you really think I should go?'

'Undoubtedly! What have you got to lose? Look at it this way, when fate steps in, who are we to question it?'

'There might not even be a ship called Princess Grace...'

'There might not, but do you really want to spend the rest of your life wondering, *what if?*'

'I'm going to do this! I have to, don't I?'

'I think so.'

'Thanks Suz.'

'I'll give you a call tomorrow evening for the next instalment.'

'There might be nothing to tell.'

'And there might be a whole new chapter about to begin. Take care and good luck. Hope whatever happens, it's what you want.'

'Chat tomorrow. Bye.'

Ripley pulled her jumper up around her neck as a shiver ran through her. Deep down she believed there was a ship called Princess Grace and Joe would be on board. Tomorrow seemed so far away. What did she hope to achieve? What did she want? She wanted Joe to run towards her, to hold her in his arms, to say he never should have left, and he had loved her all these years, as she had loved him. That scenario was her ultimate dream which would make her world complete, but she also knew Joe had made no attempt to contact her; her vision was a fantasy and in reality the most she could hope for was a pleasant reminisce of past love and a promise of staying in touch, which would never materialise. There was no choice. She had to go. *What if* and other questions had haunted her for far too long and now at long last she had a chance of finding some answers.

After a sleepless night, Ripley busied herself with her animals. She took a long ride on the beach and then showered and changed for her visit into the unknown. She had played through every scenario she could muster. Rekindled love, anger, frustration, a row, tears, friendship, or nothing at all, because he refused to speak to her.

Ripley parked her car on the east cliff and from the top of the hill she could see a large ship docked in the cargo area. She walked down the winding road towards the harbour, aware that each step took her closer to her destiny. The harbour wall led to the cargo area and now the ship loomed before her. She could see the writing on the side was certainly a longer word followed by a shorter one and found her pace quickening to try to make out the ship's name.

Princess Grace! She gulped and continued to walk. Should she slow down and put off the outcome a bit longer, or should she run to him? She settled for a steady pace, so as not to be out of breath.

A man was walking down the gangway, the last of a small group who were walking away from the ship towards the cliff steps. Ripley hurried towards him. What if Joe had already left the ship? She should have arrived earlier.

'Excuse me. I'm looking for Joe Kingsman.'

The small Chinese man stared at her for a moment. 'You are the most slim, beautiful woman. Joe is on the ship. Don't move, wait there.'

The man raced back up the gangway, looking back as he reached the top to make sure she had stayed put. Ripley waved to him and he waved back, making her smile. *Most slim, beautiful woman*; what a strange thing to say. The wait seemed like an eternity and then like a vision, Joe came into view. She would have recognised him anywhere. Still the same tousled brown hair and the high cheek bones. He certainly hadn't lost his looks. She looked for giveaway signs of pleasure on his face when he saw her, but all she saw was the look of shock that flooded over him.

She shouldn't have come; it had been a big mistake. He had stopped dead in his tracks and the Chinese man was speaking to him and tugging at his sleeve. She turned to walk away.

'Ripley, wait.' He walked towards her as the Chinese man scuttled away after the men who had by now disappeared. He stopped again a few feet away from her and stared blankly.

Ripley had rehearsed her first words a hundred times, but when her lips opened the words were not what she had planned.

'Why? Why didn't you even say goodbye?' She felt the tears prick her eyes as he stood motionless before her. 'Why Joe? I loved you.'

He took three long strides and pulled her into his arms, nestling his face in her neck. She could feel him trembling with emotion and they both began to cry.

'We'll go up into town and find somewhere to talk. I'm sorry; I wouldn't have hurt you for the world.'

'But you did. You said you loved me and...

'I did love you...'

'But you left me.'

'I had to. We'll find somewhere quiet and I'll explain. How did you know I was here?'

'The Major, would you believe?'

'May's ghost? You're kidding.'

'No, I'm serious. I live back at Cliff Top Manor now and he visited me yesterday and said you'd be here.'

Joe shook his head in disbelief. 'Incredible. And you still wanted to see me after all this time? I see you're still wearing the necklace I made.'

Ripley brought her finger and thumb to the mother-of-pearl's smoothness. 'Guess so. There's so many questions I need answered. You left me deeply wounded, in fact it's affected my whole life, really.'

'I didn't come out unscathed myself. Is your dad still around?'

'Yes, he doesn't live in Crompton but I see him regularly. I knew he frightened you off that night.'

'He didn't frighten me.' Joe stopped walking. 'Here we are, this looks cosy.' He ushered her into a small café with gingham tablecloths and an array of cakes in a glass cabinet.

'My dad used to come in here for croissant and coffee when he could. He loves this place.'

They chose a table looking out onto the gardens at the back. A waitress took their order and there was an awkward silence.

'Ripley, you mustn't think badly of your dad.'

'It's been a long time. I forgave him ages ago.'

'Forgave what?'

'Making you leave. Taking away the one thing in my life which was so precious to me.'

'Did he tell you why?'

'No. We never really spoke about it. I distanced myself from him for years and then when we started talking again it seemed pointless to bring up the past.' The waitress put the coffee on the table and went back behind the counter.

'I've never stopped loving you, Ripley...'

'I've always loved you too. There's nothing anyone can do to stop us being together now. Joe, you'll never know how long I've waited to hear those words.'

'It's not like that.'

'Do you have someone else? Are you married?'

'No...'

'Well that's...'

'Ripley stop. Stop right there. I'm your brother.'

'Brother? What do you mean, you can't be!' The fear rippled through her voice.

'Your dad and my mum were kids. He ran away. He always provided for me and that's how mum came to be working at the manor,'

Tears began sliding uncontrollably down Ripley's cheeks. She pulled a tissue from her sleeve, which she'd placed there earlier for such emergencies. She shook her head. 'I don't believe it.'

'You have to believe it. I never knew and May thought the money he sent each month was his contribution towards the running of the place. When he came to see me that night he told me, and said it would tear your family apart if the truth came out. I had to go. I couldn't lie and tell you I didn't love you anymore; I wasn't strong enough to stand before you and see your heart break.' His eyes welled up.

'Brother and sister.' Ripley searched in her bag, pulled out a fresh tissue and handed one to Joe. 'I thought you said your dad was a sailor and he died at sea?'

'That's what my mum told me. She probably felt too embarrassed to tell May the truth, so she had to tell me the same story.'

'I feel like my heart's broken all over again.'

Joe nodded. 'So have you got a husband, or children...?'

'No. I did get married, but it didn't work out. It was never meant to be. Not like us.'

'We were never meant to be either. Nothing else in the world would have taken me away...'

'I know. It must have been difficult for you. I suppose we have to be brave and get on with it now.'

'So tell me about the manor. Oh God! That's May's charm bracelet. I gave her that letter J.'

'I know. She told me the day we left Crompton.'

'So you still left. I thought with me out of the way you'd have stayed.'

Ripley and Joe sat for four hours in the café before Joe looked at his watch and leapt up. 'I need to get back on board. They left without me once before and no one even knows where I am this time.'

'I'm going to miss you all over again.'

'We'll keep in touch. After all, we are family.'

'I hope we will. I'd like that.'

Joe paid the bill and they stepped outside. 'I still love you, Dimps.'

The pet name brought tears to her eyes. 'I love you more than you'll ever know,' she said. He stooped down, hugged her tightly, kissed her lips for a second, then with his eyes watering he strode away, and out of her life once again.

She stood watching as he hurried down the road and turned the corner. She wanted to run after him, she wanted to hold him and never let him go, she wanted to share the love they used to; but it was not to be. Those times had to be forgotten and cast away as forbidden love. She brought her hand up to her necklace and sobbed.

Joe could hardly see as he made his way back to the ship. The tears blinded him and got worse each step of the way. What he wouldn't give to run back into her arms and stay there forever. There had been so much he wanted to tell her and find out about her. He would definitely write to her, but could he bring himself to meet her again when the ship returned to Whiteleaf? He doubted that very much, it hurt as bad as it had the first time he walked away. They couldn't keep breaking each other apart.

Chapter 23

By the time Ripley returned home, the place was in darkness. Her tears had stopped as the truth of the situation engulfed her mind. In robotic fashion she gave the animals their last feed of the day, closed their doors for the night and went to sit indoors.

How she wished the Major hadn't made the visit. He must have known there could be no happy outcome; it was almost cruel. Why would he have done that?

Ripley looked at the phone when it rang through her head. She couldn't speak to anyone. Tonight she needed to wallow in self-pity and then tomorrow, start again. This time she didn't feel heartbroken as before; she had a numbness and an emptiness which overwhelmed her. May sat on Ripley's lap, sound asleep, while her head was absentmindedly stroked.

Dawn broke and Ripley didn't want to leave her bed. She heard the horse kicking the stable door and reluctantly pulled herself up. This morning she didn't look down at the stables as was tradition; instead she pulled on her clothes and routinely attempted the morning's tasks. She didn't feel like riding; today the horse and donkeys could have a day in the paddock. She made herself a coffee and sat in May's old armchair staring out through the window. She needed to pull herself together, but she didn't have the will-power.

The phone rang incessantly throughout the day until eventually Ripley answered it.

'Ripley, it's Susie, are you okay?'

'Fine.'

'You don't sound fine. Tell me what happened.'

Ripley told her sorry tale and Susie listened in silence. 'All these years I've held a torch for him and now I find out he's my brother. Things could have been so different. I wanted to be in love, I wanted to play happy families and have my own children and instead I held on to an impossible dream.'

'I know there's nothing I can say to make you feel any better, but now at least you know why he left and it wasn't because he didn't love you.'

'He's never loved anyone else either. We've both spent lonely, miserable lives yearning for something we couldn't have.'

'The only difference between yesterday and today is the answer you've always wanted to know. Nothing has actually changed, he was your brother from the day you were born, only now you know. That isn't so bad,' Susie said sympathetically.

'I feel all the stuffing's been knocked out of me. I've got to go, I need an early night. Bye Suz.'

'I'll ring you tomorrow. Take care.'

Ripley went through the next few weeks in limbo. Why did she feel so bad? Why couldn't she let this go? Deep down she knew why. She still loved him; not as a sister loves a brother, but the same shameful love she'd held for him since the day they met.

Joe had returned to the ship and gone straight to his cabin. Everyone ate ashore on land days, so there were no meals to prepare. He pretended to be asleep when Chen came into the cabin; he could hear him rustling around getting changed for bed.

During the following week Joe kept very much to himself. He carried on with his chores, ate with the other men and when the tasks of each day were over, he returned to the solitude of his cabin.

One night Chen followed him back before he had an opportunity to pretend to be asleep.

'Joe, I know you are not sleeping so quickly. I know most slim, beautiful woman has broken your heart again. She must want you; she came to find you. Why do you not stay with her?'

'I couldn't. She's my sister.'

'Ah! I thought she was most slim, beautiful woman.'

'Who is most slim, beautiful woman? I don't know what you mean.'

'When we met I tell you I have big, large woman to get away from and you tell me you have most slim, beautiful woman.'

Joe smiled. 'Yes, you're right. It's the same woman, but I found out she was my sister after I fell in love with her.'

'Ah. My uncle, he fall in love with many women.'

'But for me there is only one.'

'Then you should go to her. My brother and sister live in the same house. Why not you?'

'Quite. Why not me? It's a bit different.'

'Only different if you make it different. Bill tell me life too short for regret.'

Joe nodded. 'Bill talks a lot of sense. Good night, Chen.'

'Good night.'

Joe tossed and turned for most of the night. No one knew they were related except them, and Richard of course. Could they live together? It was illegal. He took a deep breath; it was a truly impossible situation, they had to stay apart.

Just before dawn, Joe sat upright. He was going back. Nothing illicit or illegal, just two people sharing a life in all but the intimate side. Chen was right, it was a perfectly natural thing for a brother and sister to do. He would give anything to have her in his life again and if that meant celibacy then so be it; he'd already been celibate for years, it was no big deal.

Joe had to stay on board for the next two weeks until he was replaced and then he joined another ship which would take him back to England. When he arrived in Hull he caught a train to London and from there one to Crompton. In all the journey took a day and a chilly night on a platform, but Joe didn't care, he was on his way to see the woman he loved.

Ripley had put off her father's visits; she couldn't face him yet, she was still too cross with him again. One Friday night the darkness crept in while she stabled Shimmer. She patted his nose, gave him and the donkeys a carrot and went indoors. 'Come on little May, I think we might have to have the heating on tonight.' May ran around her feet as usual, nearly tripping her over, and then dashed up the passage to the hall and yapped furiously at the front door, and then the bell clanged. She looked at her watch. *I bet this is Dad fed up with being put off and wanting a peaceful weekend away from Mum.*

Ripley drew a deep breath and braced herself to stay in control and talk reasonably with her dad about how she felt. She had come to terms with the shock and knew there was nothing that could be done to change the situation, so she might as well make the best of it.

She confidently pulled open the door and shrieked like a child when she saw Joe on the doorstep.

'I wondered if you could make any use of a gardener, or someone to help with the horse and other animals you've acquired?'

'Joe, I can't believe you're here. Come in.'

He dropped his bag to the floor and hugged her. 'Couldn't leave my little sis to cope in this big house all on her own, now could I?'

'Do you think we really can be brother and sister?'

'Well, I've been celibate for so many years I figured it's not going to make much difference. Should be a doddle.'

'I'd rather have you as a brother, than not have you at all.'

'Can I come in? It's freezing.'

Ripley laughed and stood to one side. 'You've made me the happiest woman on earth.'

'And I'm the happiest man. I've missed you so much, even worse since our last meeting.'

'Have you eaten? I've got some chilli simmering away.'

Joe picked up his bag and followed her indoors. 'I almost feel like we've always been together. This feels so right. I can't believe I'm back here after all these years.'

'I can't either, but I'm glad you are.'

Joe opened the wine while Ripley served up the meal. They sat, two people hopelessly in love, but knowing it was forbidden.

It was three o'clock in the morning before their eyelids could stay open no longer. 'You can have Aunt May's old room, it's all been renovated. I haven't even shown you around.'

'No, I think I'd better stay in the cottage. It'd be sort of proper.'

'It might be cold.'

'I'll be fine. I'll make do for tonight and then sort it out tomorrow.'

'I feel bad. I don't want to think of you down there all cold and probably damp. No one's been in there for years. Stay here for tonight then tomorrow we'll sort it out together.'

'Only tonight then. We need to have boundaries if this is going to work.'

Ripley nodded. 'I'll get some clean sheets and make up the bed.'

Joe hardly slept a wink; his adrenalin was flowing. He was back home with the woman he loved. He hadn't dared to dream about this day ever becoming a reality.

Ripley stayed awake most of the night in unbelievable bliss. All her dreams had come true. The love of her life had returned and a new chapter had begun; she had a feeling this chapter was going to be the best one of all.

Chapter 24

The next day Ripley and Joe were up at the crack of dawn, eager to begin the first day of their new life together. They fed Shimmer and Joe was introduced to Ethel and Doris along with rest of the furry and feathered friends.

'I can't believe you've got a turkey after the way May's used to chase you.'

'I sort of tried to recreate what we had back then. It made this place feel like home again. I have to say he's much politer than the other one.'

'I'm impressed with all your renovations. This is what May wanted to do when you moved here. She hoped your dad would oversee it all. She would have loved the way you've kept all the original features.'

'Are you ready for some breakfast? I've got some bacon, and eggs, if you want to pop into the chicken house and collect them. Do I need to show you how?'

'Very funny. This is role reversal, you showing me around the place.'

'We'll have some breakfast and then I want to take you to see some horses. We need another one for you.'

'I can't tell you how good it feels to be back here with you and all this.' He waved his arm, pointing to the grounds. 'Thank God I made the decision to come home.'

Ripley linked her arm through his, silently sending up a thank you to whatever, or whoever, had helped him reach his decision. For that moment there were no problems; only two happy people without a care in the world.

For the next two weeks Joe and Ripley lived in blissful harmony, laughing catching up and getting to know each other again. They almost fell straight back into the routine they had previously shared. Riding and tending to the livestock and grounds at the manor took most of their time; they were rarely apart, preferring to share the tasks and work together.

Joe loved helping with the children who came to the farm for a special day and suggested it could be a more frequent event now there were two of them to organise things. He had insisted on moving back to the cottage saying that he felt more comfortable there; after all it had been his home for more than twenty years. He also felt that having his own place would keep temptation at bay.

Joe now had his own black stallion, Shadow. Although he had been brought up with horses, and able to ride whenever he wished, Shadow was the first horse he'd owned.

One morning Ripley and Joe rode their horses to Crompton, then sat on the sands and began to reminisce about the time spent there all those years before.

'It feels like I never left,' Joe said, sitting up on his elbows with his legs outstretched on the sands.

'I wish you hadn't.'

'Don't you think it's strange that neither of us ever wanted anyone else?'

'Well, I did have my little faux pas with Alex, but you're right, all I ever truly wanted was what we'd shared.'

Joe turned to look at her. She'd taken off her riding hat, allowing her hair to move gently in the breeze; she was truly beautiful. Her green eyes entranced him and he quickly looked away. 'We'd better head back before the sun goes down.' He scrambled up and held out his hand to help Ripley. She stumbled and almost fell into him. 'Whoa! Steady on there,' he said, holding her arm and then quickly released it again. 'Do you fancy a hot chocolate?' A surge of electric raced through his veins; he had to control his feelings.

'Sounds good. We can ride up the sea front and tie the horses up outside on the bike stands where we'll be able to keep an eye on them.'

Ripley had felt an uncomfortable shudder as Joe held her when she stumbled. How she loved that closeness. She thought the yearning inside her would never diminish.

Joe hoisted himself up onto his horse. 'Race you there,' he chortled.

'You're joking? Up Crompton front?' She screwed up her nose when Joe took off. Ripley hurriedly mounted Shimmer and raced behind him.

Joe quite often volunteered to cook dinner; he'd picked up a lot of recipes and tips on board the Princess Grace. One evening he left a curry simmering on the stove and went for a quick shower. He returned to the kitchen to find Ripley bending her head over the pan shovelling a spoonful of curry into her mouth.

'Hey! No tasting before it's ready. That's cheating.'

'I had to make sure you weren't giving me some awful concoction before I put it on my plate. I might have had to cook myself egg and chips for supper.'

'You cheeky...'

'You're lucky, it wasn't that bad...'

'Right!' Joe picked up the tea towel and chased her around the central breakfast bar, slapping it onto his hand to show he meant business.

Ripley shrieked and raced for the door. Along the passage way he managed to gain ground and let the towel give her a sharp whip on her bottom.

Ripley kept running. 'Ouch!'

Joe managed two more hits across her buttocks before grabbing her shoulder and stopping her.

'Now, what were you saying?'

'The curry is absolutely gorgeous and I've never tasted better.'

Joe laughed aloud at her sincere expression. They were breathless and Ripley started to giggle. For a split second their eyes met, for a moment there was a stillness and a calm before they were locked in an embrace.

As their lips met, both melted into each other's arms and what began as a gentle touching of lips became a need. Their passion held no boundaries. On the rug, in the middle of the hallway, they tore at one another's clothes releasing all the years of love and frustration.

Joe lifted himself and rolled onto his side, rested on his elbow, and took in her beauty. 'We shouldn't have done that.'

'I know. I think the years of dreaming and wanting caught up with us...'

'The heat of the moment...'

'A glass of wine on an empty stomach...'

'It wasn't empty...'

'One spoon of curry doesn't count.'

Joe looked sad. 'If this is going to work, we need to keep control.'

'We will. That's the last time. Maybe we just needed to get it out of our systems.'

Joe nodded. 'So, curry then.' He stood, pulled on his clothes and went through to the kitchen.

Ripley slowly dressed. Her feelings were confused between wanting him back, rekindling their former relationship, and a feeling of disgust at herself for wanting to make love to her brother. Feeling him inside her had brought her body alive and nothing had ever come close to making her feel so whole again; for that moment her world had been perfect bliss even though their illicit love was forbidden.

Ripley ran her fingers through her hair and took a deep breath, before going to the kitchen. 'I can smell burning...'

'At least you tasted it before it was ruined,' Joe said. 'The rice has all but dried up.'

'I don't care. The food can be burned, dried, ruined! Nothing else matters so long as I have you here.'

Joe held her tightly in a bear hug for a moment and then reached into the cupboard for the plates. 'You open the wine and I'll dish up. I'll pop the burned bits on your plate seeing as you don't mind them.'

Now it was Ripley's turn to grab the cloth and do the whipping.

'Careful now. You know where it led last time we played this game,' Joe mused, trying to hold her arms at bay and make light of the situation.

Dinnertime chatter was lacking the usual banter. Instead they kept to matters concerning the farm and the next children's visit. Ripley stacked the dishwasher while Joe fed the dog.

'I'm a bit tired, I think I'll go over to the cottage and have an early night.'

'Okay then. I might catch up on a bit of sleep too. We've had a few late nights.'

Joe sauntered back to the cottage feeling low. He sat in the armchair by the window and watched the swaying of the leaves on the trees, silhouetted by the moonlight. He'd promised himself never to let that happen. They had two choices. The first was to live a lie and continue their illicit affair, and the second, to get a grip and make sure they stayed strong enough, so it would never happen again. His passion for Ripley wanted the first option, but he held too much respect for her to live in falsehood, worrying that a slip of the tongue or a look could give away their secret. They were two decent, law-abiding adults and they had to behave in an appropriate manner so as not to jeopardise their future; he couldn't bear to leave her again because of accusations and gossip.

Ripley rested back on her pillow, but sleep was not forthcoming. Her feelings of guilt overwhelmed her. How could they have done that? Would she ever be capable of not wanting him physically? Could they really go back to the way things had been and pretend nothing had happened? What if Joe didn't want to stay at Crompton because he couldn't forgive what they'd done? He'd been pretty quick to escape to the cottage after dinner. Maybe at this very moment he was packing his bags, ready to leave again. She pulled back the covers and raced to the window. The grounds were in darkness.

She pulled on her robe, ran down the stairs and hurried over to the cottage. Joe saw her pass the window and opened the door as she approached.

'Are you okay?'

'Oh Joe, I had an awful feeling you might have gone...'

'Gone where?'

'Away... Like last time...'

He wrapped his arms around her. 'I'm not going anywhere. Come in, I don't know why we're standing on the step.' He motioned her past him into the house. 'We need to talk. I'll make some hot chocolate.'

Ripley looked tearful. 'Thanks. I felt sick. I can't lose you again.'

Joe filled the kettle and stood two mugs on the side. He turned to face her. 'How do you feel? How do you really feel?'

'Like I love you with all my heart, but I'm not allowed to...'

'Like your heart is being ripped out every time we touch or catch each other's eye.'

Ripley nodded. 'I can't go on if you're not right by my side.'

Joe put the chocolate powder in the mugs. 'The way I see it, we have two choices. To live a lie or to control our feelings. It doesn't matter what happens, I'm never leaving you again.'

'Inside I feel bad, because what we did was wrong, but it felt so good.'

'We feel the same, so that's a good thing. Would you be happy to live a lie and hide the way we really live?'

'I'm not good at lying; I never have been able to hide anything.'

'Nor me. So we'd be under enormous pressure to remember not to let anything slip.'

Ripley was thoughtful for a moment. 'I'd feel bad about myself. Sort of guilty that we were doing something we shouldn't be.'

He handed her the hot chocolate. 'So we need to decide once and for all what we're going to do.'

'What do you want?' In her heart she wanted the forbidden love which was such an easy and fulfilling option, but her head told her differently.

'I think the burden might put too much pressure on us and we'd be unhappy. I'd rather we were happy and felt good about ourselves. That's not to say I don't want more, but my sensible head is telling me to do the right thing.'

Ripley heaved a sigh. 'I think that's right. I'll never stop loving you.'

'I hope not. Brothers and sisters are supposed to love each other. Give us a hug.'

She put her head on his shoulder as he held her tight. One blip could be forgiven; they just had to make sure it never happened again.

'Come and sit by the window. The trees look magnificent by the light of the moon.' He pulled another chair over and they sat looking out into the stillness of the night. They felt strangely peaceful after the torment they'd felt a short time before. Both felt they'd made the right decision and now it was time to put the past behind them and move on.

Chapter 25

One evening, Ripley and Joe were watching a film when the phone rang. Ripley paused the film and picked up the receiver. 'Hello... Dad, haven't heard from you in ages... Fine. Fine and dandy, actually. I took on some help with the place, so I'm not run off my feet now.' She cast Joe a raised eyebrow. 'Yes, next weekend will be great. See you Friday evening then.' She clicked the off button and looked at Joe.

'You've done it now. What do you think he'll say?' Joe looked worried, not for himself but for Ripley.

'I don't care what he says. This is my house and I'll do as I want.'

Joe laughed. 'Have I ever told you how beautiful you look when you're angry?'

Ripley threw a cushion at him. 'I mean it. He's not ruining anything ever again. Anyway, we both know the truth now, so there's not a lot he can say.'

Ripley decided to sort out the one remaining cupboard in her aunt's living room, which until now she hadn't touched. Most of the shelves were filled with dusty, chipped ornaments and Ripley hated the job of binning the precious items her aunt had tucked away years ago. As she worked her way through the shelves and regarded the items, she found herself wondering what sentimental value they held. Possibly trinkets left behind from when Ripley's grandmother had been alive, or presents. She couldn't think who would have sent May presents, she'd had no family except for Richard and they hadn't spoken for years. Ripley felt a sudden sadness at the loneliness her aunt must have felt.

Joe put his head around the door. 'How you doing, Dimps?'

'Ah. Look at all this stuff. I feel quite guilty chucking it all. Do you think May was lonely?'

Joe chortled. 'You can't be serious. She never had time to be lonely. Always something or someone to sort out, and then of course the animals. She had only slowed down a few months before you moved in, so you never really knew her lively side. She rode the horses every day and walked the dogs the length of the beach. That old, rusty bike in the tack shed was hers. She used to cycle into Crompton and get the shopping in the basket on the front. Never a dull moment. Oh, I remember buying her this one Christmas.' He picked up a small china basket covered in delicate roses.

'We'll put it out somewhere when I've washed it. Is there anything else you recognise?'

Joe picked up a shell and rubbed it between his fingers. 'I gave her this. I found it on the beach. Why don't you take what you don't want to the charity shop? Better than throwing it out.'

'Good idea. I will.' Ripley pulled herself up from her knees and put a small pile of papers on the table. 'I'm going to make a cup of tea and then I'll have a look through those. Do you want one?'

'Yes please. I'll be back in a minute. Just got to check the horse's water.'

Joe walked back in a while later and saw Ripley throwing some paper into the bin. 'Oh you're back. Here. This is for you.' She handed him a letter.

'This is my mum's handwriting.' He swiftly ripped open the envelope and took a few moments to read the letter, before his eyes went back to the top and he read it again. 'Look at this.'

Ripley took it and read it.

My dear Joe,

If you are reading this, then I know my time with you has passed and I have given this to May to give you. Firstly I want you to know you are the best son a mum could wish for. Your loving thoughtful ways will stand you in good stead when you find the right person to share your life with.

I always felt bad not being able to tell you the whole truth about your father. It is true that there was a sailor, whom I believed to be your father. Only he didn't die, he went off to marry his Dutch fiancé, who he had neglected to mention, until the day he left England for the last time before leaving his job. His ship used to dock every three months, so our relationship was a long-distance one.

When I found out the truth, I was devastated and I'm afraid I took solace in the arms of Richard Bradford. I have to now confess the truth that there is a possibility he could be your father.

I'm sorry not to have told you the truth, but I felt while we were living in the family house, I didn't want to jeopardise our home and the life you had come to love.

Richard always supported us, although he made no further contact after he knew I was having a baby. I hadn't had a chance to tell him about Arne Baars and I have to admit with our home and my job on the line I couldn't risk him knowing.

I hope you can forgive my misdemeanour and I'm so sorry to break this news after I have left you; I guess I'm a coward.

I love you more than words can say and I wish you a happy life ahead.

My love always,
Mum
xxx

Ripley looked at Joe, almost unable to contain herself. 'So my dad might not be your dad after all.'

'That's what it sounds like.'

'So we could...'

'Whoa! I don't think we should get too excited until we know... But yes, what if?'

'Oh God! How do we find out? I want to know now.' Ripley saw the look on Joe's face.

'Sorry. I'm babbling on. This must be a bit of a shock.'

'I've spent so many years not wanting him to be my father and now... I don't really know how I feel. I might be related to a complete stranger.'

'We don't have to do anything if you don't want to.' Her heart beat faster as she waited for a moment before Joe spoke.

'Are you kidding? Of course I want to know. Unanswered questions are always worse than the truth.'

'My unanswered questions hit me like a bullet.'

'This is a bit different. Nothing can hurt us, it can only get better.'

A while later they sat in front of the computer searching for information on paternity testing and then Joe made a phone call.

Ripley impatiently tried to listen into the call, but without success. After what seemed like an age, Joe hung up.

'Tell me!'

'They might be able to tell if Richard's *not* my dad just by the blood.'

'What, so we could ring and ask him what blood type he is and then we'll know? I'll ring him now.'

'No. It's not quite that simple. We'd both have to give samples and then they might tell straight away, or they might have to do some tests, but there's no guarantees. They should have a sample of my mum's blood or DNA too, but of course that isn't possible.'

'What if they can't tell?'

'Then I suppose we'll have to go in search of Arne Baars. I'm sure he'd be pleased to find out about me after all these years. They said most of the time it's easier to tell who the father isn't rather than the other way around.'

'Oh my God! This is so exciting. I can't wait; I want to know now, right this minute. Why hadn't May given you the letter?'

Joe shrugged his shoulders. 'An oversight. She must have forgotten she'd got it.'

Richard turned up at seven o'clock on Friday evening. Although Ripley still held her stance of being strong and putting her father in his place, inside she was a quivering wreck as she opened the front door.

'Hi Dad. Good to see you. You remember Joe, don't you? He lived at the cottage with his mum.'

Richard cleared his throat. 'Yes, of course.' He put his hand out for Joe to shake, but he looked uncomfortable. Ripley closed the front door and Richard gave her a hug. 'I thought we might go into Crompton for a meal...'

'I thought you might suggest that, so I took the liberty of booking at Pinkies,' Ripley said.

'Pinkies has reopened then?'

'Yes. New owners, but the food's as good as it used to be. Joe and I have been there a few times.'

'So you'll be joining us then,' Richard said, almost glaring at Joe.

'I'd love to. Thanks for the invite.'

Ripley had to turn to stifle a giggle. 'Why are we chatting in the hall? We'll have a drink before we go. Do you want to change, Dad?'

'Yes, I'll pop in the shower. Can you pour me a Speckled Hen?'

'Sure will. You having a beer, Joe?'

'Don't mind if I do.' Joe followed her down the hall into the kitchen.

Richard stood staring after them, unable to believe his eyes. How had those two met up again? He'd paid Joe off; he should have been long gone. He'd have to have a private word with him. At least Ripley had no idea of the truth.

Ripley and Joe stood in the kitchen and squeezed hands. The worst bit was over. They had debated long and hard about how to introduce Joe and then decided to take the bull by the horns and get it over with straight away.

A little later, after some stilted chat over a drink, they ordered a taxi so they could all have a drink at the restaurant. Although nothing had been put into words, individually they all felt they needed a drink to ease the tension.

'Oh, I have to get back tomorrow. Your mother arranged a dinner party.'

'That's a shame.' Ripley was now under pressure, with only a short time to get her father to agree to the test.

Richard started the evening on whisky and Joe followed suit. Ripley drank wine. The regret was that no one had bothered with lunch and soon the drink took hold.

They were shown to their table and all studied the menu carefully, allowing themselves a break from making polite conversation.

The waitress took the order and walked away to get more drinks.

Ripley took a gulp of her wine and a deep breath. 'Actually Dad, I need to tell you that I know Joe is my brother.'

Joe spat the mouthful of drink he'd just taken all over the table, while Richard knocked his glass over as he placed it down.

'Right.' Richard thought for a moment and cleared his throat as he looked around the restaurant searching for something to say.

'She needed to know,' Joe said, mopping up the drink with his napkin and keeping his eyes down to the table.

'Quite.' Richard looked embarrassed.

'As brother and sister, we share the house and the chores. Joe still stays in the cottage and it seems to be working out well. No one knows the place like Joe does.'

Richard looked at Joe. 'Quite. So how long have you been back?'

'Just a few weeks. Ripley needed some help; it's a big place to manage on your own.'

'Quite.'

'Don't worry, your secret's safe. Mum won't ever know,' Ripley said.

'Quite.' Richard nodded looking thoughtful and turned to Joe again. 'You know me and your mum were only kids. I took the cowardly route and ran. I'm not proud of that, but I always supported you, financially I mean. You have to understand, I couldn't spring something like that on Clarissa; she'd never have understood, even if it was in the past.'

'It might have saved a lot of trouble if you'd been truthful from the start,' Ripley said.

'I know. Don't you think I berated myself a million times for letting you down and breaking your heart? I knew it wasn't the same with you and Alex; you'd lost that sparkle in your eyes. I only realised it after we left Crompton and I never saw your eyes look so pretty again. Can you forgive an old fool for causing so much trouble?'

The waitress returned with the drinks and walked away. Ripley twiddled with her napkin. 'We both forgave you a long time ago.'

'I'm sorry, both of you.'

'I had a lovely home and a wonderful upbringing.' Joe looked down at the drink in his hand. 'The last few years have been difficult, but it's turned out alright.'

Richard fiddled with the lapel on his jacket. 'I'm so glad to hear that. Here come the starters... I'm famished.'

The meal progressed on a lighter note, with Joe telling of his untimely stay in Guatemala and Richard explained about a new business in the money market he had undertaken. Ripley heaved a sigh of relief. The two men in her life were getting along.

Once the main course was finished, Joe handed Richard the letter. 'What's this then? I'll need my glasses.' He fumbled in his jacket, which hung on the back of his chair, and eventually retrieved the said spectacles. He frowned as he read the letter and then cleared his throat.

'All those years I paid...'

'Dad! That's history. Joe's found out that if you and he take a test they might be able to tell him if there's a possibility you are his dad or not.'

'Oh, I see. I don't like blood tests. Does it really matter after all these years?' He looked at Joe optimistically.

Joe cleared his throat and met Richard's eyes. 'Well yes, it matters to me. I would like to know. And it's not a blood test; they can do it with saliva.'

'Well, I'll have a think about it.'

'Dad. You have to do this. Joe has a right to know, it's his family history he wants to know about.'

Richard nodded. 'Ah. The dessert menu. Wonderful.' He smiled appreciatively at the waitress.

Ripley and Joe had decided it might be best not to tell Richard the real reason they wanted to know, in case he didn't approve of the liaison and tried to keep them apart again. They had to know. The days they'd waited already had been like a torment hanging over them.

They ordered dessert and as the waitress walked away, Ripley could hear the persuasive, almost desperate tone in her voice.

'So you will do it, won't you? It won't make any difference to you, but at least Joe would know his true heritage.'

'Why has this only come to light now?'

'May had the letter in her cupboard. I only found it this week.'

Richard raised his eyebrows. 'Typical. Batty old woman right to the end.'

Ripley had to hold her tongue and keep Richard from changing the subject.

'So, you can have the test done locally. We've got the paperwork and everything you'll need.'

'Will you give it a rest? I said I'll think about it.'

She glared at him. 'I think it's the least you could do after all the trouble...'

Joe slightly shook his head and threw Ripley a look which told her to leave it. How could she leave it? She'd never been so desperate. Her dad had to do this. If he wouldn't, she'd have to tell him the truth and hope he knew about true love. Somehow she doubted that. The relationship he had with her mother was definitely not one born of love.

Richard had a sleepless night. The pillows weren't right, he was hot, then cold, and couldn't get comfortable. Why had Joe turned up again after all these years? How had he known Ripley lived here? He thought he'd put an end to his past many years ago and now it was back to haunt him. Bloody man should have just stayed away; Guatemala would have been far enough.

Saturday came around quickly and Ripley stood at the front door ready to wave her dad off. She hadn't had enough time to talk to him again and now the opportunity had passed her by. Richard started his car, was thoughtful for a moment, then opened the door and climbed back out. He stood looking at his daughter for a moment.

'What?' Ripley looked quizzical.

'I'm glad you're happy. The sparkle in your eyes gave you away at the starting post. Take care and enjoy yourselves... You know life's far too short for regret, or for not taking a chance when it comes your way. Take care, I'll see you soon.'

'Does that mean you'll take the test?'

Richard nodded. 'No getting upset if the results aren't what you want.'

'I won't. Hold on, I'll fetch the paperwork.' He watched her race inside.

He'd loved seeing her face light up and felt good that he could still have that effect even as old as she was. Although deep down he knew the look was due to the possibility of finding out Joe wasn't her brother. Clarissa would go mad again if those two ended up together. Oh well, one of life's little ups and downs; he should be used to them by now.

Ripley held out the papers. 'Look, that's the address. You can just turn up, it's all paid for. Do you know where that is?'

'Yes. I know. How long before you get the results?'
'I'm not sure.'

'I hope it's quick. I don't think poor Joe will be able to put up with your excitement for too long... Don't set yourself up for a fall, Ripley. Love is a splendid thing, but it can also hurt.'

Ripley felt her eyes well up. 'I love you Dad, thanks.' She watched and waved until the car drove out of sight and then went to find Joe in the lounge.

'My dad knows we're still in love. Apparently the sparkle has returned to my eyes and it gave us away. He's going to do the test.'

Joe looked up from the DVDs he had been looking at. 'Great! Although it suddenly feels a bit scary. I'm almost not wanting to find out in case it's not the right answer.'

Ripley sucked in her lips. 'I know what you mean. At the moment there's hope, but it could be gone and we'll be back to where we are now.'

'That's not so bad, is it? We still have each other for the rest of our lives.'

'It's not bad at all, but it could also be heaps better.' Ripley's mind flitted to the dream she held of waking up next to him each morning, making love and sharing so much more than the rules allowed now.

'Shall we take the horses out? I could do with blowing a few cobwebs away,' Joe said.

They took the usual route into Crompton, but rather than the lively chatter they always shared, both were lost in thoughts of the future and what it might hold.

After days of tension, Joe received a phone call. Ripley stood at his side and tried in vain to read his expression. 'Yes... Okay... No, there doesn't seem much point... That'll be great. Thank you for letting me know. Bye.'

'Was it them?'

Joe nodded. 'Ripley you mustn't get upset. We knew from the off that there was only a slim chance it would be the result we wanted.'

'Oh. At least we tried and we've had a few nice dreams on what might have been.'

'I know. So it looks like you're stuck with me.'

'I love being stuck with you.'

'Come and give me a hug.' She took a step towards him and he took her in his arms, with her head resting on his shoulder. Not for the first time, she felt like her heart had broken in two.

'Ripley Bradford, will you marry me?'

'Marry you?' She pulled back, looked into his smiling eyes and the truth hit her. 'We're not... He's not... Is it true?'

Joe picked her up and swung her around. 'As true as we're standing here; we are not related. My blood can't have come from your dad.'

Ripley shrieked, her eyes open wide with excitement. 'I wanted this so much... Too much, and I kept trying to say it didn't matter, but it mattered more than anything else.'

'You haven't answered my question.'

'Yes! Yes, I will.' He picked her up and held her in a hug. When he released his hold, their tears flowed.

Joe took a breath. 'I want to stay in this moment of my life forever. I only have to look at your face to see how much you love me. All the stars in the night sky don't sparkle as brightly as your eyes. I love you, more than the world, more than the universe.'

Ripley looked into his eyes. 'We can stay in this moment and we're going to. Love has found us and I know we won't lose it ever again. I love you more than the stars in the sky, more than anything'

'So we have a wedding to plan. That'll please your mother.'

Ripley laughed. 'It'll please my dad too knowing he's off the hook after all these years, but my mum... I never said anything would be easy. What would we do without a few challenges to deal with?'

'I'm marrying the girl of my dreams. I didn't dare wish for this outcome. We'll have babies, lots of them, running all over the place.'

Ripley lost her smile for a moment. 'If I can. Remember...'

'Dimps, we'll adopt. Hundreds of them, and bring them up in the most beautiful home, and they'll have wonderful times on the farm and the beach.'

'Joe, I love you so much.'

He pulled her close and held her tightly. 'This is how it was meant to be. You and me, always and forever. I love you, Ripley.'

Want to find out more about Ripley and Joe? After the trauma, did everything turn out the way they planned?

Get a free bonus chapter by typing this link into your browser:

https://BookHip.com/TNSTKHK

I'll add you to my reader's group and send you news of new releases, sneak peaks, and offers. You can leave at any time.

If you liked Ripley, you'll love:

A Family for Sophia
by Davina Penn

Marrying one man and in love with another…

Sophia Wallace has lost hope in finding true love. The man she secretly loved left town leaving her with an aching heart. Years later, working as a children's nanny, she is about to be married to their father. She loves the children and she loves their father, but not with the sizzling passion she once held for her first love.

Gio had to run. He needed time to forget Sophia, his best friend's girlfriend. After years of imagining Sophia happily settled down with his friend, Gio returns to his hometown. A chance meeting reignites the chemistry they both fought so hard to forget.

Sophia has finally turned her life around and her future looks good, but thoughts of Gio dominate her days. Will she marry the dependable man who can provide the stability she yearns for, or will Gio recapture her heart?
Life was never meant to be this complicated.

If you like romance and second chance novels, you'll love Davina Penn's heart-wrenching story.

Acknowledgements

Thank you for being one of my awesome readers. If you enjoyed Ripley, help others discover my books by leaving a review.

If you liked my book, recommending it to your social media groups and friends is a great conversation starter and might help them find their next read.

My heartfelt thanks to Vickie Phillips, Glinys Graham, Judith Cook, Nola Cooper and Caz Finlay for their continuous help and support.

Most of all I thank Tim, my sounding board, my inspiration and my friend.

Huge appreciation to everyone who helped make this book great.

Edited by Ethan Clarke at Silverjay Editing

Cover design by Get Covers

Layout by Dee at The Productive Penn

Printed in Great Britain
by Amazon